The Long and Winding Road

-

The Long and Winding Road

Mark Karnegie

mondomagik press

The Long and Winding Road

mondomagik press
an imprint of mondomagik publications

For information address:
mondomagik press
7501 Ulmerton Road #1823
Largo, FL 33771

ISBN-13: 978-0692424612

Printed in the United States of America

For Mom

LEAD IN:

"How can I go forward when I don't know which way I'm facing?"

I didn't say that. I wish I had said that. John Lennon said that in a song he wrote. I just thought it was a very profound thing he said, considering what I've gone through. My name is Thomas Moore. Actually, that was my name on the day I was born. It was Tommy after that until my eighteenth birthday. It's been Tom ever since then. Except for the brief time I was known as Moon Cat. (Well, I'll tell you about that later.)

In the course of our lives, if we want to get some place, we have to know which direction to head. Have to get a road map, so to speak, and plot our course to our destination. I figured I should do that when I had to start making the decisions that would affect my life. I knew where I wanted to go, but I didn't know of any direct routes. So I had to work out a plan.

I didn't have to make many choices until I graduated high school. My family—my father, mostly—made a lot of the decisions to get me into a position to do whatever I wanted. Then, at that point, everything would be completely up to me. I eventually would have to figure out how to get where I wanted to go. I didn't have grandiose plans, really. I was going to go to college to be an engineer. I was going to marry my high school sweetheart and have a few kids who would eventually be better off than I was, as my father had done, working hard to put me in a position to be better off than he was. There was one thing that loomed on the horizon of my future, however, that could cause a detour to any plans that I might make: Vietnam.

Every generation seems to have its own obstacles and problems to deal with which might alter one's course. My father's generation had World War II. My generation from the Sixties had the Vietnam War. I wasn't sure how it might infect my dreams at the time. Going to war was not in my plans, and as news of escalation started drifting in through the television during my junior and senior years in high school in 1966 and '67, I wondered if I had to plan on avoiding the draft. The only thing I figured I could do at graduation time was to get a deferment by going to college and hope that would delay things long enough for the war to end.

Even though I knew I didn't want to go to war, however, it didn't mean I decided I would not go, and to take positive actions to evade the draft. I was raised to be a good and law-abiding citizen. I didn't know if I could burn my draft card knowing that I could go to jail for five years and be fined $10,000 because of that action. I loved my country, and I did think it was my duty to fight to defend it, as my father had done his duty fighting to defend this country in World War II. But something told me it wasn't my duty to fight this war. I recalled seeing television news coverage of a draft-card-burning demonstration where a reporter asked an unidentified young man why he was doing what he was doing, and didn't he think he should have to fight when his country was at war? And the young man replied, "I would go off to fight if my country were at war. But as of this moment, the United States is not at war with North Vietnam. The United States military is, and for this reason I will not go." It was this bit of logic that kept haunting me whenever my father would give me his speeches and lectures on duty and patriotism.

My generation had many voices to listen to, all wanting to help guide us along our distant and curvilinear paths with their messages and advice on how we should act and behave. "Make love, not war;" "Turn on, tune in and drop out;" or "Don't trust anyone over thirty." Because, I guess, it was decided somehow that we were all going to act differently from any previous generation. At the time we didn't know how we were supposed to be different. We just had to be different, by God.

The voices that I listened to the most back then were of poets and singers John Lennon and Paul McCartney of the Beatles. And I think it has served me well. I thought they wrote some quite meaty things in their songs, and had some of the most useful and positive messages (if you listened to their music forwards, that is). I suppose I thought so because what I wanted most of all was to be a songwriter. I wanted to say profound things that people could easily grasp, thereby spreading the wisdom which I've accumulated. If Lennon and McCartney were born in another time and couldn't have been pop music songwriters, I think they would have been dandy philosophers or sages.

As naïve young people, we listened to the other voices, too, not knowing a savior from a fool on the hill. Like that bit about not trusting anyone over thirty, I look back now and realize that they were the only ones who have truly seen the future.

"She was just seventeen, and you know what I mean,
And the way she looked was way beyond compare."
Lennon-McCartney

"And when I touch you I feel happy inside,
It's such a feeling that, my love, I can't hide, I can't hide."
Lennon-McCartney

One evening at the beginning of November 1966, I stepped briskly down the sidewalk in my hometown of Warwick, Rhode Island, on my way to my girlfriend Allison Lambert's house for a semi-regular dinner with her parents. I wasn't late, but I beamed with a bit of excitement that propelled me along. Actually, I was trying to arrive a little early, and out of nowhere, for a few steps, I skipped like a happy-go-lucky child. Being a senior in high school, I couldn't remember the last time that I skipped.

I had just talked to my father, and he approved of the plan Allison and I had discussed which would allow us to go to the same college the next year. Part of my exhilaration was restrained by anticipation, however, as that night Allison and I were going to ask her parents to approve of our plan.

The temperature was still mild for the middle of the New England autumn, but as the afternoon sun already had faded by the dinner hour and the breeze off nearby Narragansett Bay had swept in, I clutched my jacket tightly around me.

When I came to the Lambert house on the quiet, tree-lined street, a playful idea struck me, and I paused instead of going straight up the walk. I glanced around to see if anybody might have been watching me. After I saw that all was clear, I vaulted the waist-high, wooden fence and scampered behind a large oak tree in the front yard. It was a moonless night, but a nearby streetlamp and the front porch light helped me maneuver around. From previous expeditions, I already had my course planned. I jumped up to grab a branch, then walked my feet up the trunk until I was safely in the notch in the middle of the tree. I picked my way up one sturdy offshoot until I got to a branch that hung close to the house. After grasping it firmly with both hands, I let my feet dangle in the air and walked hand over hand until I hit the railing to the second-floor veranda. I swung my legs up over the railing, let go of my branch and stood safely on the deck.

There were two bedrooms with windows on that side of the house, Allison's and her little sister's. I tiptoed up to Allison's window and peered into her lit room. She was lying on her stomach on her bed with her feet kicking up in the air, as she read a book.

She looked so beautiful, I thought. I watched her for a moment as she twisted her silky, mahogany brown hair around her finger. The tail of her blouse was pushed up for me to glimpse the creamy small of her back. And I could easily make out the gentle-sloping curves of her buttocks through her tight, Capri slacks. I nearly was hypnotized as I watched her rump flex then relax as she scissor-kicked her legs. Refrains of the Beatles' "Yellow Submarine" emanated from her room.

I rapped on the pane trying to draw her attention. When she looked up and recognized me, she came over and pulled open the sash.

"You crazy— ," Allison started to say as I climbed through her window.

"I'm sorry, I just had to see you before I *arrived* for dinner tonight,"

I whispered as I embraced her, then I kissed her intensely. We had been going steady for two years and were at the point of planning our future together. I had climbed the tree to her bedroom a few times before and spent the night with her twice without her parents knowing that I was there.

When we separated from our tight clinch, I was about to say something else, but she put her index finger to my lips and said, "Just a second." She stepped over to her record player and turned the volume higher. When she turned back to me, she said, "I just got the new Beatles album, *Revolver.* This is about the fifth time I've played it through already. It's really out-of-sight."

"Well, you'll have to invite me over sometime to listen to it," I said with a smile, thinking that I wasn't *officially* there yet.

"So what's up?"

"Oh, I just wanted to tell you how it went with my dad today. I talked to him just before I came over, you know."

"What did he say?" Allison took hold of my arm and looked eagerly into my eyes.

"Well, what he said was—" I paused for dramatic effect. "He said yes. He's going to let me go to college in Boston next year."

"Oh, Tommy! That's so wonderful." She gleefully hugged me again then kissed me on the cheek.

"I really wasn't sure he would go for it. I know he wanted me to go to Providence College or the University of Rhode Island so that I could still live at home. I'm sure he's going to be lonely without me."

My father was a widower. My mother died from kidney failure when I was twelve, but he hadn't remarried.

"But I have to strike out on my own sometime. He even told me, though, if I could get accepted, that he would try his best to pay my way through Brown to keep me close to home."

"Did he ask you why you wanted to go to Boston so much?"

"Yes. I told him I already decided to major in Aeronautical Engineering, and the program at Boston University is the closest school. It's exactly what I'm looking for, but I wasn't sure if he would take it seriously, though."

"But he knows about your avid interest in the space program?" Allison offered.

"Of course. He probably started it. My dad used to buy me these toy rockets and spaceships when I was a kid. And he bought my first telescope for my thirteenth birthday."

"And he told you it was so that you could look for your mom up in heaven. He was so sweet." Allison looked as though she might start to cry.

"Yeah," I said. I felt as if I might start to cry, too, when my mother's face flashed back in my mind for a moment. "I wondered if he thought that I was just dreaming about space, you know, like most kids dream of being a space adventurer like Buck Rogers or something. And I think he expected me to pick something more typical, like law or medicine."

"But you told him how serious you really are?"

"Yes, and he said he realized that I never asked him for much. So, he finally agreed. Now the trick is getting *your* father to agree. I think we should bring it up tonight at dinner. He's bound to ask me about my college plans."

"But I don't have a specific reason to go to that school other than to be with you, Tommy."

"That's why we need to come up with a little strategy."

Allison gestured to me to be quiet again as the album side was finished. She went to the record player, moved the arm over to flip the disc to the other side and set the needle onto the first song. Then she led me over to the bed, and we sat down to talk.

"What kind of strategy?" she asked.

"Well, we have to say something like you need to go to a big city college to expand your horizons. You know, you have to start seeing the world as it really is. You need to start meeting a whole new set of people, with different ideas."

"That's good, Tommy. I like that."

"Boston is such a worldly city. There's just so much more going on there. I swear, it is so provincial around here. I mean, what can Providence show us that we haven't seen already? Or Kingston? We can't learn about life from books alone. We have to experience it. Live it."

"And Boston is not as if it's so far away," Allison said, getting into the spirit. "Just far enough, right?"

"Exactly. I like the way you think." I put my arm around her, squeezed and kissed her on the cheek. She responded by putting her head on my shoulder as I held her.

"It's going to be great being there with you. Boston is such a romantic city," she said dreamily.

She felt so wonderful next to me that I was getting lost in the moment. I started caressing up and down her arm, and then made a move with my hand to her breast. She still had the look in her eye that showed me it was okay. Because we figured that we had a long future together, we already talked about taking fewer risks and how we weren't going to sleep together again until after high school, at least. But we mostly were getting by at this point with a lot of making out and some heavy petting—whatever we had the opportunity for. At that moment as my hormones started to rage, I thought it looked like a good opportunity to me.

I let my hand drift down and stop between her legs, and I could feel her through the light material of her slacks. "Not now," she said softly as she put her hand over mine, but didn't push it away.

"Why don't you let me give you one?" I asked.

"You're supposed to be arriving for dinner right now," she said playfully. She didn't move to stop me, but instead, she began nuzzling me.

"I guess you're right. I mean, how would we explain that far away look in your eye and the big smile painted on your face at dinner?"

Maybe it was the thrill of having that secret from her folks because suddenly she said, "Okay." Allison took her hand off mine and hugged me harder as I started to caress her. She swung her feet up on the bed to be in a reclining position. I brought my hand to the top of her waistband and went inside, gliding down her smooth abdomen to her coarse patch of hair. I was mesmerized in the moment as my whole focus was trained on finding her sweet spot. But my trance was quickly broken by a knock on her bedroom door.

My hand shot out of her pants as if it were stung by a bee, and I jumped straight up, as did Allison, when we heard her father's voice through the door.

"Honey! Your mother wants you to help her set the table," the voice bellowed over the music. "Your guest should be arriving any moment now."

Mr. Lambert knocked again, and then the door handle started to jiggle. I knew Allison had been in the habit of locking her door since I had started making my clandestine visits, but, for an instant, I didn't know if she had this time because I had arrived unexpectedly. But I was in luck.

"Allison, honey!" he yelled to get her attention. Hopefully he thought that she was just listening to her loud rock and roll again.

"Oh, sorry, Daddy. Just a sec!" Allison shouted back through the door. Then, as I stood frozen in fear, she whispered to me, "Quick, get in the closet." I did so as she turned off her phonograph and opened the door for her father.

"Sorry, Daddy. I was just studying to some music," I heard Allison say through the closet door. It was pitch-black, save for a crack of light at the bottom of the door. I stayed as still as I possibly could and tried not to breathe too loudly. I hoped I wouldn't sneeze from smelling Allison's perfumed hangers in there.

"I don't know how you even can study with this racket, anyway," I heard her father say. "What's with the locked door?"

"Oh, I was just trying to keep Bobbi the brat out of here." Bobbi was Allison's eleven-year-old sister. "You know how she's always pestering me."

"Well, anyway," Mr. Lambert said. "Did you hear what I said? Your mother wants you to help her set the table and finish up with dinner."

"Okay, thanks, Daddy."

"Is that what you're going to wear for dinner?" he asked.

"Yes. What's wrong with my outfit? I mean, it's only Tommy coming over."

I could have been insulted, I guess, but I knew what she meant. I was a familiar sight at the Lambert house, but maybe not quite familiar enough to explain my presence in the closet.

"I just thought it would be nice to see you wear a dress a little more often," her father said.

"Oh, Daddy." I only heard a few footsteps walking away for a moment, then Allison's bedroom door close and lock again. Allison opened the closet door, and I squinted in the brighter light.

"Come on. You're late," she whispered. "You've got to get downstairs and arrive for dinner."

"That was close," I said. I grabbed her and kissed her as if I were not going to see her again for a long time.

"Come on silly. We almost got caught once." Allison pushed me closer to the window.

"Bye," I said sadly. "I'll miss you." She smiled her sweet smile at me, and then I opened the window and climbed out.

As the window closed behind me, I paused a moment, standing alone on the veranda. I scanned the neighborhood before me and thought, "Lord of all he surveys." I was so smooth at times that it was starting to get scary. I mean, I considered myself a nice guy, as did most who knew me, but I was able to take advantage of that perception more and more and get away with things that someone less reputable wouldn't. So, I thought I should take more precautions in regards to risk-taking before my reputation was changed for the worst.

After I refocused myself on the moment, I stepped over the rail and took hold of the branch and scaled my way down to the ground. I was sweating a bit from my exertion and realized I was somewhat unkempt. Instead of going up to the door, I hopped back over the fence and leisurely strolled around the block to compose myself. With my handkerchief, I tried to wipe away any remnants of tree sap and grime I had on my hands. I tugged at my jacket to straighten it, smoothed out the fabric of my trousers and combed my hair. By the time I was back in front of the Lambert house, I was ready.

A moment or two after I knocked, Mrs. Lambert answered the door.

"Well, hello, Tommy," she said, smiling. "Come on in. Right on time as usual."

"Hello, Mrs. Lambert. Thank you," I said while stepping through the threshold.

"Here, now. Let me take your jacket for you." She closed the door behind me, and her hands went out as if to catch the jacket as I slid it off my shoulders and arms. When I handed it to her, she hung it with care in the foyer closet.

"I must say, Mrs. Lambert, that you look quite lovely this evening." She was still wearing an apron from her dinner preparations in the kitchen, but it was a lacy one covering an elegant evening dress. I wasn't kidding her, but I felt a lot like Eddie Haskell after I said it. I truly thought she was a stunning woman, regardless of her age—which seemed over-the-hill to me at the time, even though she was only in her late thirties. When I saw Mrs. Lambert, I knew where Allison got her beauty.

"Thank you, Tommy. You're too kind. Allison is helping me in the kitchen with a few final details, but I'll let her know that you're here. If you want to have a seat in the living room, she'll be out in a few minutes."

"Thanks," I said as she turned to go back to the kitchen. I stepped into the living room to wait. I sat in my favorite chair, which I guessed must have been designed for reading. It was big, comfortably padded and reclined slightly. The large room was furnished with a number of chairs and two sofas, and was arranged to foster discussion, I supposed, as some of the seats were angled to face each other, and there was no television set, which was the focal point of most living rooms I had seen—as if it were the object of living. Artsy paintings adorned the walls around the filled bookcases, and a stack of magazines fanned across the coffee table in a fetching display. I was about to peruse one when Mr. Lambert entered the room.

"Tommy, I'm sorry. I didn't know you had arrived. How's it going, my boy?"

"Very well, sir. Thanks." I had jumped up to shake his hand as he strode across the room to greet me. He was a large man, and his massive hand always overpowered mine. Maybe it was a none-too-subtle reminder of the hierarchy in our relationship. While he grasped my hand this evening, the image of where it had just recently been suddenly entered my mind. I hadn't had a chance to wash up as of yet, and I guiltily yanked my hand back as quickly, I imagined, as I had yanked it out of his daughter's pants only a few moments ago. Mr. Lambert gave no indication that my actions were abnormal or suspicious in any way, but being a lawyer, he didn't need any possible evidence handed over to him, so to speak.

"Allison must be in the kitchen still, helping out the Mrs. I'll go check on how it's coming along. Be back in a sec."

He left me standing alone in the room. I paced a little, absently looking at different things. Mr. Lambert always had been warm to me. I was never sure if that was an actual sign of his approval, or maybe he could've been relieved that his daughter hadn't ended up with someone, shall I say, less desirable, or totally unacceptable to him. If I didn't know he liked me, his size would've been quite intimidating. He had a bold, aquiline nose and a square jaw with a tiny cleft in it. He was the type to have his hair trimmed weekly, always well-groomed and clean-shaven—except at this time of day when he had a bit of a shadow. For dinner, he was wearing a dress shirt with tie and trousers from a tailored suit. His only signs of relaxation came from removing his cufflinks and rolling back the sleeves, unfastening his top button and loosening the tie.

Mr. Lambert was a corporate lawyer for a large paper mill in Providence. He was a proud man and had provided very well for his family. And even though I might've entered into his trust, he still was very protective of his daughters. I expected him to be a tough negotiator when I presented my plan that evening, so I needed to be sharp. It may have entered his mind that his daughter's future would eventually belong with me anyway, but I surmised he wouldn't let it go easily.

"Tommy, long time no see," Allison said as she came up behind me, locking her arms around my waist. I spun around while still in her grasp and greeted her with a kiss.

"Hello, Precious. You're a sight for sore eyes," I said, then kissed her again. I suddenly got the feeling of being watched. I looked up while still in lip contact and saw Allison's kid sister Bobbi spying on us.

"Oooh, I'm telling Mom," she said and then disappeared around the corner.

Allison sighed and said to me, "I sometimes wish I could twitch my nose and make her disappear."

Next, poking his head into the room, Mr. Lambert said, "Okay, kids. Dinner's ready."

Allison looked to her father, and then said to me with a sly grin on her face, "Oh, I just got the new Beatles album today. After dinner, you'll have to come up and listen to it."

"Far out," I said, as I was allowed to be with Allison in her bedroom, but only with the door open, of course.

After making a pit stop in the washroom, I joined the Lamberts in the dining room at the formally set table. I thought it was nice that they had a regular family meal. With just my father and me, we ate on the run a lot, in the kitchen or on the sofa in front of the television.

"Something smells wonderful," I said as I took my seat next to Allison.

"It's my famous rib roast that you like so much," Mrs. Lambert said.

"Mmm-mmm," hummed Mr. Lambert as he settled in at the head of the table. "My favorite."

Mrs. Lambert placed the dishes of food on the table, and Mr. Lambert carved the pieces off the roast and doled them out.

"So, Tommy," Mr. Lambert said. "You must be getting ready for the basketball season."

"Yes, sir. We start practice next week." I dolloped whipped potatoes on my plate and passed the bowl around, as I was being handed the vegetables and bread.

"Do you think you can beat Pawtucket this year?"

"We should have a chance. I think we'll have a very good team this season." I was only a second-stringer, medium height, who only played for fun. Mr. Lambert seemed to follow the school's success more than I did. But maybe he was thrilled to have another male in the house to whom he could talk. Sports was our usual topic of conversation.

When we all had our portions, we held hands in a circle and bowed our heads while Mr. Lambert said a short grace. I looked over at Allison and found her glancing at me. We smiled when our eyes met.

"Allie and Tommy are making goo-goo eyes at each other again," Bobbi said.

"Oh, don't be embarrassed, Tommy," Mrs. Lambert said. "I think it's sweet. And, Bobbi, it'll only be a year or two before you'll be wanting boys to make goo-goo eyes at you."

"I doubt it," Bobbi said. "That's just icky."

"So, Tommy," Mr. Lambert started again. "How are your college plans coming along?"

At least it was going to begin early. I had to swallow a bite of food first, then I answered, "Well, I talked it over with my dad, and I decided to go to Boston University next fall, if I can get accepted."

"You'll get accepted, dear," Mrs. Lambert said, "with *your* grades."

"Wow," Mr. Lambert said. "That came as a surprise. I thought you'd be going to Providence or URI. They're both good schools. And you're not even going to try to get into Brown?"

"I might have, but Boston has the program in aeronautical engineering that I want to get into."

"Really? Very impressive," Mr. Lambert said.

"My goal is to work for NASA someday."

"That certainly is a lofty dream, son." He paused to take a sip of his drink. "So how do you think you'll like living away from home?"

"Actually, I think I'll enjoy it. It'll be a chance for me to experience a bit of independence, but yet, it's not too far away. It's only a couple hours away by bus."

"Yes, I suppose," Mr. Lambert said. "I guess you could come down to visit Allison just about every weekend if you wanted."

"Well, Daddy," Allison piped in. "I was hoping to go to school wherever Tommy went."

"But I thought we discussed this, honey. You were going to go to one of the local colleges so that you could still live at home."

"I know," Allison said, "but now that Tommy wants to go to Boston, I want to go, too, to be with him. Even though it's not that far away, you must realize how hard it would be to carry on a relationship while living in different cities. Besides, college is supposed to be a chance to broaden one's horizons. I've lived here all my life. I'd love to start seeing new places. Boston would be so fresh and exciting that I think it would be a great place to broaden my horizons."

Good girl, I thought. I was hoping she wouldn't forget that part.

"If Allie goes to Boston, can I have her room?" Bobbi asked. "It's a lot bigger than mine."

"Just you never mind about that now," Mrs. Lambert said to her.

"College is a big step," Mr. Lambert said. He looked at Allison, then to me, then back to Allison. "I know you and Tommy have been going steady a long time, but I just hope you're not letting a decision like your education be influenced by a relationship. Is this something you've given much thought to?"

"Yes, Daddy."

"And do you know if this is going to be a good school for you?" he continued. "It may be a fine school for engineering, but what about for what you want to study? What was it again that you decided on?"

"I want to be a teacher," Allison replied.

"And do you know if this is a quality school to become a teacher?"

"Um, if I may say so, sir," I interjected, "the School of Education has a very fine reputation. And the university is quite highly respected. Did you know that Dr. Martin Luther King went to school there?"

"Really. I didn't know that," Mr. Lambert said languidly. I thought he looked a little annoyed at me for intruding. "My point is that you have a number of good schools to choose from, and you shouldn't make your decision based on just one issue."

"Do you want us to break up or something?" Allison asked, possibly trying to uncover her father's hidden agenda. I looked across the table at her mother and Bobbi, who, like me, were eating slowly, while listening intently to the dinnertime debate between father and daughter.

"No, not at all," he replied forthrightly. "You know that I have the utmost respect for Tommy, here. But if you think about it, it might be beneficial for the both of you to go to different schools that are still nearby. With Tommy in Boston and you here, you could see each other all you wanted every weekend. But during the week, you could concentrate on your studies without—um, distractions. Your mother and I went to different schools, and it worked for us."

"Daddy! You went to a men's college and Mom went to a women's college," Allison responded.

"That's beside the point," he said.

"It's just that if we live apart, there's a chance of drifting apart. And I don't want to risk that. Besides, Tommy's not the only reason I want to go to Boston. I've been thinking a lot about it, and if I want to teach kids, I have to know more than just what's in the books. I need to have experience to draw from to help guide them if I can. I need to live life before I can lecture about it. Boston would be new and exciting, a great way to experience life, meeting new people every step of the way, seeing all new things, instead of feeling like I'm in a rut because I know where everything is, having the same friends from high school who are all playing it safe just like me."

"There's nothing wrong with playing it safe," her father said. "I see that you've given much thought to a variety of issues, but there are a number of other things I don't think you have considered."

"Like what?" she asked.

"Like being alone in such a big city that's unfamiliar to you. Boston can be a dangerous place for a young girl like you."

"I won't be alone. Tommy will be with me."

"And another thing, college campuses all over the country have been attracting a lot of radicals and troublemakers lately. You've seen what's been going on, demonstrations turning into riots, bombings, shootings, people drugged out of their minds."

"Most of that stuff is going on in California, not around here," Allison said.

"It's spreading everywhere," Mr. Lambert told her, and then he turned to me. "But I guess I should be glad that you don't want to go to school out there. It's just insanity. I hope that they get smart in California and elect that Reagan character next week. He sounds as if he'll put a stop to all the nonsense out there."

"Come on, dear," Mrs. Lambert joined in. "Don't start getting into politics at dinner. You know how worked up it gets you."

"I'm just saying Allison needs to consider things before traipsing off to Boston. Would you pass me the potatoes?" he asked me, and I obliged. He started fixing his seconds, as he was eating as heartily as he was trying to make his point. He then continued the debate. "I mean, you've got people like that Carmichael character going to college campuses all over the country, always looking to stir up a hornet's nest of trouble. What with the war, civil rights, women's lib, it seems like every beatnik, pinko subversive is trying to indoctrinate the minds of American youth when they're at their most impressionable."

"But don't you think the war might be over soon?" I questioned. "President Johnson just came back from Manila with a very strong peace offer that included withdrawal of American troops."

"I don't think the North will jump at it," Mr. Lambert replied. "Sure, it would give us what we want, which is the status quo. Things would be back to the way things were, and we'd have our way out of the mess. But the status quo isn't what the Communists want."

"But don't you think that by now they've realized it's a war they can't win with U.S. involvement?" I probed deeper, curious to find out another adult's view on the subject, besides my dad's.

"I just don't know if they've realized it or not," he said. "I wouldn't put too much faith in the peace process, though. You know what will end this war quicker than any peace talks? Invading the North."

"Wouldn't that simply strengthen their resolve against us?" I pushed.

"It's the only way to convince them they can't win. You can't negotiate with them. I'll just give you one piece of advice, son, that my father gave to me, 'Don't ever trust a communist.'"

"You act like the war is coming to Boston," Allison said.

"There are people out there who'll make you think it is," he replied.

"But you can't try to protect me my whole life," she said. "You'll just have to place your trust in Tommy to protect me." I was surprised at how much input Allison was giving, which wasn't all at my prompting. Perhaps she truly felt strongly about this and didn't just want to tag along after me to Boston.

Mr. Lambert looked me over again, grinned and clapped me on the back with his massive hand. "I must admit that he is a very trustworthy young man." Then he turned to his wife. "What do you think about all this, hon?"

"I was looking forward to still having Allison around for a few more years," Mrs. Lambert said. "But she is going to be an adult. I think we should let her make her own decision about her life, even though we'll miss her very much."

"I guess it's hard to see Daddy's little girl as all grown up," he said.

"But I am." Allison reached across the table and placed her hand atop her father's.

"It's still a way's off," he said. "I'll tell you what. Apply to Boston and the schools around here, first of all. You still need to get accepted. Out of the schools that accept you, we'll be able to make a decision then. How does that sound?"

"Great! Thanks, Daddy." She seemed to take it as tantamount to his approval.

"You'll have to keep your grades up, you know," he cautioned.

"I will." Allison reached under the table to squeeze my hand as a signal that we had been successful. It was looking that way. In the next few months, we both had to make sure nothing happened that would change his mind. As we were finishing up our dinner that night, I thought I might have more of an opportunity to work him, schmooze him and make him comfortable with the idea of me as a possible future son-in-law.

"I just remembered," Mr. Lambert said to me. "A couple of my colleagues and I got tickets for the Clay-Williams fight coming up. I got an extra one for you. Do you want to come along?"

"Yes, sir," I said enthusiastically. "Thank you." He had invited me twice previously for a sort of boy's night out to watch his favorite boxer, Cassius Clay, fight on closed circuit television at a little place in North Attleboro. Maybe I was like the son he never had.

I think at the moment I felt as close to being an adult as I could get before graduation. I was with the girl I eventually thought would be my wife; an adult was treating me like one of the guys; and I had made my first important decision about my life. It was also the last time that one of my life choices was contingent upon someone else.

CHORUS:

Allison and I both got accepted to Boston University a few months later. I just missed being salutatorian of our class by percentage points. It only meant that I didn't have to give a speech at graduation, and so I didn't mind at all.

Mr. Lambert came through and let Allison go to Boston with me. Allison seemed to think it might have had something to do with an associate of his letting her daughter go to school up there after she had been accepted at Radcliffe. Mr. Lambert almost changed his mind when he heard about a race riot in Roxbury a couple weeks after graduation, but he kept his promise. I didn't think that would be a big worry. Boston had been fairly quiet compared to other large cities at the time.

That year, 1967, was a time of major changes and upheavals for so many people, as well as for me. I don't know if we were all simply caught in the convergence of a swelling tide and swept along by unseen forces, but there came a point for this generation when change was no longer something to be resisted, but rather a goal to be strived for. I wondered that maybe, for me, my age made it purely happenstance.

I began the year as a minor child and left it as an adult. I asked people to call me Tom because I thought it sounded more like a man's name. Tommy was too childish. That was a small but abrupt change meant to facilitate the transition to adulthood. Other changes, however, were more gradual as I may have been trying to hold on to some of my innocence.

I had followed the progress of the space program with wide-eyed wonder as we were getting closer and closer to reaching the moon. But at the beginning of the year, astronauts Grissom, Chafee and White were killed in an Apollo I ground-test explosion. I thought at the time it might cause an end to space exploration, or, at least, a lengthy delay. But by the end of the year, things seemed to be right back on track to accomplish the goal set forth by John F. Kennedy of putting men on the moon by the end of the decade. I had thought that it was so important for us to win the race. If we didn't get up there soon, the Russians would get there first, and that would make us vulnerable to them. But, equally importantly, we set the goal for ourselves, and if we couldn't accomplish what we set out to do in space, then what other lofty goals were beyond our reach: the war in Vietnam, the war on poverty, the war on racism, the Cold War? Many people were beginning to doubt we could finish any of those races. After Apollo I, I began to question, at what cost was joining this race? Was it that important? At least, what was the hurry?

The Beatles were changing. Their Sergeant Pepper album came out in April, and I remember being knocked out by it because it was so different from anything else I had been hearing. We had no way of knowing at the time, but it has been said that the event of Sergeant Pepper changed the way rock music was made, particularly the way albums were made from that point on. My friends and I would play it over and over, trying to figure out what we thought were hidden meanings in the cover design and in the lyrics that were printed on the back cover. Talk started that the Beatles were being influenced by drugs, especially psychedelics. I didn't know much about that scene, as it was still basically underground at that moment. Although, it was that "Summer of Love" when it began to spread more widely. Though my friends and I didn't or couldn't fully understand the Beatles, somehow we felt as if we did.

Relationships were changing. After graduation, my best buddy from high school told me how he was going to spend his summer. He said he was going to hitchhike to California to attend the Monterey Music Festival, and then to San Francisco to "just groove and check out the scene" he had heard about there, before heading off to college at Notre Dame in the fall. Before he set out, we hugged, and he promised he would write and tell me everything he saw. But I never heard from him or saw him again after that day.

Allison and I went to a graduation night party to say goodbye to a lot of people we fully expected to never see again, as we all would be going our separate ways in life. And to celebrate the shedding of the shackles of childhood, so to speak, Allison and I made love that night, our third time, and I think we both realized it was the first adult decision we made *as* adults. Technically, we could've gotten married at that time. We had sex because we wanted to. Then, after that, we stopped again because we wanted to.

Still, we spent many days that summer seemingly clinging to our carefree childhood ways, putting off the responsibilities as long as we could. I worked part-time for my father's plumbing supply company during that summer to have a little mad money, but I had plenty of free time for myself where I still felt free. Many summer days were spent jaunting around with Allison, hiking and tree-climbing in Lincoln Woods, exploring the beaches on the southern shore of Rhode Island, or quahog hunting around Narragansett Bay, sometimes hopping the ferry to Block Island to gad about like tourists or spending the day at the Rocky Point amusement park, stuffing ourselves with clam cakes and saltwater taffy. It was a time I felt closest to Allison.

I felt closest to my father, as well, during that same time. Working for him was a pleasure because I got a better understanding of what life was like for him. And he always had this proud look on his face as if he were showing me off to everyone and saying, "That's my boy!" Maybe he was sensing he would be losing me, or, at least, seeing me a lot less often. But that summer and autumn, we religiously followed the pennant drive of the Boston Red Sox together. It was an easy way for us to connect. As lifelong Sox fans, we both thought it akin to a cosmic experience. My dad was about my age twenty-one years before when Boston last won the pennant, when they were led by Ted Williams.

We would watch the games on TV when we could on Saturday or Sunday afternoons, or listen to the radio when we were at work. And when I went away to school in Boston that September, he would call often and al-most exclusively talk about the race and Carl Yastrzemski's triple-crown chase. Then, when the World Series came around in October, my father was able to get tickets, and we attended each game that was held at Fenway Park. We were devastated when they finally lost, but we also realized how magical it seemed to experience it together, to watch them come so close when almost nothing was expected from the team that year. I sometimes look back at that moment as a last grasp at childhood innocence and the past, as the adrenalin flow and excitement were part of the desperation of trying to hold on for as long as I could, and the loss was the letting go, a quick and clean break from the child-ish past, and all that was left was the future and whatever it would hold.

But there was another sports story which occurred that year where I felt I had lost a lot of my innocence and naïveté and truly had begun to change my perspective of the world around me. Muhammad Ali, the world heavyweight boxing champion, was convicted of refusing induction after he was drafted. He was my favorite boxer, the same hero I had watched fight months earlier with Mr. Lambert, and I had followed his career since the Olympics in Rome. He always seemed like such a fun person, but those were serious events that year

At first, I was extremely disappointed with what he did. I thought he was using his new religion as a cop out. He certainly wasn't opposed to violence as a boxer. It seemed to me he was just another celebrity looking for special treatment. But when I heard people defending him saying that race was the issue, I began to see how they could be right. If he were a white celebrity, he almost undoubtedly would have been given some sort of special treatment. And after his conviction, he got the maximum sentence, while the average person usually got the minimum, or wasn't even tried. I saw that the system was trying to make an example of him as a black man, as a message to black America, that they better not question or defy authority—white authority, in essence. I saw there really was a white America and a black America, separate and unequal, as I had been hearing about for a while, but didn't quite understand.

Watching Ali make his stand and his statement helped change the way I viewed the world that I lived in, that I was a part of. It got harder and harder to listen to people tell me what the real world was like after that point. I wanted to see for myself. The real world was out there. All I had to do was open my eyes.

VERSE 2:

As I approached the door to my dormitory room one February afternoon in 1968, choruses of the Beatles' "Magical Mystery Tour" drifted to my ears in the otherwise quiet hall, and the faint but distinct acrid aroma of marijuana smoke wafted toward my nostrils.

I cracked the door open slightly, only allowing myself enough room to squeeze in, and then quickly closed it behind me, trying not to let out any air if possible.

"I thought I asked you to please not smoke that stuff in here," I scolded my roommate, Rolf Gunderson, who was sitting on the floor, legs crossed in the lotus position, painting slogans on placards. "Do you want to get busted? Never mind that, get me busted?"

"Um, hey, I'm sorry, man." Rolf looked up at me sheepishly as though he were a child just caught doing something bad by a parent. "I thought that since you were out, you wouldn't mind."

I had been out looking for a hardware store to pick up some scrap lumber sticks and tacks for handles for the signs that we were making up for a protest rally later that afternoon.

"But I could smell it out in the hall," I told him. "If you're going to insist on doing it, can't you at least open a window?"

"But it's thirty-five degrees outside," he replied.

As I looked across the room and through the beam of sunlight streaming through the window, I could see a definite smoky haze. "Well, I guess we're going to have to suffer and shiver for a few minutes to clear the air in here." I handed Rolf his coat that was hanging on the rack by the door. "Here, put this on and open the window in your bedroom."

As he went off, I stepped to the window of our common room that was between our individual bedrooms. He and I really lucked out being freshmen and getting such a prime dorm room. The building was converted from an old hotel in Kenmore Square, situated on a narrow, triangular city block, which dictated the shape of the building. Our room was located at the point of this cheese-wedge structure, and the view from our tenth-floor room offered a panorama of downtown Boston. Rolf's window faced south, and Fenway Park was right in his sight line. The playing field wasn't visible because he looked at the backside of the Green Monster, but I got a kick out of seeing our dorm hall beyond that famous left field wall when Sox games were televised. My bedroom window offered a view to the north, where I had one open sector between buildings where I could glimpse the Charles River. The common room window peered straight up Beacon Hill and the downtown skyscrapers.

I opened the window wide and braced myself for the cold, but I figured as the heat flowed out, the smoke and smell would be sucked right along with it. When I started to see the vapor of my breath inside, I thought that should do it and closed the window. "Okay, Rolf!" I shouted to him. After shutting his window, he came out of his room hopping up and down and rubbing his hands together. I sat on the cast-iron radiator to warm myself back up.

"Do you want me to light some incense to maybe cover up any last traces?" Rolf asked.

"No, that's okay. Don't worry about it." I wasn't much of a fan of the incense odor either. Even if I hadn't smelled anything, I usually could tell if he has smoked weed. He always became extra mellow, or he sometimes got these confused looks on his face, as he had now.

"What's up?" I asked.

"I was just trying to think of something I was supposed to remember to tell you, but, man, I don't know what it was."

"Was it something important?"

"I think so, but maybe not urgent, you know what I mean?"

"Well, you'll think of it sooner or later," I said, wanting to relieve the pained look in his eyes. He squinted as if he were looking for the answer, literally.

"How are the signs coming along?" I asked. We each had come up with our own slogan, but since Rolf had the more artistic hand, he painted them.

"Finished," he said, and held them up to view. "Take a look."

Rolf was immersed in the underground culture, and his use of peace symbols, psychedelic colors and designs, reflected that he was one of *them*, belonging to the sub-culture. I felt there must be some kind of code in the using of the symbols, and that if I had painted the signs—I might have been able to copy the outside shell of the symbols, but not fully understanding the meanings yet—I was bound to be identified as a faker. Rolf even tried to initiate me at times, offering me hits of pot (which he even suggested would give me some kind of deeper insight), or discussing his politics. He had tried to convince me to join, or at least attend meetings of the campus chapter of

Students for a Democratic Society, a political organization that had been in-volved with the student demonstrations against the war. I told him I wasn't very political. What I didn't say was I had heard the group was extremely left-wing, bordering on communistic, and I didn't want to get involved in a group where I would be labeled as believing something the group did without know-ing what that was. Rolf didn't push it, like some other SDS people I ran across. He said he understood, and that people usually don't get involved un-less things directly affected them. But he countered with saying that what the government was doing was going to directly affect me eventually. I did a lot of sidestepping until recent developments.

The demonstration that we were preparing for that afternoon was a protest against the university's policy of giving grades of individual students to the Selective Service System for the purpose of determining whether a student deserved his deferment, or simply was dodging the draft. In essence, the SSS was saying that if a student maintained a high grade-point average—and we weren't sure what exactly constituted a high level: A average, B aver-age, perhaps—he was considered a "serious" student and deserved the opportunity to finish his education, while someone on the low end was on the fringe, bound to drop out anyway, and, therefore, should be made eligible for the draft right away.

I didn't like the idea of the war, mostly because I felt it wasn't my fight. But being Rolf's roommate, he started supplying me with more reasons to oppose the war. And I easily could realize that this policy could directly affect my life, so I felt I could not simply stand by any longer. One bad exam could lead to a low grade, which might drop me below their arbitrary level. All of a sudden, I could find my deferment canceled and be shipped off to Vietnam.

Rolf did convince me how little disagreeing in principle would get me, and that I could not just disagree in principle anymore, but that I must disagree in deed as well and voice my opinion to be heard.

Rolf held up the sign with my slogan, which read: Send No More Graded Meat to the Slaughterhouse—which I thought made a good analogy. But I liked Rolf's even better, which read: Pass, Go Collect Degree; Do Not Pass, Go Directly to Vietnam! The back sides of both signs had the same slogan, kind of an SDS over-theme Rolf took home from the last meeting: No Grades! No War! No Way!

"These look great," I told him.

"We just need to tack on the handles now."

I took out my bundle of sticks and nails and began tacking on handles to the placards.

"What time are we supposed to head over to the rally?" I asked.

"Three o'clock."

I looked at my watch. It was 2:45. "Hmm. Wasn't there something else going on at three o'clock today?"

"Not that I know of, man," Rolf replied.

I pondered for a moment, searching through the loose debris of my mind that had been getting about as cluttered as my room. "Shoot. I just remembered. I'm supposed to meet Allison at the library at three to study."

"Oh wow, sorry, man. I just remembered what I was supposed to tell you. Allison called."

"Thanks, Rolf. What would I do without you," I said sarcastically.

"That's too bad, I guess. You'll miss your first demonstration. It would've been a gas to have you there."

"I'll still make it. This is important. I just have to stop off at the library to tell Allison I'll study with her later tonight or something. You want to take my sign, and I'll meet you over there?"

"No problem," he said. We quickly bundled back up for the cold weather and headed down to the street. Rolf looked like a soldier in his green army jacket and the signs perched on his right shoulder as if carrying a rifle.

"I'll meet you there in a few minutes," I said. We were both heading in the same direction across campus, as the library was on the way to the registrar's office where the rally was going to be, but I took off running to catch Allison. It hadn't snowed in a couple of days, but there were still some leftover piles from the last storm, particularly between the street and the sidewalk where the plows had deposited them, and also a few patches of ice covered the walkway. It was awkward trying to run in boots, but from my winter experiences as a kid, to have a little fun, I took a couple of calculated slide steps on the ice patches.

When I got to the library steps, I stopped to catch my frozen breath before searching for Allison. She found me first.

"Tom! There you are. I've been looking all over for you." She gave me a kiss that I could barely feel due to the numbness of my face. Running had made the wind bite a bit harder. I also could barely feel her hug through the layers of our clothes. "Let's head inside so that we can warm up and get started."

"Actually, I was just hoping to catch you here to ask if we can get together later tonight to study. Rolf and I were headed over to the registrar's for a protest rally this afternoon."

"What?" An incredulous look appeared on her face.

"It's a big demonstration to protest them giving out grades to Selective Service."

"I know," she said. "I heard about it. But why do you have to go?"

"Because, it's important for me to voice my opinion to be heard on this issue. I just can't sit back forever and expect things to work out the way I want without ever taking any action myself."

"What has gotten into you lately?" she asked. "You already forgot about meeting me for lunch last week. Now, you've forgotten again and made other plans, haven't you?"

"I didn't forget," I said, not being entirely truthful. I could've said I didn't forget completely.

"What's the matter, then? Don't you want to see me anymore?" Now she was looking hurt.

"Of course I do," I said, trying to reassure her. "But things like this protest are important. There are bigger issues than just you and me, and they are bound to affect us. We have to stop being provincial in our thinking and start seeing the big picture."

"What big picture? And how does any of this affect you, or us?"

"It definitely affects me, and because it does affect me, it will affect you, too. You don't want me to get drafted, do you?"

"No, of course not. But you have your deferment. You don't have to worry about getting drafted now."

"But I do! With the current policy in place, if my grades slipped, I could be subject to the draft."

"But why worry about it?" she pleaded. "Why not study hard, like with me today, and keep your grades up so that you won't have to worry about the draft?"

"Because, it's so arbitrary. When Selective Service needs a bigger draft pool, and they will need one for as long as the war continues, they'll simply change the standards and close loopholes. And that's what they did with the deferments. It used to be that they didn't even look at anyone going to college, but they're desperate for men and are looking for ways to find more all the time." I realized how much I was sounding like Rolf when he was trying to convince me to get more involved. I was repeating a lot of the same arguments he used on me, but they were true, and me reflecting these points back to Allison made me think how right it was to be involved in this fight.

"And even if I did as you say," I continued, "and got straight A's and didn't get drafted, how could I, in good conscience, sit back and watch the hundreds of students who will be affected by the policy get shipped off to Vietnam, while I'm safe and cozy in my dorm room? That's why when we win this fight, we have to continue to the next one and get the draft abolished all together."

"Do you think you'll be able to do that?"

"We definitely won't if we don't take some action and at least get our voices heard. You know this war could still be going on when I graduate, and I could be drafted and sent off to die just as I'm starting my life, when I'm ready to start a family, with you. But, you know, I need to stop thinking just about how this affects me or us. There are people dying over there today as we speak. We have to stop being selfish and see if we can't do something about the people who will surely die tomorrow. There are rights and wrongs involved here. And this war is definitely wrong."

"I-I never heard you talk this way before," Allison said, taken aback a little. "I never knew you felt like this before."

"I didn't know that I did either, until just recently, when I started really thinking about it. I kind of avoided thinking about it mostly. And I can't do that anymore and be Pollyanna and say everything is going to be okay."

"Well, I can see how important this is to you. Go to the rally and tell me all about it later. You still want to study later?"

"Yes, absolutely," I said, hopefully reassuring her that it wasn't a choice between her and the demonstration. "I still need to study to accomplish all my goals, and our goals." I smiled at her until she smiled back. "How about eight o'clock tonight at the study hall in your dorm?"

"Okay, I'll see you then, my little rabble-rouser."

At that moment, I thought how wonderful it was to have her as a girl-friend, so supportive and understanding. I mean, I thought I was finally beginning to act like a man, making stands on issues and such. And I left her at the library in good conscience to head off to the demonstration.

I only had a few more blocks to go down Commonwealth Avenue. When I saw the crowd of people in front of the Registrar's Office, I was impressed by the turnout. It wasn't too hard to locate Rolf in the throng because of the signs, and I followed them to him. He was talking with a few other people when I walked up.

"Tom! You made it," Rolf said. "Great. Things are just getting started." He handed my sign to me.

One of the guys in the group told me, "Good sign, I must say."

"Oh, Tom," Rolf said, "these are a couple of friends of mine I met at SDS. This is Bill, Nelson and Reefer." To the others he said, "This is my roommate, Tom Moore."

"Reefer?" I questioned as I shook his hand. The other fellows looked like typical college kids, like myself, limiting their signs of rebellion to letting their hair grow a little long, but this guy had wildly tousled hair, round, silver-framed spectacles and a Vandyke beard that made him look a lot like Leon Trotsky.

"That's what everyone calls me," he replied. "Actually, my name is Henry Riefenstahl. But Reefer fits." He grinned as the others chuckled. "So how come we haven't seen you at any meetings yet?"

"Oh, I guess I'm still trying to get acclimated to university life," I said without going into detail about my real reasons.

"Well, you should stop in next time with Rolfie, here," he said, trying to recruit, as I heard they often do.

"I just might," I said, still not sure how involved with them I wanted to get, but I did want to do more and know more about the anti-war movement.

"So, what are you studying?" Reefer probed me.

"Aeronautical Engineering," I told him proudly, almost expecting him to be somewhat impressed. "I hope to work for NASA someday."

"Boy, you must surely want to become one of *them*, don't you?" he said.

"What do you mean?" I asked, not sure what he was insinuating.

"You know? *Them*." He gestured vaguely to the Registrar's building. "The problem. The power structure. The military-industrial complex, man. I mean, what do you think aeronautical engineers do, anyway?"

"Well, they can do different things, but I'm interested in it as a scientific endeavor. You know, space exploration, things like that." I felt as if he thought I might be some sort of spy.

"Maybe you should wake up and smell the bacon, buddy boy," Reefer said incredulously, not mean-spirited. "They design planes and rockets, which are tools of war. Like weapon delivery systems. That space exploration bullshit is just a smoke-screen. They're snowing you if you think they're spending billions of dollars on the idealism of scientific research."

"Hey, man. He's not like that," Rolf piped in, defending my honor. "He's cool, or he wouldn't be here."

"Of course, of course," Reefer said jovially. "I don't mean nothing by it. If Rolfie says you're cool, you're cool with me. Besides, you're a freshman. What do you know? You'll learn as you go, though."

It was kind of a shock for me to think that what I wanted to do wasn't respected by my peers, so to speak. I didn't take offense to him, but I was stunned, and he got me thinking that not everyone sees things from my perspective. But I was eager to learn people's different viewpoints and their unique realms of consciousness. He had no lack of conviction, either, as I had at times, and I admired him instantly for that.

The crowd was beginning to swell in size now. Our little sub-group joined the picket-procession-line that marched back and forth in front of the office doors. Partly, it may have been to keep warm, but also to garner the attention of anyone walking in or out of the building and plead our case. I wouldn't have known which person we needed to seek out.

A couple of students led the crowd in chants, and as I joined in, I felt exhilarated by the degree of unity our voices achieved. At first, I basically spoke the sing-song phrases being offered up, but as I felt the energy of a hundred or more voices along with mine, I fed off that power and shouted forcefully. We came to be heard, after all, and they were going to listen, or we'd continue to vociferate until the metaphoric walls of Jericho came tumbling down.

The small patch of lawn in front was becoming more tightly packed, and we were no longer a picket line anymore, but re-merged into a crowd, and I got slightly separated from Rolf and the others. Some people in the rear of the multitude spilled off the walk in between the parked cars on the street.

Someone from inside the Registrar's Office came out of the door and tried to speak to us, but I couldn't hear what he said. From the reactions of the people up front, it wasn't positive. When he walked back into the office, a couple of the student leaders followed and waved for others to join them, while the word filtered back that we were going to have a sit-in to force the issue, which I thought was a pretty big step. We simply weren't peacefully assembling anymore; we were moving on to trespassing, an offense susceptible to arrest.

Not everyone followed inside the office, and a majority, including myself, remained outside, waiting for some kind of impulse on what to do next. We were there to argue our points, but since there was no one to listen, we weren't sure of what to do. Different small groups were chanting their own slogans, but mostly they canceled each other out.

Then, as the crowd was just beginning to lose its group dynamic, the police showed up to galvanize this mass back into shape. The cops suddenly became our *raison d'etre*. At first, they were trying to clear people off the street, as they were partially blocking traffic now. Then, as the officers filtered to the front of our little swarm to assess the sit-in situation, they urged us to disperse. There were at least twenty cops on the scene that I could see, preparing to restore order to the structure of the world we lived in. They probably weren't even aware of why we were there. They just knew we shouldn't have been there right then.

A police front man got up on the steps to the office to speak to the crowd, as a phalanx of other officers formed behind him. "Listen up!" he said, his authoritative voice crackling over his hand-held loudspeaker. "We are asking for your cooperation here. You are being asked to calmly and peaceably disperse this gathering." He lowered his bullhorn by his side and looked out over the crowd for its reaction. Mostly we looked back at him blankly. A couple of people shouted something at him, but it was unintelligible to me.

"This is an illegal assembly," he began again. "If you do not disperse immediately, we will be forced—" Something distracted my attention for a moment out of the left corner of my eye. An object flew through the air, and once identified, my scientific mind automatically judged speed and trajectory to determine the likely point of landing. The officer was still speaking when a medium-sized snowball came from beyond his field of vision and hit him squarely in the jaw. The impact tilted his head like a boxer had just landed a solid left hook.

"What the—? Who threw that?" The disoriented and stunned cop looked at the crowd in disbelief and then to his men behind him. Either his face was ruddy from his blood boiling or the icy snow made his face raw.

Laughter erupted from our mob of protesters, and, to my amazement, a dozen more snowballs were launched in the direction of the policemen. I thought, are those people nuts? They were throwing injurious projectiles at men who had weapons of mass destruction. If I wasn't a bit frightened by that fact, I think I would have laughed at the notion that our lofty, idealistic protest degenerated into a snowball fight with the cops.

The police started grabbing people, and I'm not sure if they were going after people they had thought were the throwers. The less-dedicated amongst us began vacating the scene. I was one of them, but being in the middle of the throng, I couldn't move immediately. I thought that this definitely was not what it was about for me. Some people were taking parting shots from behind me. I heard shouts of "Eat snow, pigs!" from the rear as another snowball sailed over my head. I slowly backed my way out, still watching the unfolding drama before me when I was plunked with a snowball. I thought, forget the drama, and I dropped my sign to leave more quickly.

In front of me now, my escape was interrupted by one guy who had just eluded the grasp of a cop, who was looking quite peeved for missing. Cold air vapor streamed from the cop's nostrils like a raging bull, and he looked my way. He was a mountain of a man, and I turned to run, but I slipped on a patch of ice. I was face down on the ground when I felt a meaty hand grab my shoulder, and it lifted me back to my feet, and for a moment, I actually was lifted slightly higher than my feet could reach for the ground.

"That's enough. Get up," the cop said gruffly. "And drop that snow."

I looked down at my hand and saw the snow he was referring to, that I had clutched when I landed on the ground. I shook it off as if it were an insect crawling on me.

"I wasn't throwing any of the snowballs, I swear." Right after I said that, I understood why pleas of innocence often ended up sounding so lame.

"Tell someone who cares," the officer replied. He pushed me ahead of him, holding on to the collar of my coat as if I were a little puppy dog being lifted up by the scruff of the neck after soiling a new rug, and he deposited me in front of the police paddy wagon on the street. He frisked me and told me I was under arrest for disorderly conduct, unlawful assembly and assault on a police officer.

"I didn't do any of that!" I protested. "I was just in the crowd." He only responded by cuffing my hands and leading into the back of the wagon. My mind was in a state of disbelief. I actually was going to jail?

"Tom! Bro, over here," a voice came from amongst the other people in custody in the wagon. I looked through the faces and finally recognized Reefer. "You made it," he said, as if he were expecting me to show up there. "Hey, man, make some room," he said to others sitting next to him, and they moved so that I could sit beside him.

"I can't believe it. I'm going to jail," I said more to myself than to Reefer.

"Don't sweat it, man," he told me. "I've been arrested a bunch of times like this. It's nothing."

"What am I going to tell my father?" I said aloud to myself again when that thought suddenly occurred to me.

"Hey, listen. When you get your phone call, do not call your old man," Reefer told me emphatically. "I have a cousin who's a lawyer who helps me out in these situations. I'll get him to help you, too, so that you won't have to tell your old man a thing if you don't want to. My cousin can post bail for us if we need it. But, you know, most of the time they drop the charges before the night's through, anyway. Just don't sweat a thing. Relax."

"I can't believe it. I'm actually going to jail," I said again, as if I didn't even hear a word of what Reefer had just said. "What am I going to tell my father?"

VERSE 3:

"I once had a girl, or should I say, she once had me."
Lennon-McCartney

*"Somebody calls you, you answer quite slowly,
The girl with kaleidoscope eyes."*
Lennon-McCartney

Basically, things worked out just as **Reefer** had explained to me. When we were placed in lockup, we were offered our chance of making a phone call. I passed. Reefer called his cousin, and we waited for him to arrive. For the first time in my life, I experienced intense claustrophobia in our cell, which we shared with ten other people. I felt the urge to walk out of the room, but knew I couldn't. I was caged.

Reefer finally met with his lawyer cousin, who said he was preparing to bail us out, but when he started talking about *habeas corpus*, the police dropped the charges, and we were released outright.

Rolf, who hadn't been arrested, had come downtown to check on us with Reefer's other pals, Bill and Nelson, and we gathered on the outside steps of the police station. The three non-jailbirds seemed impressed with our incarceration, and pumped us for information. Still, I was stunned by the ordeal and didn't say much, while Reefer felt triumphant and regaled them.

"My easiest stretch of time yet," Reefer concluded.

"Hey, Tom, how was it, man, your first time?" Rolf asked me.

"I'm just glad it worked out in the end. I'd hate to have that on my record simply for trying to make a statement."

"Hey, whatever it takes, my man." Reefer put his arm on my shoulder. "Sometimes you have to stand up to the power, face it down, even if it means being beaten down and jailed by the pigs, before they'll listen to what you have to say, man. There are a lot of people out there," he swept his hand outward to the surrounding city, "who don't believe in freedom of speech, especially when the voices happen to disagree with theirs. It takes sacrifice and sometimes you even have to lay your body on the line. That's what our brothers in 'Nam are doing, and if we fight with the same principles and determination of soldiers, we will eventually win."

I was enthralled with the strength of his convictions, and he was swaying me to be more steadfast myself. In comparison, I knew I was being soft, and was almost ready to shrink away after my first confrontation of theory versus reality. At that moment, I was worried that I was just another liberal intellectual who wanted my ideals to fit perfectly into my theoretical world. But no one lived in my theoretical world except for me.

"Hey, Reef," Nelson addressed him, "there was an executive committee meeting, while you guys were in, to get regrouped and update the progress of the demonstration, and they got word that there's a group of professors who'll join in the protest if the policy isn't changed. They say they'll give everyone of their students A's because they don't want to be responsible for being the difference in a guy being drafted."

"That's great news, man." Reefer turned back to me and said, "See what I mean about laying it on the line? See what a little civil disobedience and resistance can do? You slow down the wheels a little bit, some sand in the gears, so to speak, and eventually they are going to stop."

"A bunch of guys said they're heading over to the Pink House for a little soiree," Bill said.

"We are there, my friend," Reefer announced and bounded down the steps, as the others followed.

"So, I'll see you guys later." I turned to walk back to my dorm. Rolf turned back to me, and the group waited a moment.

"Tom, you're invited, too, man. It's a party up in Cambridge. It'll be a trip."

"No, thanks. I think I want to head home and go to sleep after everything today." I looked at my watch. It was 9:30 p.m., but I was beat.

"Tom, my man," Reefer interjected. "You've just been liberated. You've been set free, and you're going to cage yourself back up. Come on. Think of it as a little victory celebration of a good day's work. You were a big part of it. I'd like to introduce you to some people. Maybe you can get a better idea of what we do."

It felt nice that I was being considered part of their group now. If I felt on the fringe at the moment, however, maybe going to the party might help me get involved a little deeper and strengthen my resolve. So I accepted.

We took the Red Line of the MBTA subway to cross over the Charles River into Cambridge. I simply followed the crowd as we left Harvard Square and traveled a few blocks into the residential area surrounding the Harvard University campus, eventually stopping before a large, pink house. I later learned that before the building was painted pink, it was still called the "Pink House." It had been an old fraternity house from the Twenties and Thirties, and when the frat boys eventually moved on to newer digs, the place was sold to one of the leading Socialist activists in the area, who turned the house into an informal party headquarters, which earned it the name the "pinko house," or "pink house" by sarcastic neighbors, who heard rumors about the goings on there. The owner took the moniker to heart and subsequently painted it a shocking pink to remove all doubts. After the woman died, and ownership changed hands a few times, the house still leaned to the left, so to speak, and served as a kind of haven or outpost for bohemian types, poets, writers and musicians. Politics may have waned during the Fifties and early Sixties, but the house was thought to be returning to its roots in recent years.

When we arrived, a few partygoers who occupied the front steps and porch were openly smoking marijuana cigarettes and drinking beer. Reefer led the way into the house, as he waved to this person or acknowledged that person. The main room was large, with a high ceiling and a winding staircase in the middle leading to the different living quarters upstairs.

An unnerving mix of sitar music and Grateful Dead songs came from different directions. The subdued lighting was multicolored and transmuting, while a projector cast images of free-flowing amoeba-shapes onto one wall, and a smoky haze hung in the air.

Rolf leaned close to me and said, "Hey, if anyone offers you a drink, you should probably stay away from the Kool-Aid."

"Okay," I responded. But my only thought at the time was how funny it seemed for the hip crowd to be serving such an innocuously square beverage.

Reefer introduced me to a few people who were there. They would ask me what my politics were, and I would say I'm not sure that I had any yet, and they would say that I should attend this meeting or another, and that they could always use more people. I would say that I might just do that. Then I was left to mingle or wander when discussions between Reefer and his pals got deeper and more concentrated. I looked around for Rolf to chat with, but I didn't see him. I went to get a draft from the beer keg and walked around feeling lost and slightly out of place.

As I squeezed past one group engaged in a discussion, my attention was grabbed by the woman ostensibly holding court there. There were a number of women at the party, but they seemed more a part of the decoration, while the men were involved more in the group discussions. Most of the other women were quirkily gyrating to the music, or hanging out, looking a bit spacey. This woman's guise wasn't much different than the others, yet she seemed quite unusual, in an attractive way. She wore hip-hugging corduroy jeans, a loose-fitting blouse with long, flowing sleeves, and her midriff bare. Several strands of love beads draped around her slender neck, and a brunette mane of wanton, tempestuous curls framed her resplendent face.

She sat cross-legged on a velvet pillow, took a drag from an Indian-style peace pipe and passed it off to the group seated in a semi-circle around her. As I slowly ambled by, I heard what she was saying, in a way, lecturing.

"If the U.S. views the Tet offensive as a futile and last-ditch effort by the NVA and Viet Cong, they are in for a rude awakening," she surmised. "If they only think of body counts and objectives attained or defended, they will fail to see what looms on the horizon, or better yet, what lies below the surface of the horizon. Tet is just the tip of the iceberg."

"But won't the losses mount up to eventually lead to a breaking point?" one of the engrossed listeners countered.

"The losses mount up to eventually lead to higher resolve and determination," she said.

"Won't higher fire power eventually overcome higher resolve in the end?" another parried.

"Tet shows that this is not a frontal war. The U.S. might have the bigger fly-swatter, but when it swats at a swarm of gnats, it has little effect other than to stir the swarm. They won't be allowed to sit safely in the South. Let them draw a line, call it the DMZ, and say don't cross this line. The gnats are swarming, my friends." She spoke in a professorial tone that gave the impression of a deeper understanding of the situation.

When she wasn't speaking, the woman had a beatific look on her face, as if she were totally at peace. As I sashayed on by and back across the room, I found myself glancing back toward her angelic visage. Reefer walked up to me and asked if I was enjoying myself.

"Yes. It's a very interesting place," I said. "I was just wondering, though, who is that over there?" I pointed to the Buddha-esque woman who caught my eye.

"Ah, you have a good eye," Reefer said. "That's Lorelei. She's one of the residents here. She's sort of the 'Queen Bee' of this 'Hive.' I should introduce you to her. She really knows the score."

Reefer waved to the woman to come over as Nelson and Bill joined us. She broke up her little flock and mingled with our group.

"Lorelei, my lady love. How have you been?" Reefer embraced her and kissed her on the cheek.

"Not bad, Reef. Are you being a good boy and getting into trouble?" she replied.

"Yeah, as a matter of fact, I got busted today, stirring up the masses. We had a good demonstration before it was broken up, but I think we got some action going on it. And I'd like to introduce you to someone who was active with us and in jail with me. This is Tom Moore."

"Oh, Thomas Moore, like the Irish poet?" Lorelei said.

"Yes, I guess so, although I'm not really named after him." I was aware of my namesake through high school English, but didn't know much about him. "Sometimes people will say, 'Oh, like the guy who wrote *Utopia*, which of course is Thomas More, but I'm surprised you've heard of the other."

"Yes, I'm a fan of *Irish Melodies*, but also, More has had quite an influence on me," she said.

Nelson lit up a joint, took a drag and passed it to Bill, who passed it to Reefer.

"I haven't seen you around before, but you're involved in the movement?" Lorelei asked me.

"Well, I guess you could say that I just got my feet wet today." Reefer passed the joint to Lorelei, who took a hit, held her breath and slowly exhaled the smoke. She then handed it to me but I didn't reach for it.

"You smoke?" she asked.

"Actually, no. I never have."

"Never?"

"No." I was already feeling a little light-headed from all the smoke around me, but it felt the same as when I first tried regular cigarettes in high school. I heard that marijuana was a hallucinogen, so I wasn't sure if I was getting any of the same effects as from smoking it, but I had been reluctant to try it to find out what the difference was.

"You aren't a narc, are you?" Lorelei smiled broadly, so I thought she wasn't actually suspecting me.

"No. I just decided not to use it, as a personal decision. Like not smoking regular cigarettes."

"That's cool," she said and took another hit, before passing it back around the way it came. "But I find it lets my mind loose to think about things in all new ways. Are you in college?"

"Yes, BU. Freshman."

"Ah, you've got a lot to learn. But just like you're going to college to expand your mind, pot is just one more way to expand the horizons of your thinking. The problem with college is that they will try to expand your thinking only in the way they see fit, while our movement wants to expand people's minds in any direction they choose, or multiple directions."

Lorelei leaned close to me, smiling a bit flirtatiously, "If you ever change your mind, as John Lennon says, 'I'd love to tur-ur-ur-n you-ou-ou-ou ow-ow-ow-on.'"

I just stood there a little dazed. I was surprised that I was turned on to her charm. She excused herself from our group and disappeared into the crowd. Even though it was a brief flash, it was the first time I thought of someone else besides Allison. Then that made me think of Allison, and for the first time that night, I remembered that I was supposed to meet her again to study. Being in jail distracted me so that I forgot all about it. I knew that she was going to be steamed the next time I saw her. I finally spotted Rolf dancing with another hippie chick. I didn't want to spoil his evening, but feeling a bit guilty, I wanted to tell him I was going home. He said he understood, and I left him there to practice his psychedelic mating dance.

Allison was quite upset that I missed our study date that evening. That I was forcibly detained tempered things somewhat, but she still felt that I should have thought enough about her to call. I did feel bad about that. The incident gradually faded away into the past as the semester continued. But as I did become more involved in extracurricular activities, eventually going to an SDS meeting with Rolf and various protest rallies, which Allison didn't wish to participate in, she and I drifted apart as our interests diverged.

Allison wasn't totally blind to what was happening around us, though. She talked about the both of us working for the campaign of Robert Kennedy. We didn't follow through during the spring because, we wondered, how much help does a Kennedy need to win in Massachusetts, anyway? But if the campaign moved into the fall, we still contemplated the idea, as we might be able to offer some kind of help in a national contest.

Allison was also visibly saddened when Martin Luther King, Jr. was assassinated on the Fourth of April. She attended a candlelight vigil with me mourning Dr. King that evening in the Boston Common. We couldn't understand what was going on in recent times, why people with true vision were thought to be so dangerous that they had to be killed, especially why men of peace had to meet such violent ends. I knew that Dr. King took inspiration from Gandhi about non-violent protests, and I wondered if it was simply inevitable that he had died in the same fashion. I felt close to Allison that night as we held each other and sang plaintive songs to his memory. But when the semester ended later that month, Allison told me she wanted to go back home for the summer. I told her I wanted to stay in Boston because there was so much more to do, and I wanted to get even more involved with the protests.

She didn't participate in a national boycott of classes that April because she was too concerned about how it might affect her grades. She didn't seem to understand how important it was for me, and she barely said a word to me as I saw her off at the bus station. I told her that I would come home in a couple weeks for a visit, but she acted as if she didn't care whether I did or not.

To stay in my dorm during the summer, I had to take at least one class, so I signed up for a required American literature class. Just a light summer of reading, I figured, and I would be freer to pursue my other ventures.

The first part of May was a rather quiet time in Boston. The city didn't have the kind of unrest from the black communities as in other big cities like Chicago, Detroit, Baltimore. I spent a lot of time with Rolf, hanging out or going to more meetings. As I had been fraternizing more with Rolf's crowd, I had been thinking for several weeks that I wanted to try marijuana, which was pervasive in the group. I had been reluctant in the past because I didn't like to smoke to begin with, but I was a bit afraid of it, not knowing what it truly did. But I likened it to the first time I tried alcohol. I couldn't fully understand the feeling it gave without experiencing it for myself, and then I could make an informed judgment on whether it was worthwhile or not. Having seen its effects on Rolf and others who used it very casually, I equated it with alcohol, and the fear factor subsided. It was an illegal substance, however, but still not much different from alcohol, as I was still not of legal drinking age at that point, but had imbibed for a couple of years, back into high school. So, I approached Rolf with the idea of trying some as a very controlled experiment. I didn't want to do it at a party where I might be self-conscious being a first-timer in front of veteran smokers. And public spaces had their own dilemmas of being surprised by someone out of nowhere. Even though I had reservations about it, our dorm room was the only place I could feel comfortable enough to try it.

The night that I was ready, Rolf set up the room for atmosphere as we sat in front of the open window, the warm, spring air gently flowing from Rolf's bedroom window to the common room window with the aid of a fan. He set a few of his record albums to play—the Who, Rolling Stones, Jimi Hendrix, Bob Dylan and the Beatles—and used red lamps to dim the light, giving me the impression of a darkroom for developing photos. He took an album cover in his lap and piled on some grass from his stash, and showed me how to separate the seeds from the weed with a playing card. He also brought out a bong, as he reasoned that since I didn't normally smoke, the water pipe cooled the smoke before inhaling it to mellow it out. I had seen a few people using the bongs before, and the gurgling noises that they made with the water made me think they were slurping some kind of beverage from a straw. But Rolf demonstrated first as he packed the bowl, lit it on fire and took a hit. He coached me on proper procedures, like inhaling deeply and holding my breath for the quickest effect.

I drew my first toke, as Rolf had to help me light it. I began to feel the burn as I trapped the smoke in my lungs. I thought, how cool can you make smoke anyway? I fought the urge to cough it out, and released it through my mouth.

"How is it? Pretty good, huh?" Rolf asked after I exhaled. I didn't experience the good yet, but I responded, "Yeah." We took turns, trading the bong back and forth. While waiting for any effects to kick in, I saw the lights from Fenway, and I wondered if my dad was watching the game on television. He was a bit disappointed that I hadn't wanted to work with him that summer as I had the last. But I felt I was just starting to grow, and if I had gone home for the summer, I would regress and feel like a little kid again. And I didn't want that feeling anymore.

The first change that I experienced was that all the anxiety I was feeling beforehand about concealing the fact that I was going to smoke marijuana simply melted away. I don't think I felt anything more than a light head, but I felt very relaxed about everything: Allison, my father, school, the war. I

wasn't consciously thinking about those things, but I knew the way I was han-
dling them was the right way. I was in control of my life. I didn't feel like a
naïve adolescent, oblivious to the nuances of the world. I could get what I
wanted in life if I just stayed in control.

Rolf and I just shot the bull about nonsensical stuff, Arthur Fiedler
conducting guest soloist Jimi Hendrix, Bill Russell lacing up a pair of skates
and playing for the Bruins, Topogigio flipping off Ed Sullivan, having sex
with Linda Bird Johnson. Other moments we were silent, listening intently
to a particular song that was playing. At one point, I looked out the window
up at a sliver of the moon and thought about the Russians who were orbiting
it at the time. It didn't frighten me as it did some other people. I thought
about floating in weightlessness, about looking down from the cosmonauts'
perspective. Going to bed a little later that night, I dreamt of trips I might
make in the future to build a moon station, where we would eventually launch
missions to Mars or beyond. Each step we made now in space exploration
would be a building block to make such things possible, I thought, within my
lifetime.

After that night, I would not decline the next offer of reefer at a party
or a rally, but nonchalantly would take a few drags to show I was hip to the
scene. If I wasn't offered any, I didn't go looking for it. I enjoyed the sensations it provided, but I hated the smoke, which may have doomed me to being
square. Although, as I soon found out, there were other ways to turn on.

Hanging around Rolf and his pals led me to another party at the Pink
House early that summer. It had been a few months, and I hadn't thought
about Lorelei while going in, but when I spotted her there, I recalled our previous meeting, and again I was mesmerized. My eyes followed her around
the main room as she flitted about.

She wore an Indian buckskin dress with leather fringes, more beads,
moccasins and headband, lacking only the eagle feather sticking out from the
back to complete the costume. I felt a little childish as I would quickly avert

my eyes if she would cast a glance my way. She eventually worked her way around the room and approached me anyway. I wanted to say something to her again, and was about to come out with something lame, such as, "Hi, do you remember me?" She caught me by surprise, though, when she warmly greeted me.

"Ah, Mr. Moore, our Utopian," she announced.

"The Irish melodist, actually," I said. "But you can call me Tom."

"Of course, Tom, I remember. I was just kidding you. I haven't seen you around here in a while. Have you been staying active?"

"I suppose you could say so," I told her. "I've been going to different meetings with my roommate, doing some pamphleteering around campus, that sort of thing, but I'm not real active yet, I guess."

"If you're interested in something *really* active, some of the guys around here are organizing a trip to Chicago this summer for the Democratic National Convention. They're expecting a major convergence from all over the country to show up there to finally get the message through loud and clear to these namby-pamby politicians to do something about stopping this war. I guess going to the Republican Convention is a moot point. Republicans never met a war they didn't like."

"That sounds like an excellent idea," I said, at the time thinking that it was. But I never got enough gumption to say that I was going to go, and inadvertently avoided getting swept up in a very ugly scene there that summer. But I still sounded interested. "You can't get much more political than that."

Lorelei took out a joint from a pouch in her dress and fired it up, and after taking her tokes, offered it to me. When I calmly took the cigarette and took a drag, I looked for a reaction from her, but perhaps she didn't remember my anti-smoking stance, or else she remembered but didn't care to comment as she continued to share back and forth as we talked.

"So, you're part of the BU crowd, right?" she asked.

"Right. I'm sort of on summer break, but I am taking one class while

I'm trying to get more involved."

"What class are you taking?"

"American Literature, 19th Century."

"Who are you reading?" she asked while holding an inhale of smoke.

"The usual, I guess, Cooper, Melville, Twain."

"So typical," Lorelei said in exhaling stream. "Like it would kill them to teach anyone with some semblance of relevance. Are they teaching any Thoreau?"

"Not this particular class. But in high school we read a few passages from *Walden*. 'The mass of men lead lives of quiet desperation,' and that sort of thing."

"What should be required reading for every student in any college today should be Thoreau's essay, 'On the Duty of Civil Disobedience.' 'The mass of men serve the state thus, not as men mainly, but as machines, with their bodies. They are the standing army, and the militia, jailers, constables —' Do you read anyone more current and relevant? Kerouac, Ginsberg, Burroughs, Kafka, Sartre, Camus?"

"Are you a student?" I questioned, eager to know a few more personal details about her.

"I was," she answered, mystically leaving blank a bit of her history. She only added, "I was a conformist once. When I went to college like all the other good little girls and boys, they failed to teach me anything useful, so I decided to teach myself."

"Well, no, I haven't read those authors yet. But I have read a few more recent books by Hemingway, Steinbeck and Salinger."

"Agh, they're all so safe, no doubt approved and endorsed by your friendly, neighborhood English teacher freak who wouldn't want to risk allowing a garden-fresh thought to enter your head. I could give you a short reading list that would completely open your mind to new possibilities and teach you to think for yourself, and, thus, you would learn more than you ever could in that class you're taking now."

I dumbly looked around the room, not knowing how to continue the conversation, when she smiled coquettishly at me and said, "Have you ever listened to 'White Rabbit' while taking psilocybin?"

"No," I said, perhaps not making clear that I had never taken psilocybin mushrooms, instead of never listening to the song while doing it. Lorelei didn't ask me if I wanted to, but she took me by the hand and gently tugged me along as she said, "Come on with me. It's a pretty cool trip."

My mouth didn't protest or object, nor my legs. I continued to follow submissively behind her in silence, as she led me through the mass of people and then up the stairs to her room. I hadn't consented yet, either, but I was torn between the fear of taking a psychedelic drug with unknown consequences and the excitement of exploring a new world of wonder with this beguiling female guide.

The room that she brought me into reminded me more of the inside of Jeannie's bottle than a bedroom. In place of actual furniture were satin-covered cushions grouped on the floor, and a variety of warm-colored chiffon draperies adorned the walls. Also, I had my first sighting of a lava lamp. Lorelei seated me on one of the cushions as she made some preparations tending to a tea kettle on a hot plate.

"I know a lot of people just eat the mushrooms," she said, "but I've brewed my own special 'tea' from them, if you'd like to try it?" In keeping with Alice's tea party, I supposed.

I was getting too close to the point of no return, and I felt I needed to confess my naïveté, lest it become embarrassingly obvious. "Um, in all honesty, I've never actually tripped before. I'm not sure about this."

"Really? No 'shrooms? Acid either?"

"No."

"Angel dust?"

"No."

"Silly me for assuming then. But there's nothing to worry about or anything to lose, except for rigid, old-fashioned thinking. But I'll tell you what, for your first trip, I won't trip with you, so that I can guide you along. I sense that you are an adventurous spirit and a seeker of truth and knowledge, and I can show you an interesting little side path to take. Besides this is the best thing to experiment with. I'm not big into the other psychedelics because they are man-made chemicals, and you can't always trust them. Mushrooms are natural stuff, though. People have been taking them for centuries. It's just that modern man has forgotten how to coexist with nature, and has lost a lot of ancient wisdom. Now there are a few people who have found how to tap back into that store of knowledge, and it seems even more wondrous because of the depths the spirit has fallen."

I just looked on dumbly as Lorelei poured me a cup of tea. After returning the kettle to the hot plate, she pulled out her copy of the Jefferson Airplane's *Surrealistic Pillow* album and placed it on her phonograph.

"It'll take a few minutes for the effect to really kick in, so I'll play the song when you've started your trip. It's kind of cool knowing I'm welcoming a neophyte on his first journey to a higher plain of enlightenment."

I looked up at Lorelei and down to the mysterious brown liquid in the cup. I knew that whatever I experienced, I would not be the same person I was going into the party that night. And that suddenly appealed to me. I had no way of knowing if this was the first step down the slippery slope of other drugs, but I was trusting I was strong enough to resist that path. And seeing that it seemed not to have any detrimental effects on the provocative woman who stood before me, my scientific side was willing to delve into the experiment, which is not to say I still was wholly eager. A certain amount of trepidation still remained when I brought the cup up close to my lips, and I may have noticeably trembled before sipping that pungent potion. While expecting the more familiar mushroom taste, instead I sensed the flavor of tree bark, although I had never ingested that either, nor desired to.

"You'll really need to finish it up to get the good effects," Lorelei instructed me. I blew a few times across the surface of the steaming tea to where I could take a few more healthy swigs. I almost gagged on the smell and taste of it nearing the bottom of the cup, and after ingesting it all, I looked down at my stomach and wondered if it would rebel against me. I think I was trying to be aware of any new sensations I was about to feel.

"It takes a few minutes to experience the first effects," Lorelei told me. "You should just relax. Lie back a little bit. Let it come to you. Just let me know when you first start to feel something."

I did just that, resigned to the fact that no matter what I did now, something was going to happen to me. I couldn't stop it if I wanted. So, I lay back and waited. The only sensation I experienced in the first couple of minutes was revulsion of the aftertaste still left in my mouth. Lorelei looked the part of mad scientist, looking me over, waiting to see how her experiment turned out. I looked up at her and then noticed something peculiar. It was as if I were looking down a tube or a tunnel at her, with my peripheral vision being stretched out and lengthened, while she was in focus at the center, but she was a bit smaller now, though I sensed that she was still seated across from me.

"Whoa, I think it's starting to work," I said, noticing a slight echo as well. "You look so far away."

"Excellent. No, I'm right here. Just continue to relax. I'll just play some music for you."

She went to the turntable and I lifted my head a little to try to follow her with my eyes, and the tunnel effect was gone. I saw a more normal view of the room again. I looked around and the lava lamp caught my interest. The orange glow that emanated from it was amazingly vivid, as if I never had seen that color orange before. And the way the room was decorated starting making sense to me, as the array of colors were meant to intensify this phenomenon. Everything seemed more fascinating. I brought my hand up in front of my face, and it was as if I were looking at it through a magnifying glass. With astounding clarity and acuity, I viewed the ridges of my finger-prints in awe. If this was what it was about, I didn't know why everyone wouldn't be eager to try it. The eerie marching beats of the snare drum stepped into my head. I watched as Lorelei lit a joint, and I was fixated by the glowing red tip, watching it burn brightly then wane as she stopped in-haling. A smoke ring floated out of her mouth, and it looked like fun. I wanted to float just like that. It looked like something substantial, as if I could reach out, touch it and hold it. When I heard the word "caterpillar" in the song, the smoke ring turned into a caterpillar, and I withdrew my hand. It just smiled back at me, as it puffed on a water pipe. Visually, I wasn't in Lorelei's room anymore, but just some odd space with a checkerboard floor, but everything was at skewed angles. Different characters, such as the Red Queen and the White Knight, were inviting me to play a giant game of chess, where we served as the pieces. When the White Knight spoke, I saw words stream out its mouth with the letters spelling the words backwards. It seemed when I got some kind of suggestive image from the song, my mind created it visually, quite vividly. I felt a sense of panic when I felt as if Lorelei wasn't with me. I called out to her, but I couldn't even be sure if I did it vocally, or if it was just in my mind. I closed my eyes because I wanted to stop seeing things, but I still saw strange line patterns moving and flowing on the canvas that was the back of my eyelids. That changed to fractal patterns of intense colors and brightness, as if a kaleidoscope were in my head. A gnome-like voice called out to me, "We have been waiting for you to come. We have many interesting things to show you. Come, follow me." I couldn't even say if my eyes were open or closed at the time, but I saw the faint image of a little man-like creature ahead of me waving his arm, beckoning me to come forth. Then I saw a group of them, giggling and trying to coax me along. They dispersed and disappeared from view. I felt as if I were floating along, and I had the urge to look backward, and I saw the earth shrinking behind me as if I were heading out into space. I took a tour of the universe, but it was as if space weren't the usual black void, but rather alive with color. I zipped past planets and moons and comets and suns and stars. I freaked out a little later that year when I saw the motion picture *2001: A Space Odyssey* and witnessed strikingly similar sequences at the end, and I surmised that someone in the making of that film assuredly had taken a drug-induced trip. I visualized examples set forth in Einstein's Theory of Relativity, and I sensed that I understood them completely, how the faster I traveled to the speed of light time slowed down, and how my volume of matter increased toward infinity, and that I would become, literally, one with the universe. When I reached the speed of light, time stopped, and I stopped, and everything was eerily still. Nothing could move, because time was locked. I felt panicky that I was stuck in time forever. But my mind was still racing. If I were motionless, then I couldn't be traveling at light speed, and thus time would function as normal. But maybe I was still traveling at light speed, and perhaps I finally went beyond light speed because things began happening in reverse. In any event, time lost all its meaning. I don't know how long the trip took from start to finish, but I felt as if maybe years passed when the effects started wearing off.

When I recognized that I was still in Lorelei's room, I looked up and saw her gazing at me, smiling. I said, "Hello," as if I really had left and had just rejoined her. Then I felt so excited, and I talked her ear off as I wanted to try to relate everything I had witnessed. She told me a few things also, how I reacted at some points, that the trip lasted all of about 30 minutes. We talked halfway into the night. Looking back on the experience, though, I talked of the sense of learning deep things, feeling more enlightened at the time, but I realized that I really didn't learn anything that I could quantify and explain to someone else. I felt dumb trying to explain my impressions of that trip. I became convinced that it was simply the perception of enlightenment that was given by the mushroom, and it basically tempered my desire to try it again, as

I have yet to meet anyone else who could tell me anything they learned from a trip that made any sense, also. But at the time, I felt good about my bravery at facing the unknown and surviving intact. Although, I had to wonder, if say an Egyptian farmer in ancient times stumbled across some mushrooms growing out of his cattle's dung and he experimentally ingested them, what kind of visions would a man like that encounter? Wouldn't it blow his mind if he saw things he couldn't relate to his natural world? Perhaps in his visions he saw a pyramid shape for the first time, and it inspired him to create such a structure, thinking it was a message from the gods. Was what I experienced just an extension of my dreams of space exploration? Or does it bend perception in such a way to create new ideas. Was it magic mushrooms that helped cave-dwelling humans break out of their animalistic existence to imagine new and wondrous things, and thus strive for them into the future? It seems like progression of knowledge and imagination is self-perpetuating. As I feel most of what I know is based on the imaginations of all who have come before me, and I would feel no more able to take a step further into the realm of space travel than a caveman would without others setting me up on the platform of their prior knowledge.

As we both tired after talking of heady stuff, Lorelei suggested I simply crash where I was for the remainder of the night. I wondered how a trip like that would affect my dreams, but I think my brain was exhausted and took the night off. I slept soundly.

In the morning when I awoke and found Lorelei up, munching on a shredded wheat biscuit and sipping what I assumed was regular tea, I was about to thank her for a stimulating evening and head back to my dorm, but she asked me if I wanted to accompany her on a little errand.

"I find I'm in need of replenishing my supply of mushrooms, and there's this place I know where I harvest them, a quaint little cow pasture north of town. Would you like to join me, to keep me company?"

"Sure, I've got nothing else going on," I told her.

"Why buy from someone else when I know a place to get my own. And if I didn't harvest them, they might just go to waste."

"Of course," I said. She led me back downstairs, through the now deathly still house. It was just past the dawn hour, and it was the first time I saw the neighborhood in the light. The house revealed its wrinkles, so-to-speak, showing its age in the flaking paint and rusty screens. I could only imagine how disheveled I looked as we approached the lima-bean green Karmann Ghia she drove. I raked my fingers through my hair a couple times when she wasn't watching, as I didn't want to seem that vain, but rather as carefree as she seemed to be about her appearance.

As we drove off and then north on Route 3, I pondered about how refreshing it seemed for Lorelei and me to basically spend the night together, but without the encumbrance of sexual desire or participation. Still, I doubted that Allison would understand that if I told her about it. If that's all there was, I might be tempted not to mention it to her, just to save the hassle. But after we got out into the countryside, turned down a dirt side road and found the farm she spoke of, the prior night took on a different perspective for me.

Lorelei bounded out of the car, spread her arms as she twirled a couple of times and took a good hearty draft of country air. Maybe I didn't appreciate it as much as she did, as I took a whiff and only detected the combination of manure and skunk. She vaulted over a waist-high stone wall and urged me to follow suit. "Come on, don't be shy," she said with a gleam in her eye. I hesitated a moment, not sure about venturing onto what looked like private property. She just hopped and twirled away, like a rabbit saying, "Catch me if you can."

"Follow me!" she shouted as she skipped and danced across the field. I figured I should play along. I chased after her as she crossed a line of trees and began descending into a glade of dandelions and clover, and as I got closer she turned as if to taunt me, but instead smiled and laughed, and then began shucking her buckskin, simply tossing it aside, and then she darted away before I could get a good look at her naked body. I don't know what came over me besides getting the gist of the game, and I quickly glanced around and saw how shielded we were from the view of the road, and then I also discarded my clothing as I continued to chase. Lorelei appeared totally carefree and uninhibited as she rolled herself down a gentle slope of a cool, green, clover-covered hill, with her creamy, still winter-white flesh marking a sharp contrast. I followed suit and understood her reveling. The morning dew having just evaporated left the clover dry and cool to the touch. My body tingled all over with the new sensations reaching previously dormant areas. I felt so invigorated and incredibly aroused when I came upon Lorelei lying still on her back, gazing longingly up at the azure sky. I caught a few breaths, and she sighed pleasantly, causing her breasts to heave and capture my attention. Seeing in amazing detail her contracted aureoles and erect nipples and her shock of velveteen pubic hair against her smooth skin—being the first time viewing such things in the harsh reality of daylight—heightened my level of excitement. I reached out and traced my finger around her left breast, almost afraid to touch or damage something so delicate. But she responded in kind, caressing my back and shoulder. Then all my inhibitions ran wild and maybe frolicked around with any inhibitions she might have let loose in that field, as we locked in an embrace and passionately made love to each other, virtual strangers though we were.

I could hardly regret anything that felt so alive and beautiful at that moment, but as I learned in physics classes, every action had a reaction. All I could do was wait for the recoil which was bound to kick me in the face.

CHORUS 2:

"I think I'm going to be sad, I think it's today, yeah,"
Lennon-McCartney

"She loves you, and you know you should be glad,"
Lennon-McCartney

I didn't know what to make of my encounter with Lorelei. When she drove me back to Boston that day, we didn't discuss what it meant to each other. For myself, I wasn't sure what it meant to me. Lorelei simply said, "You should come by more often," and I said, "Okay, sure." Whether that meant she wanted to continue as lovers, I did not know. Besides, Allison still was my girlfriend.

A week after my trip, I decided it was time to take a jaunt back home, to visit my father, but mostly to talk with Allison. I supposed I could have pretended it never happened and continued on with her. But I didn't want to be a cheater. I don't know how long I could have gone on hiding it, wondering if maybe she could tell anyway. I had to face her and the consequences of my actions.

On a Saturday morning, I walked over to the Lambert house. I had called ahead of time, to let her know I wanted to see her. Allison was excited at first, but perhaps sensed that I was simply being direct and a bit distant, not wanting to reveal too much before I got a chance to see her first.

Mr. Lambert was working in the yard pulling weeds when I approached. I was hoping to avoid him in particular, but, in reality, anyone else besides Allison. Watching him grasp and choke a weed with his meaty hand made me think how he might be in the mood to choke me when he found out I broke his daughter's heart. But at the moment, he greeted me heartily.

"Hello, son," he called upon seeing me enter the gate. "It's been a long time. We haven't seen you since New Year's I think it was."

"Yes, sir," was all I could muster to say.

"How's life in the big city? Allie told us you were staying up there for summer school. Been keeping you busy?"

"Yes, sir."

"Well, it's good to see you again. We'll have to have you over for supper one night before you head back."

"Thank you very much," I said, not expecting I'd have a chance to actually accept the invitation once I broke the news. "Um, I just came over to see Allison."

"Of course. Allie!" he shouted, expecting to be heard through the open windows. "Tom is here!"

I waited another few awkward moments there silently until Allie finally appeared. She came over and hugged me warmly.

"Hey, Tom, welcome home. What's up?"

I didn't want to appear rude to her father, but I suggested we go elsewhere to talk. "Do you want to take a walk down to Sylvester Park with me?"

"Okay." She walked over to her father and gave him a peck on the cheek. "See you later, Daddy. I'm just going out for a walk."

"All right, see you kids later."

Allison took my hand as we walked down her street to the park. She told me what she was doing during her summer break, but I didn't say much, only responding enough to keep her talking. I wanted to wait until we were settled to talk seriously. The park was across the street from an elementary school, and it didn't get much use on the weekends, so I knew we would be alone there. I led her over to the set of swings, which were nothing more than a leather strap for a seat attached to two rusty chains. I took a seat on one, and she took an adjacent one.

"So what's up?" she asked, as I was still silent, idly kicking the dirt just to make the swing move haphazardly. "You seem like you have the weight of the world on your shoulders."

"I think that maybe it is. I did something that I'm not very proud of."

"What, did you go and get yourself arrested again?" she said with an essence of humor in her voice.

"No. That I could probably deal with better."

"So what is it then?"

"Well, it all started with Rolf trying to get me more comfortable with his crowd dragging me to one of those parties he goes to, and there was this girl, and you see, she's like heavy into the scene, and, well she did offer me some drugs, but it wasn't just that—" I rambled.

"Whoa, you tried hard drugs or something?" Allison's expression turned to amazement. "I can't believe you did that. I never even saw you try pot. Which one was it?"

"Well, she did give me some mushrooms, but that's not what I'm trying to say."

"What are you trying to say?"

"What I'm trying to say is, that, well I, I slept with another girl." Now her expression turned to shock and disbelief. She looked as if she were gathering to complete her thoughts for a retort, but I didn't want her to think it was my aim to hurt her, so I kept going. "It just sort of happened, you know. It's not as if it were planned. I wasn't after her. I mean, I guess it seemed you and I were growing apart and all."

"And you thought that made it all right to start looking around for somebody else?"

"No, that's not what I was thinking. I don't know what I was thinking."

"Well, I'll tell you what I was thinking. I was thinking of sharing my life with you—my whole life—with just you. But I guess you weren't thinking that way." Now I saw the hurt in her eyes, and heard a slight tremble in her voice.

"But I was too. It's just—I don't know. It's just that you're the only one I've known, and I wanted to know if it would be any different with someone else. How am I supposed to know if you are the right one for me if I never know about anyone else? But I'm not saying you're no good for me now. I still love you. You're a wonderful person. But I guess I was beginning to doubt whether we would continue to grow in the same direction."

"I have to say the thought crossed my mind lately, too. It's just that it seems you've changed a lot. Things haven't been the same as they used to be."

Allison didn't say it, but perhaps she thought a breakup was inevitable, which didn't leave her devastated. She wasn't crying.

"Yes, I've changed. But you should expect that of me. I'm not going to be the same high school kid you grew up with for the rest of our lives."

"But I thought we would be able to work through it, if you loved me enough. I loved you enough not to run around while I was here."

"But I love you very much," I said. "I'm just going through a very confusing time right now, and I don't know what I want. It's not as if I'm choosing someone else over you. I'm not leaving you for someone else. I don't even know if I can have a relationship with that girl. It was just something that happened. To tell you the truth, I can't even say for sure that I'll ever see her again."

"You really have changed. Are you into 'free love' now, too? You think you can just sleep with a girl and not have any emotional attachments?" Allison's tone was very biting.

"Well, it goes two ways. I don't know that she wants me. She might be into free love and may never want to see me again. I don't know. I don't know her very well, and honestly, I'm not exactly comfortable with that. That isn't me. But I don't even want to be concerned with that right now. I have to figure some things out about myself first. I have to find out what I really want. I feel lost, and I think I have to find myself."

"So what happens then, when you 'find' yourself?"

"I don't know. But I will know once it happens. When that day comes, I could come to realize that, absolutely, you are the right one for me. But I can't expect you to wait around until that happens."

"You've got that right."

"Because it could be tomorrow, ten years from now, twenty years from now, or I may come to realize for certain that it was better off this way. I wouldn't want to stand in the way of you finding someone else who's possibly better for you." Perhaps I was trying to make her feel that what I was doing was the noble thing to do so that it wouldn't be an acrimonious breakup.

"The thought of finding someone else doesn't exactly sound appealing to me right now. I'm not the one who is confused, remember?" Allison tried to choke back the emotion coming through in her voice now, but tears had yet to fall. "I know that we haven't been as close as in the past, but being together right now isn't the most important thing to me. If we were to separate today, there's not a whole hell of a lot to miss right now, is there? But what you promised me—that we would grow old together, raise a family together—that's what I'm going to miss. How can you jeopardize all that now, just because you're unsure of yourself?"

What she said hit me squarely in the face because an idyllic kind of family life with her in later years did appeal to me; it *was* what I wanted, too, and if I was wrong in my judgment today, I was risking the possibilities of it ever happening. But my vision was clouded. "But how can you be so sure that is how it will turn out—you and me and baby makes three and we all live happily ever after?"

"I trust my judgment. I guess you don't. I am willing to work hard to get to that place. But I guess you aren't. I could wait around for you to 'find yourself,' or whatever, but I can't wait for you to decide if I'm the right one for you, when I've already decided that you are the right one for me." Tears did roll down her cheeks now, and Allison got up from her swing to turn away from me so that I wouldn't look at her. I felt awkward about it, even though I had always wanted to comfort her, but since I seemed to be the cause of her pain this time, I paused a moment before walking over to her and putting my arm around her.

"I know that I'm probably making the biggest mistake in my life, and I could regret it every single day to come, but I can't risk hurting you worse later on." I'm not sure what she took that to mean, as she could have thought I was referring to my inclination to cheat, and how it might not completely cease in the future, but rather I was thinking—though could not bring myself to say—that I was afraid I might yet get sent to Vietnam and make her a widow in the end. I could not see as clearly what my future held.

Allison quickly dried her eyes when I embraced her, not likely because I consoled her, but most likely because she didn't want me to see her that way.

"I don't even know why I'm crying," she said. "You didn't come here to break up with me, but to tell me why I should break up with you." The warmth her body usually gave off when I touched her turned into an icy chill.

"Do you want me to walk you home?" I asked a question that did not need to be asked only moments before because the answer would have been obvious. But now, I didn't know what to do. Allison was no longer my girlfriend.

"No. Please don't. I'd like to be alone right now." So, I watched her slowly walk away, not turning to take a last look over her shoulder, as I dumbly sat there upon a picnic table. I knew that we were going to break up, but I couldn't call that a successful conclusion. I was feeling rather mournful. Certainly, I said goodbye to my past at that moment, but unclear was whether or not I also said goodbye to my future.

VERSE 4:

"Hey Jude, don't be afraid, You were made to go out and get her,
The minute you let her under your skin, then you begin to make it better."
                                                              Lennon-McCartney

"And now these days are gone, I'm not so self-assured,
Now I find I've changed my mind, I've opened up the doors."
                                                              Lennon-McCartney

About a week after I returned to Boston, after muddling through my normal routine like an aimless vagabond, I decided I needed to see Lorelei again. Even though she left an open invitation to me, I debated whether I should wait until the next party at the Pink House and just be very casual about it, as she appeared to be. But I hadn't heard of any more parties just then. For some reason I was nervous and reluctant to simply show up on my own, to reveal that Lorelei was my express purpose of visiting. I only could manage to get there in steps. First, I convinced myself to go to Cambridge, then once there, I could finally convince myself to walk towards her neighborhood, then once I was that far, I could convince myself to knock on the door. Actually, I didn't have to do that because a guy was sitting on the porch, smoking what looked to be a normal cigarette. His presence almost caused me to walk on by, but I was certain that he noticed me, paying attention to the house, that I wanted to go up, so I did.

"Uh, excuse me, is Lorelei here today?" I asked as I approached. The bearded fellow hardly seemed bothered by my intrusion into his almost trance-like state.

"Yeah, she lives here. Inside." He jerked his thumb over his shoulder after pulling the cigarette out of his mouth.

It may have looked like I reacted to him as if he were a cobra, coiled and ready to strike, since he did not move to make much way, and I had to gingerly stepped past him and then into the house. I avoided any further embarrassment of asking Lorelei's whereabouts when she appeared before me, perhaps upon walking from one room to another.

"Tom-Tom, the piper's son! So good to see you once again," she greeted me. No one had ever greeted me that way before, but I was struck at how close to accurate she was. I had never discussed my father with her before, but I was indeed a sort of pipe-man's son.

It suddenly dawned on me that I should have a reason for appearing, and I thought of something quickly.

"Hello, Lorelei. Uh, I was in the—well, I wasn't exactly just in the neighborhood, because I did want to come visit you. I, uh, was having a slow summer, not much to do and a lot of free time on my hands. I wanted to start reading some of the books you suggested that I should take up. You know, to expand my mind, gain more practical knowledge, that sort of thing."

"Wonderful. Reading is a great way to let your mind venture past the confines of your own skull. And I have some favorites that should do the trick. You are welcomed to raid my personal collection for books, if you promise to return them, of course."

"Of course," I said thankfully. And thus, she took me to view her stacks, plucked out well-worn copies of *Walden* and *On the Road* to loan me to start, and that's how I spent most of that summer keeping in contact with her. I would read the books she gave me, and then, I would have the built-in reason to visit her again, to return them, and she would suggest one or two that I would take home with me, and so on. My mind was very captivated by the volumes she graced me with, and I read rather voraciously. So I had an abundance of time to be with her, which I enjoyed greatly. We would get in long, stimulating discussions about the books I had just read, and thus, revealed more about ourselves to each other—at least the way we thought. It seemed rather awkward to ask her out on a date, despite how intimate we had been a couple weeks before, and I still couldn't be sure if she considered us a "couple." Actually, I was a bit fearful of defining things too precisely. She seemed so comfortable in not defining our relationship, and I wanted to be comfortable with it also, perhaps contrasting how completely defined my relationship with Allison was—Allison and I had even got to the point of discussing and agreeing on the number of children we wanted to have together: two. I couldn't explain why, but at that particular time, it felt good not to know how the future was going to play out.

Perhaps trying to convince myself, as well as Lorelei, that I wasn't some sort of cad who simply wanted her body, I played the platonic angle as well as I could manage, and didn't make a move to sleep with her again. Also, Lorelei had made the first move, and I wasn't sure if after being with me, she decided that I wasn't very good, or she had enough of me already after only one time, so I decided to wait to see if she made a second move. I didn't have to wait long.

At first glance, the second time we made love seemed as spontaneous as the previous time. Although, looking back, I had to wonder if perhaps there was some sort of premeditation, mostly because of the similarities. One afternoon, when we were discussing Thoreau, Lorelei, with a sudden gleam in her eye, suggested that we take a ride out to Walden Pond itself, which was about twenty miles west of Boston, to come even closer to communing with the spirit of Thoreau than could be obtained simply by reading his elegant words. The idea sounded like fun. I had been to several historical sites in downtown Boston—Paul Revere's House, the Old North Church, the Boston Massacre site, the Old State House—and I felt a connection to those people from the storied past when occupying the same space that they had, and perhaps their ghosts still inhabited. If not ghost-spirits, there seemed to be some kind of ghost-shadows that their presence in those locations had cast. My mind would often transport me back in time, and gazing across some piece of real estate caused me to try and think what it would have looked like, felt like then. On the way to Walden, we drove past the Lexington and Concord battlefields and I became a farmer-soldier, angry at growing injustices, impelled to the point of revolution. Lorelei pointed to an attractive, old house in Concord and said, "That was Ralph Waldo Emerson's house," and I became a neighbor of the great nineteenth century writer-philosopher. But a few miles south of Concord, I became Henry David Thoreau, himself, as I walked the same grounds where he lived for two years around Walden Pond. He described it so completely, and there it was before me, and it would have been hard to imagine how it was much different than it was one hundred years or so earlier.

The woods surrounding the pond was a state preserve. After we parked the car and crossed the paved road, we crossed the threshold back into nature. The area was not entirely pristine, as we found a well-worn path that seemed to circle the water. I could only wonder how many other captivated readers were inspired to trek to this literary locale.

We made a beeline to the water's edge to take in the vista of the glimmering body. I took a hearty draft of the pine and maple scented air. Lorelei also seemed to find serenity in her surroundings. After a few moments, she headed back to the woods saying she wanted to show me something. She pranced away, and I followed, as she blazed her own trail, like a doe being chased by a lusty buck. I caught up to her after a healthy hike through the trees; the pond was now just out of view, but I knew where it lay. We stopped at a small, knee-high monument of stacked stones.

"This was the site of Thoreau's cabin. Can you believe it?" Lorelei said to me rhetorically.

"Really?" I said in amazement. I looked around to perhaps find any left over inspiration. In one sense, what I saw was nothing extraordinary. I had been in woods almost identical in Rhode Island, and, truthfully, I think Mr. Thoreau could have ended up at a number of similar ponds in the area and still have been inspired to write as he did. Even the name Walden seemed to hold some kind of magic, but if it had been called another name, no matter how unassuming, wouldn't it be also lyrically enhanced by the thoughts and ideas he attached to them? No matter, it happened to be this one. And here I was also. In his famous book, Thoreau encourages a self-examined life, and as I was trying to do just that, I felt a deep connection to him, and now to Lorelei because she felt the same way.

Lorelei got that gleam in her eye again, and she darted off, inviting another chase, as she shed her clothing. I followed suit into birthday suits, and we frolicked around the forest, which wasn't as easy on the bare feet as a rolling meadow, but we managed. The chase ended at the water's edge, where Lorelei solemnly took me by the hand as we waded into the almost-sacred pond. I imagined it was akin to a spiritual experience for her as she baptized me in her holy waters, allowing me to enter her sect of hippie believers. We made love, and we both may have mentioned something about God.

We clung to each other for awhile afterward, until we were startled by a hiker who made a sudden appearance on another nearby shore of the pond. We weren't afraid or in the mood to be embarrassed, but we knew we were the ones out of place. We laughed it off, though, as we climbed out of the water, giving the gray-bearded man who stumbled upon the scene a complete eyeful to ponder, and we scampered back through the trees to our clothes.

On the drive back to Boston, a seemingly innocuous question occurred to me to ask of Lorelei, something about what I didn't know about her. Off the cuff I asked her, "What is your last name?"

"Do I need one?" she responded.

"Well, since most people have one, I just thought I would ask what yours is, considering we seem to be getting to know each other pretty well." I may have actually smirked more than smiled at her.

"What if I told you I didn't have one?"

"Everyone else I know has one?"

"You are so bourgeois, aren't you?"

"What do you mean?"

"I mean, that's probably your upbringing. I'm not saying it's your fault. It's just the way you think. It's all you know. All you know is everyone has a last name, like everyone has a mother and a father, and a house with a garage, and a white picket fence, and a tire-swing on the yard tree."

"I'd like to think I'm a little more worldly than that."

"Oh, do you, now?" she said playfully.

"Come on, I know you've got a last name. Just tell me."

"Well, if you must have one, I guess I can give you one. Let's see— my last name is—" She briefly looked off into the clouds while she drove. "Summer's Day," she said dreamily.

"Pardon me?"

"Summer's Day."

"As in 'Lorelei Summer's Day?'"

"Yes. Don't you think it's beautiful?"

"I think it's quite beautiful."

"Great," she said, and I figured that's the persona she wanted to portray, the out-of-sight Flower Child, so I let it go. She would either tell me her regular name eventually, or I would find out by surreptitious means or by serendipitous means.

Even still, I was feeling more and more comfortable then that Lorelei was accepting me into her realm. I continued to see her regularly as I borrowed and returned more books. I was there at the Pink House with her when one of the other residents announced that Robert Kennedy had been shot after winning the California primary. We and all the other residents of the house gathered around a television set and watched the news in horror. To this day I don't know which was more shocking, John Kennedy's assassination or Bobby's. JFK was president and it seemed unimaginable that a person of that stature and power could be taken away so swiftly and brutally. But that it would happen to his brother, too, only five years later, with the nation still not quite over their grief for John, seemed incredibly cruel and unusual punishment. While Lorelei said that she disliked most American politicians, Bobby Kennedy was the only one that didn't scare hellfire out of her. He seemed the only one who wanted to do right for the common man instead of himself, and who could actually lead the disillusioned to do something positive, she said. He inspired me to want to work for his campaign even though I could not vote yet, and JFK inspired me to take my interest in space and turn it into a patriotic ideal of making the world a better place. But their absence left me nothing but disillusioned and angry. If this was the world we were left with, where any bright, energetic leader who dares to be different is snuffed out, how could I not take a stand and fight to change it?

That summer of '68, I spent a lot more time with Lorelei and her friends getting more involved in different political activities. We attended a memorial vigil for Bobby Kennedy at Harvard, and, a few weeks later, a huge anti-war rally in the Boston Common. I got an incredible sense of self-vindication that what I was doing and thinking was right when 100,000 other people joined us in the park that day, and felt an amazing communion with other souls. Lorelei and I joined a sit-in at the Boston University chapel when a deserter took refuge there and police tried to extricate him. I thought I was going to be arrested for a second time, as some of the other obstructionists were, but I supposed they couldn't arrest everyone, and those of us who were left at the end of the ordeal simply had to wonder how we would be beaten down the next time we tried to make a stand for justice and free will.

My anger and frustration at what the country seemed to be becoming continued to grow that summer. Day after day, reports on television news about how the war was going simply made it all appear so pointless. Images from actual battle sites contradicted at times the official conclusions that we were winning. While I came across a few people who wanted the United States to lose this war, I did not, but I couldn't fathom how we could possibly win it with any honor.

After the wave of dissent from people in my age group came crashing down during those years, I could also see the backlash from older generations whose belief systems were now being challenged. Not only were there snide comments about men with long hair, but there was out and out discrimination for it as well, as if it said everything that needed to be said about a person. Otherwise mild-mannered and conservatively dressed men and women would hurl insults at the mostly slovenly-dressed protesters and sometimes get their hackles raised and be darn near ready to commit acts of violence on those people who were asking for peace, presumably because that threatened to destroy everything that was good for them. But even the protesters for peace grew frustrated enough to fight back. This situation played out before me as I watched on television the coverage of the Democratic National Convention that August. The pot was definitely boiling over. Lorelei was pleased in a sense to see what the police were doing to the protesters because she said it exposed the system's ugliness, and that confrontation was necessary to force people to take sides in a struggle that was too important to ignore. That concept was rather foreign to me and the way I was raised, but I had to wonder if she was right, and I tried to understand.

For all my growing anger, disappointments and disillusionment that summer, being with Lorelei helped balance the equation because she made me feel happy, enough at times to put aside the current events. Even though she gave me books which were supposed to be relevant to what was going on, I continued to experience the pleasures of literature, of reading to foster thinking, of better understanding the complexities of thought. Lorelei handed me a lot of Beat literature, and I made a real connection with Jack Kerouac. After finishing *On the Road*, I then borrowed and pored through *The Dharma Bums*, *The Subterraneans* and *Desolation Angels*. I was fascinated that Kerouac was talking about a lot of things that the current generation was fixated on: questioning long-held beliefs, searching for truth and beauty in everyday life, examining the spiritual connections and relationships between people. What seemed unique to my generation, the thought that no one else could understand who wasn't experiencing what we did, was expressed by someone ten, fifteen years earlier by Kerouac. And although the presentation styles were completely different, Kerouac sounded very much like Thoreau, whose radical, life-changing themes were expressed over a hundred years earlier.

When Lorelei saw how taken I was with Kerouac's writing, she suggested another field trip. This one was a little different, but it was also a short drive outside of Boston to the town of Lowell, Massachusetts. She drove to a nondescript, working-class neighborhood and parked along one of its indistinct streets.

"See that house there?" Lorelei pointed across the street to one in a row of two-story houses huddled next to each other, not enough space to allow much of a lawn, aged and slightly shabby, where you could almost tell the age of the house by counting the layers of paint, like counting the rings of a tree. They didn't look much different than the houses in my neighborhood in Warwick. "That's the house where Jack Kerouac grew up."

"Really? How do you know?" I asked.

"After he got really famous, it became sort of common knowledge in the area. You know, people know people who knew him. His family doesn't live there any more. Of course, he lived all across the country for most of his adult life. I think he recently moved with his mother down to Florida."

"It's interesting though that his environment growing up looks similar to mine."

"His family is French-Canadian. His nickname as a child was Petit-Jean."

"Oh, yeah? Of course, my family is mostly Irish, but I had a grand-mother on my mother's side who was French-Canadian. I called her *Memere*."

"That's French for mother. That's what he calls his mother." Lorelei seemed to know a bit about Jack Kerouac. I assumed that she read his biog-raphy.

As two children rolled by down the sidewalk on scooters, I tried to picture the as-yet-to-be man of letters as a runny-nosed youth playing on those streets. I couldn't help but think of my youth, running around my neighborhood streets. I tossed out a couple of tidbits of my family history hoping she would respond in kind. We hadn't touched on the subject yet, so I offered up a couple more of the main details of my past.

"This kind of reminds me of my old neighborhood in Warwick, Rhode Island. My dad still lives there. My mom died when I was twelve, though."

"Oh, I didn't know. I'm sorry to hear that. How?"

"Illness. Short-term. It kind of snuck up on her I guess. Influenza caused a pretty intense fever, and her kidneys shut down. She had weak kid-neys to start with, but nobody knew that before she got sick. And she was used to being the caretaker, you know, where she downplayed her own health concerns and quietly suffered sometimes."

"That's terribly sad."

"I didn't mean to bring you down or anything. It's been a while, now." I had gotten used to talking about my mother's death to other people on that level. Just state the facts. I didn't want to delve into my emotions about it yet, so I left it at that and changed the subject. "How about you? Where are you from?"

"A place exactly like this one," she said, looking out into the street instead of at me now. "That stuff isn't what's important. It's so typical; it's to the point of being dreary. Same as most people, so I decided I didn't want to be defined by those insignificant details, and I try to define myself by who I am in the present moment."

"Okay," I said. Like not telling me her last name, she must have had reasons beyond that kind of philosophical cop out. Similar to me stopping after a certain point when talking about my mother, I sensed that something in her past must have been painful, and she didn't want to elaborate and deal with the emotions at the time. So, I dropped it, trusting she would tell me when she was ready.

"Thanks for showing me this place though," I said. "It's very interesting." She looked at the house a few moments more before she restarted the car, and we drove off back to Boston.

Another day that summer, we drove down to Provincetown on Cape Cod and spent the day with some of her "party" friends who were having a cookout on the beach. Lorelei and I managed to sneak away briefly, and "we skipped the light fandango" behind the shelter of some sand dunes. We didn't always have sex in the great outdoors, but I was beginning to think she was a bit of an exhibitionist. I didn't think that the fear of being seen would be a positive thing, but it did seem to add to the exhilaration. I stayed with her a couple times at her place, and we made love there. She asked me to try a mushroom trip again. I did twice more, but I also declined a few more and watched over her as she experienced them while I smoked some pot. Without really saying so, I felt like a couple now with Lorelei. I was seeing her exclusively, but we didn't quite "date."

A few times we did go out for a night on the town to a beatnik coffeehouse in Cambridge to hear poetry readings. I hadn't read very much poetry, but I was stimulated by Allen Ginsberg's "Howl," which was also on Lorelei's suggested reading list. The joint was called "The Beat'n Path," and was located in a cramped storefront that may have housed another type of business at one time. My guess was a jeweler's, due to the look of the windows in front which looked more like display cases. An acoustic guitar and tambourine graced one window, which may have confused some people into thinking that it was a pawn shop. Inside, the narrow establishment was more of a corridor than a room. On the center of each table was a different colored candle, which combined with the subdued lighting system—strands of Christmas lights, draped along the walls. The place was almost full, but we located an empty table and sat down. There was a small "stage" area at the back of the room, where people were reading their poetry. I glanced around the room and one part of the decor caught my eye. A small, two-by-three-foot North Vietnamese flag was tacked on the wall. I had no doubts by this time what kind of crowd Lorelei belonged to, especially when she urged me to read "The Communist Manifesto," by Marx and Engels. She said she wasn't a totalitarian communist like the Russians, who bastardized true Marxism in her opinion, and, that if I went to the original source, I would see the positive ideals that she believed in. I only perused this literature, but I did see an egalitarian archetype laid out, where the spirit of the people would be raised in common glory. Although it couldn't convince me otherwise, that totalitarianism was the only way to achieve such unison. Just ask the Czechoslovakians. They found out in 1968 that all men were created equal in the communist state, except for the ones who disagreed with it. I didn't relate those thoughts to Lorelei, however. She was free to support any ideology. I thought it better not to argue over what I perceived as inconsequential issues. I wasn't scared to death of communism as some people were. From whatever knowledge I had gained to that point, I didn't equate communism as an ideology that was pure evil, just as I didn't think of capitalism as ordained by God, either. Similarly, just because I stood opposed to American involvement in the war, it did not mean that I supported North Vietnam, as some around me clearly did, or wish that they would win. I could not bring myself to think that they were morally any better than we were in the whole debacle, or have any semblance of fighting a just cause.

The place was thought-provoking, however. Young intellectuals were engaging in political discussions and artistically expressing themselves through poetry. I wanted to be thought of as an intellectual as well. Though I must admit, most of the poetry went right over my head. I probably missed most of what was an author's intended meaning, but I responded to general images and impressions given in a particular poem to say whether I liked it or not.

One fellow got up on the small stage and recited his poem as if each word had some deeper meaning if you only thought about it long enough. He was accompanied by what seemed to be a house bongo player. The poet would read a line and dramatically pause to allow the bongo player to fill in improvisational scat riffs on his pair of bongo drums wedged between his knees before going on to the next line, and so forth. It was as if the bongo man was translating each line of poetry in his unknown jazz language, suggesting that each beat held such profound meaning. The poet was selling his profundity as well, with the intense expressions on his face.

> "Stony, bony, cac-o-phony,
> Righty, tighty, God almighty,
> Roly, poly, mono-poly,
> Winsome, lonesome, win
> some, lose some,
>
> On a bender, love me tender,
> Take a seat to, take a number,
> Take a moment, disencumber,
> Lanky, spanky, Go home, Yankee
> Bless me, curse me, only thank me"

Supportive applause from the audience followed his reading, as he bowed and returned to his table. The next poet emerged from the crowed looking even more serious, dressed all in black, wearing a beret and smoking a cigarette with a holder like some caricature straight from the Left Bank in

Paris.

> "Foolish pleasures dance divine; Loco motives seem sublime
> Fright makes might stronger still; Chilly Willy sets to kill
> Freaking ice holes now do form; Mother's nature becomes the norm
> Fathers of convention steal the show; Children of the horn now do blow
> From wuthering heights did I fall; Vented spleen but had the gall
> Lethal lepidoptera bare their fangs; Spread their wings on sturm und drangs
> Icy floes that slip on by; Nicy knows and so do I
> Gothic strains of mythic cranes; Finding lust on winding lanes
> Look for meaning then find none; Night is nigh and day is done"

I had no idea what that poem was supposed to mean, but I did like the imagery. I turned to Lorelei, as we both applauded, and said, "I really admire people who can paint pictures with words."

"Yes, me too," she said.

"I mean, how some people can seem to capture a wide range of emotions and truth with a clever turn of a phrase. I always thought I'd like to be a songwriter, you know, and say something really important. But I don't know anything about music."

"So be a poet, like these people," she said. "I think it would be a great way to express yourself."

"But I guess I don't have anything important to say yet."

"Sure you do. You seem like a very perceptive guy. You feel things deeply. Say what you feel. Write it down. Express your feelings about the war. You care deeply about that."

"But I've never even attempted anything like poetry before."

"I think you have the personality of a writer. You have a very artistic soul. I'm surprised that you haven't tried to reach your creative side yet. You might even find out you're wasting your talents on engineering."

Lorelei was very persuasive with me. She made me feel that I *could* do it. And after hearing more of the coffeehouse poets, I started to feel that I couldn't do much worse than some of them who probably thought of themselves as serious poets. From the very beginning, though, Lorelei took on the role of mentor for me, trying to teach me new ideas, and inspire me to try new things. I thought that might be the crux of her attraction to me. She was looking for a protégé. I was her lump of unmolded clay. Certainly it was a point of attraction for me. I thirsted for knowledge, and she slaked me.

I decided to give writing some poetry a shot after that night and after a couple of return trips. My first attempts were almost nonsensical. I think I was trying to match some of the rhythm of rhyming patterns I heard at the coffeehouse. I'd come up with a couplet that I liked. For example, "Leapin' Lizards and Jumpin' Jehosephats, Eatin' gizzards in rednecked laundromats," or "Have you ever felt the power of a whiskey sour? Have you ever felt the anger of a Harvey Wallbanger?" My attempts to expand on them came out as something foreign to me. I couldn't even say what they meant really. I wasn't saying what I was feeling. I thought about simply trying to tell a story in a poem format. And I thought about the war angle. I wrote a first draft of one that I thought had a couple good lines, but still didn't have any unifying theme beyond "war is bad." As I crumbled that paper up and tossed it with the other false starts in the wastebasket, I let my mind wander. I visualized a battlefield. Flags were flying on each side. I thought back to being a child reciting the Pledge of Allegiance to the flag of the United States of America, and how patriotic feelings made me want to fight for my country. I imagined how my mother would cry if I told her I was going off to fight in a war. Then, I don't know if I stumbled on something myself, or if I was inspired to grasp an idea that was dangling in front of me. I thought about the red, white and blue of the flag as the three characters in my story-poem, the father, the mother, and the son who goes off to war. I started by writing a bunch of words that rhymed with red, then a bunch that rhymed with white, and blue. The structure was as defined as the trio of colors on the flag, and then it seemed to write itself. I took a couple of days tweaking a line here and there, but I was anxious to share it with Lorelei. I liked what I had said, but still I thought the poetry was almost childish. When I showed it to her, I said that

I doubted that I could get up and read it in front of a lot of other people like the others did, but she told me that if I didn't read it at the coffeehouse, she would. She liked it that much.

That prompted me to read it, but still I was nervous as I took the stage. The bongo player was present again. Perhaps he did add something after I recited each line.

I.   Once there was a man named Red
Never a follower, he always led
And these words of wisdom his father said
"Don't fear my child, go back to bed
Dreams aren't real, they're in your head
Don't be a freedom lover, they all end up dead
Oh, give us this day, our daily bread
For one day soon, you will be wed"

II.   Well, he met a girl, and her name was White
Her smile was sweet and her eyes were bright
He loved her so much, it was all so right
When she held his hand, and he held her tight
Well, they married one day as they hoped they might
Together forever, night after night
Where once it was dark it now is light
Once a man was blind, but now has sight

III.   Now Red and White had a son named Blue
The miracle of birth had blessed them too
The years went by and as he grew and grew
So did their love, it was oh so true
If there were any love stronger, there were very few
Like a triangle side supports the other two
"Wherever I go or whatever I do"
Blue said to them, "Remember, I Love You"

Time grew shorter now, Blue was a man
Time to be leaving now, and see all that he can
"Don't look behind you son, just walk out that door
Your whole life's ahead of you, so don't cry anymore"
He said, "Don't worry, Father, now for I'll make you proud
When I return home to you I won't be lost in a crowd
I will fight for the right and reject the wrong
I will protect the weak and build them up strong"
Then he turned to his mother for one last goodbye
When they kissed each other, she started to cry
"Please take care of yourself and do what you believe"

And with that he picked up his coat and started to leave
Now it was time for him to go off to war
The realities of life are very sour and sore
Why he was shooting his brothers he couldn't understand
All of this fighting and killing for one piece of land
For all of his life now he had been a boy
But from this day forward, there would be no more toys
He saw his friend shot down and all his suffering
He witnessed the final end of a once infinite thing
He tried to run away but didn't know where
He could hide from life and all the sorrows that were there

Now the war on the outside was finished and done
But the war inside of him had just begun
They called him survivor, but who really knew?
Still fighting the battles and winning few
Let's pray that his American Dream will come true
So long may it wave, His own Red, White and Blue

I received a bit of hearty applause from the patrons and a couple slaps on the back as I passed some tables back to where Lorelei was seated. "That's telling 'em, man," one said.

I don't know if they took it as an anti-American poem, as Lorelei said it indicted the system for chewing up and spitting out young lives. I said, "I think it's simply the inner conflict of someone loving his country and what it stands for, and hating what the country forces him to do, contrasting the promises the country makes and what it actually delivers." Even though I wrote it, I still had to think about what it meant, and how it could be interpreted. I don't think I had that clear a stated meaning when I started or as I wrote, but it seemed to evolve into that.

My thoughts up to that point were muddled and cloudy where I couldn't precisely express myself or my views. But laying it out in this manner gave me something to grasp onto, something to explain why I felt the way I did about the war in Vietnam. It wasn't because I didn't want to keep communism in check, or because I wasn't patriotic. I simply didn't want to be Blue. I did not want to be Blue.

VERSE 5:

"People say I'm crazy, doing what I'm doing."
                                                Lennon

"With a little luck, we can help it out;
We can make this whole damn thing work out."
                                                McCartney

As autumn arrived, I went back to my full load of classes for my sophomore year, but my heart wasn't in it as it used to be. I felt as if I had learned so much more during the summer of reading on my own than I did in two semesters of college. I was bored by the old, stodgy teaching styles in the current academia, and my lack of enthusiasm resulted in my skipping an occasional class. I had never done that before. On the traditional Senior Skip Day in high school, I was one of the few characters who actually showed up to class because I wanted to maintain my perfect attendance record. Part of my waning zeal for my studies was partly due to the fact that I wasn't taking any engineering courses yet. I still was treading through the mire of general education courses and prerequisites, and I felt I wasn't learning anything of real value.

My anger at the current state of affairs also grew. The war continued inexorably, day after day, week after week. There were some peace talks that took place, started, stopped and started again. But the war simply continued, escalated even, perhaps each side wanting to gain the upper hand before a negotiated settlement came, but I sensed that it would bear no fruit.

The coming election held no promise to me. The choice between Nixon and Humphrey hardly seemed like a choice at all. Humphrey would simply be another Johnson, I thought, and Nixon likely wanted nothing more than to be president. And we all knew what Wallace wanted. I shouldn't have cared because I couldn't vote, but that irked me more so. Now at nineteen, I was subject to the draft system, where I could be conscripted into military service (as I could hardly feel protected by a student deferment which easily could be revoked at any time), thereby forced to take on adult responsibilities with such life-and-death ramifications, and yet I couldn't vote for or against the politicians most likely deciding my fate. Because of the war, there was pressure growing to change the voting age to eighteen for those reasons, but at the time, I had to wonder why the powers that be would ever give those under twenty-one the right to vote, when they surely would not vote for anyone who would allow them to be drafted.

Even from the cozy comfort of my college campus, however, these things weighed heavily on me, to the point of affecting my school work. On the first few weeks' assignments, I noticed that my grades were slipping. I knew college work would be harder, but for an honor student in high school, I wasn't used to the B's and C's that I was getting. I knew I wasn't putting in the same effort, but it was harder and harder to get myself motivated. One class in particular had me feeling as if I were sinking in quicksand.

In another literature class, I had a teacher who wasn't like the same old college professors I was used to. In fact, he was a graduate teaching assistant. He looked rather young, perhaps two or three years older than I, and I thought that fact might help him relate to us students better, for he was still a student himself. He would often show up to class late, apologize and tell us all about the hectic life of a graduate student—how he would be attending class, then teaching class; or taking exams, giving exams; writing papers, reading papers. On the first graded assignment, I received a failing grade from him. It was the first time I had experienced such a thing as far back as I could remember. We were to read a short story and write a short paper about it. He had written vague, cryptic comments in the margins of my paper, such as, "Shows no original thought here," "What's your point?" "Where's your thesis statement?" After class, I spoke to him about what he specifically meant.

"I'm not sure what you wanted here," I said. "Perhaps you can explain a little more clearly what you were looking for."

He glanced at my paper. "I was looking for a concise, thought-provoking review of the story. I failed to see any initiative beyond a rehash of what was discussed in class. I thought your writing style was rambling and lacked direction."

"You assigned the story to read. I read it, and we discussed it. I wrote my thoughts about it, which happened to coincide with other people's opinions of the story, but it's all wrong? I'm still not sure what you're looking for exactly. You haven't taught us anything yet on how you expect the paper to be, and you give me such a harsh grade like this." Actually, I was thinking he was expecting to read the paper *he* would've written for the assignment.

"How to write a good paper about literature should have been covered in Freshman English," he said smugly. "I can't spend time going back over things that should already be learned by the time you take this class. I'll tell you what, though. If you can make an appointment with me during office hours, I'll go through your paper with you in more detail. Seeing that it's the first paper, I'll give you a chance to revise it."

My ego was wounded to think that I needed extra help, but I took him up on the offer so that I could get a better read on what he wanted. I guess I still had a hard time grasping the concepts, as I could only muster a

C minus on the rewrite. And when I got the next assignment back with a D and saw his latest comments, I felt he was trying to tell me how to think as he would. He must have written the perfect paper when he took this class, and now he compares it to his students' papers and grades according to how close they come to his paper. I never had such trouble before, and I was confident that it was simply a personality conflict. I don't know what I did to rub him the wrong way. At this rate, though, I was sure that I would fail the class and have to take it over anyway (with a different teacher, for certain, to see if my hunch was correct), so I decided that I would drop the class.

I overslept one morning and completely missed my chemistry class. I had a couple classes in the afternoon, but I decided to head across campus to the registrar's office to take care of the paperwork. While dropping the arrogant graduate assistant's class, I noticed the deadline for dropping classes without receiving a failing grade was approaching soon. I contemplated the morass I was in. According to the current trend, I was bound to get dismal grades in the rest of my classes as well, and soon they would become part of my permanent record. I knew it was a question of my heart not being in it. Perhaps it would be better to drop all my classes now and have no deleterious grades etched on my record, and then retake the courses when my heart was back in it. This ploy had serious repercussions, however, and I needed to talk to Lorelei about them.

I wandered all around the campus that day gathering my thoughts, skipping my afternoon classes as well. I hadn't taken any courses yet in the engineering building, but I found myself there, perhaps seeing if I felt as if I belonged there. In an outdoor stairwell of the building, I paused on the third floor landing that overlooked part of the campus. As my mind drifted, I absently folded a paper airplane. Right then, that was my only care in world, to see how far my plane would fly in the gentle autumn breeze. But it was quite fleeting, as my glider eventually took a nose-dive and crash landed.

Outside the library was the newly dedicated Martin Luther King, Jr.

Plaza honoring the slain civil rights leader and former BU student. I also found myself wandering outside Allison's dorm building, suddenly wanting to see her again. I hadn't run into her coincidentally on campus yet, but it probably was a good thing.

Instead of hopping the subway to Cambridge, I walked, crossing the Charles River via the BU bridge. I paused in the middle as I continued to gather my thoughts, and I tried to enjoy the scenery. Scullers and crews—they could have been from any of the neighboring schools: BU, Harvard, MIT, Northeastern—were busy rowing their crafts on the near-placid waterway. The leaves had recently changed hues to amber and crimson. In the sky, intermittent V's of Canadian ducks and geese pointed the way south.

When I finally made my way to the Pink House, I found Lorelei in the main room alone, reading a book.

"Fancy seeing you here," she said. "I thought you had a class about now."

"Yeah, kind of. I wanted to talk to you about something pretty heavy, though, and I need to ask you for a big favor."

"Sure. Lay it on me."

"Well, I've been mulling it over in my mind for the past few days, weighing pros and cons, and I think I've basically convinced myself to drop out of school for the time being."

"Really? That's fabulous." Her eyes lit up, and she smiled. She took to that news rather well. Perhaps it was an easy decision for her, but it was tormenting me.

"At least until I can really figure out where I'm at, you know. I feel as if I'm spinning my wheels there. I have to figure out exactly what it is I want, and once I do, then I can give it my full effort."

"Absolutely. I think it's the best thing for you right now. There's so much more that you can do once you're free from the shackles of the square system. Believe me. I know. I did the same thing, and I'm as happy as the lark sitting on the bough of the tree, looking through the window at his caged brethren singing for their masters."

"You're right. I do feel there is a lot more I will be able to do."

"I say it's better not to be a part of the system, but rather a part of the solution," Lorelei said to me.

"I'll probably withdraw tomorrow. But that'll leave me in something of a pickle, which leads me to the favor I need to ask."

"Sure. What is it?"

"Well, once I withdraw, I won't be able to stay in my dorm anymore. I could go home, but that's the last thing I want to do. I want to stay in Boston and stay active. And also, to be with you. I was wondering if I could stay here for a little while, just until I get on my feet again. I'll start looking for a job as soon as I can, so it will be just temporary."

"Yeah, sure. I don't mind. You can stay in my room. It'll be fun."

"I have no idea what kind of work I can get, but I guess I'll try anything."

"Just remember," Lorelei said. "There's no shame in becoming a member of the working class. It's quite honorable, actually. Welcome to the proletariat." She hugged me, and I crossed another threshold into adult life. Not only was I going to work for the first time supporting myself, but I was going to be living with a woman for the first time as well, with everything that entailed.

So, the next day, I took care of the paperwork, and I explained to Rolf what I was doing. He seemed a bit shocked, but he said he understood where I was coming from.

"I guess, I'll probably still you see you around, though?" Rolf said.

"Oh, yeah. Absolutely. I just hope you get another roommate as good as me," I joshed. We hugged, too, for a brief, awkward moment, and then I picked up the sum total of my worldly possessions, all fitting inside one suitcase and a duffel bag, and I caught the T back into Cambridge to my new "launching pad."

After settling in at the Pink House, a bit self-consciously doing so because I wasn't certain that I would fit in as neatly as the others, I began my job hunt in earnest. I wasn't sure where to start because I realized that I had no experience doing anything besides my summer internships as the boss's son. As I had let my hair grow longer, I felt the prospects of applying to many places would be a waste of time. And I hadn't considered spit-shining my image to ease my way into the establishment when I was just getting started resisting it. Poring over the classified ads seemed fruitless for the most part, but I found something that seemingly satisfied all my needs. I had no strong desire to do it, but I nearly begged during the interview to be hired as a dishwasher at a nearby restaurant in Cambridge. I figured it would be hard work, but I certainly could do the job, while it wouldn't place too many demands on me. Basically, all I had to do was show up on time every day. My eagerness probably made a good impression on the manager, and I was hired at two dollars per hour. The only thing I had trouble getting used to was wearing a hairnet. But I didn't think I could afford any pride at the moment.

I got busy working mostly twelve-hour shifts, from 1 p.m. to 1 a.m., either five or six days a week. It was a hectic schedule at first, not leaving me as much free time as I first thought when leaving all the assignments from school behind, but I wanted to pick up as many shifts as I could to build a little nest egg to alleviate some of my nervousness about taking care of myself for the first time. Once I felt comfortable pulling my weight, perhaps I could ease off a little and enjoy my new freedom.

Despite living together, Lorelei and I didn't have much time to spend together as a result, but she always seemed cool about everything I did. Mostly, I would come home exhausted in the wee hours of the morning and quietly slip into bed with her, and after I soundly slept in, I would wake to find her gone off to some such or other, to her normal activities. My rare days off, though, we did different things together to break out of the routine.

On bad weather days, we would sometimes stay in bed all day, making love, reading to each other, getting stoned. The house was something like a commune, and I would help Lorelei in some meal preparations for the whole group, although the last place I wanted to be on my off day was back in a kitchen, but she made it fun for me. There was the occasional protest rally that we could attend together, and I was introduced to more and more of her acquaintances, seemingly an endless stream of people that my head would spin and I forgot most of the names before I could say, "How do you do?"

Into November, Nixon had just won the election. It was just par for the course it seemed. With all his talk about law and order, it was just a message to all us protesters that political dissent would not be tolerated. Maybe it wasn't his intention, but Nixon made the generation gap a whole lot wider. His election just stiffened the resolve of the people I knew.

As far as my own generation gap, I still had not told my father about leaving school. I even went to great lengths to hide the fact. I had to beg a bunch of favors from co-workers at the restaurant to cover my shifts for a couple days so that I could go back home as expected for the long Thanksgiving Day weekend. If I didn't go, I'd have to explain why, and I didn't even want to mention that I had a job because it would ultimately lead to questions about school. When asked by my father, or my aunt and uncle whom we had dinner with, how school was going, I politely said that I was trying not to think about school while I was back home, thereby avoiding the subject of dropping out. I did my best to relax, watching football all weekend with my father, and I went back to Boston on Sunday evening as if nothing was out of the ordinary.

To pay back the favors, I nearly worked every day until New Years Day. One day off I did have in December, I got lucky and was able to watch some of the coverage of the Apollo 8 mission to orbit the moon. My enthusiasm must have rubbed off as most of the others in the house watched with me, and we were all amazed to be seeing live pictures from space. Being a bit more knowledgeable than the others, I was questioned about the goings on. It freaked some of them out when I told them that while the moon rotates like the earth does, its rotation exactly coincided with its revolution around the earth so that the same side of the moon is always facing us. I explained that for the very first time mankind was beginning to see the other side of the moon. Maybe they were absent that day in junior high school science class. Or smoking pot.

As pleasantly distracting as that moon mission was, the moment of truth with my father was soon approaching. Christmas break was coming up, and I was expected home for the usual time school was out. But since there was no way I could earn up enough favors to take two weeks off from the restaurant, I would have to stay in Boston, which meant I would have to explain my absence to my father. I put it off as long as possible, until Rolf called.

"Yeah, you're old man called up here, you know, and he was asking for you, but I didn't know what to tell him, man," Rolf said, "because I thought you would have told him what was up."

"I know. I haven't gotten around to it yet. I guess I'm kind of afraid he might freak out about it or something. He's definitely not going to understand."

"So, I just told him you were at the library and that you'd call him when you got back."

"Thanks, man. Thanks for not blowing the lid off just yet. I needed the time to adjust to it myself before I have to face him. But I'll call him back, and get it over with so that you won't be inconvenienced any more."

"It was no big thing. I'm just glad I didn't spill the beans without realizing."

"All right, then. Thanks again, Rolf. I'll catch you later. Bye."

"Good luck, man."

Obviously, I couldn't keep the charade up any longer. I paced back and forth in the room, and then dialed up a collect call home.

"Hey, Tom. How're you doing?"

"Oh, pretty good, Dad. How about yourself?"

"Oh, fair to middling. I guess I missed you before when you were out."

"Yeah, sorry about that."

"Oh, nothing to worry about. I was just wondering when it was you were coming home for Christmas break. Maybe I got my dates mixed up or something. It would be no problem if you wanted me to pick you up so you don't have to take the bus again."

"No, that's okay, Dad. I mean, the thing is, I don't think I'll be able to make it down this time. I, uh, got this job that's going to keep me up here for the time being."

"A job? What's that all about? Hell, if you needed a little extra money, you know you could have come to me for it."

"It's not exactly like that. There's something else."

"What?"

"Well, it turns out that I, uh—" I felt as if I were about to drop a bomb and had to brace myself for the explosion, "I dropped out of school— for now. Just for awhile, not permanently. I just needed some time to think things through, to get it all straight in my head what I want to do with my life."

"You what? You dropped out of school? Without telling me?" His voice grew progressively louder with each question, though not quite yelling, yet.

"I didn't think that you'd understand."

"You're damn right I don't understand. You've been telling me for the longest time that you wanted to be an aerospace engineer. What happened to that?"

"I still do, I guess. I don't know. It's not about that really. It's hard to explain, but there's a lot about the world that I don't know yet, a lot more about me that I don't know yet. I'm just not sure that school is the right place for me at this point. I just need to sort things out and make sure that I'm on the right track."

"But college is supposed to be the place to figure that kind of stuff out. You stick it out, and in the end things will become clearer for you. It's not so easy to take time and think when you have to struggle to support yourself everyday. Besides, you drop out of college and you lose your deferment. Have you given that any thought?"

"Yes, I've given it a lot of thought."

"And what? Are you ready to be drafted?"

"Not exactly."

"Oh, don't tell me my son is one of those long-haired ingrates who thinks their precious freedom to act as foolishly as they please doesn't come with a price tag. Freedom has to be fought for, if you want it badly enough."

"I happen to agree with you on that one, Dad, but I happen to believe that resisting a call to fight an illegal war *is* fighting for my freedom."

"Oh, beautiful. My son went to college and became a pinko."

"You can throw around all the names and labels you want, Dad. I didn't call to argue with you. I just wanted to let you know that I probably won't be home for Christmas. It's strictly because of my job. I'll see if I can get down to visit on my next day off."

"Well, don't put yourself out or anything to visit your old man," he said sarcastically. "I was wondering why I hadn't gotten a tuition bill yet for next semester. I guess it's too much trouble to tell me what's going on."

"I'm sorry about that. But now you know."

"Does this have anything to do with what happened between you and Allison? I never understood why you broke it off with her anyway. I feel like you're keeping me in the dark about everything."

"No, it doesn't have anything to do with that. I left school simply because my mind wasn't into my studies. It's not as big a deal as you think. After I take a little time off, I'll probably come to realize that college is what I want, and then I'll go back with a clear head."

"You definitely could use a clear head."

"Come on, Dad. You'll see. Like I said, I'll come down as soon as I'm able, and we'll talk more then. Okay?"

"All right."

That Christmas was unlike any other I had experienced. To the people who surrounded me at the time, it was just another day. December 25th arrived, but Christmas didn't. Lorelei said she didn't want to participate in such a commercialized, bourgeois celebration. Even though I wasn't expecting a present from her, I did go out shopping to buy some American Indian jewelry that I knew she liked. She was appreciative anyway, though a little embarrassed to add any credence to the gift-giving ritual. Her counter was always, "Why limit giving of gifts to just one day a year? Whenever it enters your heart, give then, no matter what the date says on the calendar." It was a point not without its merits. Perhaps to prove her point, a few days later Lorelei bestowed upon me the gift of the Beatles White Album, which had been recently released, and I had been eager to hear it completely through. The record raised hot topics for discussion amongst the group at the house, as a few people took their turns trying to decipher the meanings behind some of the lyrics. "Revolution," in particular, caused a bit of a ruckus. The Beatles seemed to be talking directly to this bunch when they sang, "But if you go carrying pictures of Chairman Mao, you ain't gonna make it with anyone anyhow." Most felt it was a statement that they were copping out of the real revolution by saying, "But when you talk about destruction, don't you know that you can count me out." Some were calling the Beatles cowards because it would take some destruction here and there to make changes in the real world. They weren't going to happen by naïvely wishing they would change, like the Beatles seemed to be saying, they argued. To just tell everybody, "Don't you know it's gonna be all right," defeated the purpose of what everybody in the house was working for. I could see why they mostly felt insulted. The song did sound like a satirical backhand slap to the face of these people. I didn't want to try to articulate my view to them, but I really dug the song and thought it quite accurately depicted my feelings that I really hadn't had a chance to tie together at the moment. What the Beatles spoke to me in that song was let's not lose sight of what we really want to accomplish here. Let's not try to destroy hate with more hate. Let's not tear down love in the process of this revolution that was going on at the time. Looking back, I think they were very perceptive thinking that what started out with so many good intentions was on the verge of slipping out of control into something just as bad. But I didn't offer any rebuttal at the time. My confidence lacked the iron-clad convictions of those around me, so I just nodded mostly.

I worked Christmas Eve and Day at the restaurant, so I was only able to catch some of the old holiday spirit as I walked home at night, seeing all the festively decorated homes, caught in recollections of my past seasons, especially early on, when my family was still whole. I worked solid until the day after New Year's, when I took a couple days to go back home to see my dad.

I expected the fireworks that were kept in check via the telephone would be rekindled now face to face. But to my surprise, my father avoided the subjects of school and the war and such, and really made me feel that I was missed around the place. (I can look back now and say for certain that I wasn't the only one he missed deeply, especially that time of year.)

My dad had a few Christmas presents still waiting for me to open. By then, though, he had all the decorations taken down, and again something else had deviated from the Christmas times that I was used to. But I also had to realize, I was growing up. I was not a child anymore. Things couldn't stay the same.

I had brought a few gifts for my dad as well, and so we exchanged presents despite it being the Second of January. I got him his favorite after-shave, a nice sweater to replace the threadbare one he would always wear around the house, and something I had gotten six months prior: an autographed baseball. I really had to hustle to get it. Before a summer game in Fenway, I jockeyed for position by the dugout with kids of various sizes, but I was just able to get the last one before he had to take the field, and we had to take our seats. He signed it: "To Jack Moore, Thanks for keeping the faith, Carl Yastrzemski," and tossed it back to me, while someone almost ripped the ball from my hand anyway, despite being personalized to my father.

"Wow, that's really something, Tommy boy," my father said, using my childhood name, but at the moment I didn't care. "That's not just your scribbling on here to make me look like a chump when I show this to my buddies?" I knew that he had no notions that I would actually do something like that, that he was just kidding.

"No, Dad, that's really his autograph."

"Why, you little son-of-a-gun."

"Yeah, I guess that makes you a gun, then."

He laughed and then hugged me. Then he took out my "big" present, and I was probably in just as much awe as he was for the ball. It was a huge new telescope, twice as big and powerful as the one I had still in my old room. We had some really warm moments that night. He took me to a restaurant for dinner, and I couldn't help but think of the poor schleps washing my dishes that night, which gave me a chuckle. We kept the conversation safely in the past for now, reminiscing about the good ol' days. Returning home, I stayed the night in my old room. Still adorning the walls were some newspaper headlines trumpeting different milestones in the space program through the last decade. And I noticed that they continued past the time I left for college.

The next day, my father had to go back to work. I hung around the house letting memories seep back into me before I had to catch the bus back to Boston. I left a note for my father, thanking him again. I told him where

I was staying temporarily, but I'd be looking for a new place soon, so I was going to leave my new telescope in my old room for now.

When I got back to Cambridge, I slipped back into my old routine quickly, back to work for nearly a couple months. It was the middle of March before I started to see my life a-changing—for good or bad, I didn't know, but a-change was a-coming.

On my own, I took stock of my situation. Looking at how much I had saved, I thought I'd be able to afford my own place. I felt somewhat out of place at the Pink House, and I simply wanted to feel more independent. I liked the people there well enough, but I don't know if they were the people I would choose on my own to be friends with. I loved Lorelei, though. And I thought about asking her to move in with me, and perhaps it would seem more like a normal relationship. We would still hang around with her crowd when she wanted to, but it would be more of the time she and I, a couple, a pair, perhaps, would begin to build a life together. I wanted to explore the possibilities of getting a different job that would leave me a more normal schedule, so that I could have a life. But for all the times I tried to ignore it, the Vietnam War still was going to have its say in the matter.

After not seeing much of Lorelei for a stretch of a few days, and running the thoughts around in my head, I finally had an evening off, and I was eager to talk to her about my plans. I had gone in to the restaurant for the lunch shift, and when I came home, I inquired of her whereabouts.

One of my housemates was sharing a joint with his new lady friend, whom I didn't recognize, on the main room sofa. "Hey, Morris, have you seen Lorelei?"

"No, man," he said while trying not to exhale.

"Do you know where she might be then?"

"No, man," he said, and then finally exhaled. He offered up his joint. I waved it off. "I saw your old man though."

"What? When? My father?"

"Yeah. Today, man. Earlier. He was looking for you."

"He came here?" I said incredulously. Trying to get information from someone getting stoned was like getting information from someone while their teeth were being pulled. "What did he say?"

"He just said he was looking for you, you know, needed to, like, have a talk with you man-to-man, man."

I was getting a little agitated, wondering what was up that my dad would decide to drop in on me. Although, I knew he made visits to Boston every now and then for business. But I figured he would call and let me know. "So, where did he go? Where is he now?"

"Oh, right, man. He said you could reach him at the hotel in Coptic Square, man."

"Huh?"

His lady friend giggled, and said, "No, Copley, Morrie, Copley Square."

"Oh, right, man. Copley Square."

"Thanks." I went upstairs to get cleaned up and changed. I would have to hook up with Lorelei later. I figured that what my dad wanted to tell me was serious. I was about to call the hotel, but I didn't want to talk to him on the phone. Instead I caught the subway to Copley Square to look for him.

When I went up to the desk and asked the man for the room number for Mr. Jack Moore, I thought that he was looking down his nose at me because of my long hair and mod-casual attire, which probably didn't fit the dress code of his hotel's archetypal clientele. His countenance displayed a none-too-subtle annoyance at my request for his assistance. "Oh, are you his son?"

"Yes, I am."

"I guess he was expecting you to call. He asked me that if his son called, to have the call transferred to the bar downstairs. That's where you'll find him at the present time."

"Thank you." Not only was I puzzled at my father's unannounced visit, but also that he was hanging out in the bar. My father was a social drinker as far back as I remember, but he started drinking more heavily for about a year after my mother's death. He had been straightforward and open in telling me about it later and described it as his involuntary reflex to his mourning for her. Then he thought about what he was doing and was able to stop, for my sake he said, as he knew he would have to be stronger than that for me so that I wouldn't lose both parents, ultimately. At any rate, he must have done a fairly good job at hiding it from me at the time because I don't remember much difference in his behavior. Perhaps I was lost in my own grief to really notice. After he told me about his drinking, however, I didn't think twice when I would see him have a drink or two at home, usually on holidays with other family around. Today, he could have been simply bored while waiting to hear from me and didn't want to just sit in his room, but I sensed that something was troubling him as I walked down the stairs to find him.

He sat in a corner of the barroom at a table finishing his dinner of fish and chips, but he also had a couple of beer bottles on the table as well. When he noticed me as I approached, he didn't greet me with much enthusiasm or affection.

"Hi, Dad. I had heard that you came by earlier when I was at work. Sorry, I missed you. How come you didn't let me know ahead of time that you'd be in town, though?"

"Hiya, Tom. Have a seat. Can I get you anything? Would you like a drink, or something to eat, maybe?"

"No, thanks, Dad. I'm fine. It's good to see you. You just caught me a little bit by surprise. Are you up here on business?"

"Partly, but it's nothing big that I couldn't have let someone else handle. I wanted to talk to you—you know, about what you've been up to lately. We haven't been able to talk that much. Last time I saw you, we didn't get much of a chance to really talk about things."

"I know, Dad, and I'm really sorry about that. I've been dealing with a lot of different emotions lately, and I hadn't felt like I had them all sorted out enough yet to talk about."

He sprinkled a couple of dashes of balsamic vinegar on his remaining chips, and said, "Do you have them sorted out enough now to tell me about it?"

"Some things, maybe, but there are other things I'm still working through. I've been working at the restaurant a few months now, and getting used to that. I've been staying with some friends, but I was thinking I could be on my own soon. I don't know how long I want to be washing dishes, so I might start looking for other things in the meantime."

"But why are you so eager to work? Why did you have to leave school in the first place? I don't understand that at all. You don't want to be an engineer anymore? What happened with your dream of working for the space program? The only experience you seem to be getting might let you work in the NASA cafeterias. But come on, son. You're more capable than that. You've got too much going for you, but I see that you're ready to throw it all away. And I wonder if you realize what you could be doing to your life right now." After he vented all that, he washed down the remnants of his meal with the last of his beer.

"I don't have a crystal ball, so perhaps I don't realize what I could be doing to my life right now," I said rather sarcastically, as I was starting to get defensive. "I think I would still like to be an aeronautical engineer, but I felt as if I had to stop and think for a moment. Maybe that dream was just a kid's dream, a kid who doesn't know enough about the world yet." My father interrupted my venting by motioning to the waitress, and ordering a whiskey sour. The bar wasn't heavily populated at this hour, and he was served in short order. I continued my explanation, but paused when the waitress was at the table. "I mean, what do I really know of the world to know what I'll be spending all those years in preparation to actually do? Maybe the space program is really a front for a military program."

"Come off it. You've been listening to too many of your leftist friends."

"Maybe I have, Dad. But maybe they know something. Then again, maybe they're talking out of their asses. But I think I should investigate a little more, try to learn something real so that I can make a decision for myself."

"Believe me; they're talking out of their asses."

"What do you know about them? You've never talked to them. You dismiss them like you do everything else that doesn't fit into the world of your already made-up mind."

"I've been around. I know something about the world to know someone who's talking out his ass."

"Oh, sorry, Dad. I forgot. The older generations have all the answers. And they think that they should be able to spoon feed their wisdom to the younger generation and expect it to go down easy, without question, with thanks and an eager request for more, please. Well, this new generation is choking on the pabulum being fed to it, and it wants to explore and experience things on its own to make up its own mind."

"I don't even know what you're talking about. I wasn't trying to make this an argument about different generations. I just want to know why you had to leave school."

"I didn't feel as if I could give school my full effort while I was trying to answer some fundamental questions about myself. And with everything going on in the world today, I felt that if I wasn't giving school my full effort, in the meantime I was simply hiding out."

"Hiding out from what?"

"Hiding from the draft with my deferment."

"So you have to throw your deferment away? While you're busy trying to make up your mind, it could be made for you. That's the real reason why

I came up here." He reached into the inside chest pocket of his rumpled suit jacket. "I received this at home a few days ago. I thought best to hand deliver it to you instead of forward it because I felt that you were just going to ignore it."

In his outstretched hand, he held an unopened envelope addressed to me. I paused a moment when I saw the return address. It was from the Rhode Island Board of the Selective Service System. I took it from my father with great apprehension.

"I have a pretty good idea what it is, now that you've dropped out of college," my father said. "Likely they're asking you to report to take a physical for reclassification."

I opened the letter and skimmed over it enough to confirm my father's suspicions. I had a little less than three weeks to report. I knew when I dropped out that this would be the inevitable result of my action, but I kept pushing it toward the back of my mind. I knew that I would have to face this decision, but I still hadn't come to any conclusion on which direction to go. Do I go the route of the good citizen and do as I'm told, taking solace in the fact that at least I'm not being given special treatment? Or do I go the route of principled resister, taking pride in the fact that I'm standing up for my beliefs and accepting whatever consequences may follow? I knew that agreeing to take their physical was not the same as agreeing to accept their conscription, but I felt that I would be making a stronger protest if I didn't give the impression that I was resisting to simply save my own skin. The whole system was wrong for everybody, not just for me.

"I guess I never thought that I wouldn't know the answer to this question, but are you going to go?" my father asked me, looking solemnly into my eyes as if he did know that answer all along.

I averted my eyes from his for a moment, and then I found the courage I needed and locked my gaze back at him as I replied, "I don't think I can."

"What do you mean, you don't think you can?"

"I think it would be pointless to report when I have no intention of submitting to the draft."

My father's face grew flushed and exasperated as he looked back at me in abject disbelief. "What kind of son have I raised here? Obviously one who feels he can decide for himself which laws to obey and which laws to disregard because he doesn't happen to agree with them." His voice was getting noticeably louder.

"Dad, shouldn't we discuss this in private?" But he paid me no heed.

"Do you know what you're doing? Do you really know what you're doing to yourself?"

"I think I do. I've given this a lot of thought, and I'm ready to accept the consequences for my actions and decisions."

"If you didn't want to be drafted, why didn't you just stay in school?"

"I felt guilty. Why should I be given special treatment just because I had the good fortune to be blessed with scholastic aptitude? What did I ever do to deserve that kind of break?"

"Maybe your country thinks that you've got something more worthwhile to offer."

"Than what? More worthwhile than my life? Come on, Dad. You can't be saying that my life is worth more than the next guy? I don't think that's what you taught me that this country is all about. 'All men are created equal,' and all that jazz. Well, are they or aren't they?"

"They are; of course, they are. But if you feel you're the same as the next guy, how do you feel special enough to not answer the call of your country while the next guy is doing his duty and putting it all on the line?"

"Because I don't think any of us should go and be forced to fight an illegal war. And the stronger I protest and the more people I can convince to not go, the sooner it will have to stop, and no one will have to go and die for no good reason."

"You think you've got it all figured out, and yet you're still so wet behind the ears. Maybe you haven't figured out what the reason might be. You can't trust that people in our government, with more education and experience than you, can rationally conclude that this war is the right thing to do?"

"No, I can't. I think they're lying to us. The government keeps saying that we're winning the war, but when I watch the news on TV every night, it doesn't seem like we're winning at all. And I guess I'll never understand why we have to stick our noses in other people's business. What right does the United States have to tell the Vietnamese how to live their lives? We're acting like bullies over there. Because we've got the might, we've got the right?"

"Bullies? We're over there at the request of the Republic of South Vietnam to help defend their freedom. Or don't you think it is okay for our soldiers to help defend other people's freedom?"

"We can't solve all the world's problems, Dad, and especially not through the use of military force."

"So maybe we only worry about ourselves and turn a blind eye to Vietnam. Then they lose their freedom. Maybe we'll still sleep okay over here. But what about when their neighbors lose their freedom, too? And then their neighbors, and so on, and so on? There's a free world out there, and an enslaved world out there. And if we don't want our free world to keep shrinking, to the point where freedom could disappear here as well, we have to stand up to the big red menace now, while we still have some numbers on our side."

"Listen to yourself, Dad. 'The big red menace?' You sound like a kid who's afraid of the dark and thinks he sees monsters in the shadows."

"Well, believe me, that's what World War II was about. I was there. It was a different menace, but it had to be defeated if America were to remain free. I'm shocked that you can disrespect your country so easily, but I'm appalled that you're disrespecting me, too."

"What are you talking about, Dad?"

"I did my duty. I fought for my country to give you the freedoms that you're taking for granted right now. I was ready to die for them. And you're telling me that you're not ready to do the same? You're not a *coward*, are you, son?"

I was taken aback by his question. I suppose I never had the opportunity to make it understood that I wasn't a coward. At least I thought I wasn't one. I was considering my protest as an act of courage. But what did I really know of my own capabilities in that regard?

"I don't think that I am."

"What makes you think that?"

"Well, if it were truly a matter of defending something like my family or my country, that would be clear in my head. True, I've never been faced with that circumstance. And I don't feel as if this is something like that at all. It's not clear to me. Some soldiers who have come back from Vietnam have spoken on campus, and they don't paint that patriotic picture that you do, Dad. They can't understand the reason that they were over there either. And, yeah, I suppose because I'm young, I haven't been really faced with my own mortality yet, and I'm a little bit afraid of dying when I think I have so much to live for, to look forward to. But I don't think it's that, because I imagine I would be willing to die for a just cause. You know what scares hell out of me, though, more than the thought of me dying? It's the thought that I might have to kill another human being. I don't think I could live with myself. That thought frightens me to my core. I'm not a killer. And I don't ever want to be one. I don't want to be forced to be one. It's something I don't think I could justify in this case. I would feel like a complete criminal if I had to kill somebody in this war. Just because my country says it's okay, doesn't make it right."

"So now we're getting to the nitty-gritty. You don't want to be like your old man. You're ashamed of me, aren't you?"

"What are you talking about, Dad? Of course I'm not ashamed of you. What would give you that idea?"

"You said that you don't want to go to war to be a killer. That's what war is about, unfortunately. I went to war. I fought. And God forgive me, I had to kill people."

I was stunned breathless, as if he had punched me in the solar plexus. "Wh—What?"

"You said that you couldn't live with yourself if you killed someone in war, so you're probably thinking, 'How can he possibly live with himself after killing someone?' Is that what you think of me, Big Daddy, the war-monger, the killer, the criminal?"

"No, of course not. You never mentioned that before, though. You said that you had it pretty sweet during the war, mostly mop-up duty behind the lines in Europe." I lowered my voice so that only he could hear me, hope-fully. "You really killed someone in the war?"

"Yes. It was kill or be killed. I guess I never told you because there are things that maybe sons shouldn't ever have to know about their fathers. I guess I was ashamed of myself. So I understand why you wouldn't want to be like me."

"But what happened? You said that you got to France well after D-Day and you mostly patrolled towns that had already been liberated."

"Yes, mostly that was it. But I was in the infantry. We would get ro-tated to relieve some front line troops from time to time. I was so young, and I was still in boot camp at the time of D-Day. My whole regiment was newly formed and shipped over from the States in late August of '44. We were so green, they tried seasoning us with short stints of combat. Luckily for me, things were really rolling by then, and they wanted to keep up the pressure with the well-oiled veterans, but when those guys needed R&R, my outfit was plugged in to fill their spots. We had our share of nice duty, patrolling liber-ated towns pretty much like police to keep the order. Then there were times we were sent into some small French, Belgian, Dutch and later German towns to liberate them, which mostly meant running off already retreating soldiers.

But oftentimes they fought as they were retreating. I was lucky again that I wasn't too close to the Battle of the Bulge, but around that time we got much stiffer resistance and counter-attacks. I killed six German soldiers during that stretch, and I saw each one of their faces—young boys, really, much like me at the time, much like you now."

My father choked back long-repressed emotions, which I think were being lubricated by the alcohol. He ordered another whiskey sour before he delved into the details. As he related his story, he looked as if he were fighting back tears when he came to the vivid war memories that he had safely submerged, but only now were resurfacing after 25 years. He broke eye-contact with me, often casting his eyes downward, maybe looking into his drink, then also casting them upward as if he were looking at some scene somewhere beyond my right shoulder.

"The first one was in a little village outside of the town of Sedan. It was on a road that was intended for a lot of our troops to be moving soon. Our company was checking to see if the place was secure. My platoon was just moving in on a farmhouse around dawn when we located a two-man German sentry posted outside. Others in the platoon took care of them, and as a German soldier ran out the door of the house and was aiming his rifle, I was able to shoot him first. There was a firefight with ten more soldiers who had been sleeping in the house. With shots spraying all around, I don't know if I got any more there, but the platoon killed seven and we took three prisoners. People don't die like they do in the movies, you know. They don't close their eyes as if going to sleep. Their eyes are usually wide open in a frozen stare, and a grimace of horror is sculpted onto their now stone-like faces.

"The next four were soon after in the town of Namur. It was house-to-house fighting and I was I able to toss a grenade into a window and took them out in a cluster. When I saw them afterward, they looked like raw hamburger.

"The only other confirmed kill that I had was during a battle in the forest. That was a real nightmare. The Krauts knew we had boys in the woods, and they were lobbing artillery into it. They didn't have to be too concerned about how accurate they were either. A shell could hit you directly or the ground by where you were hunkered down. But also, if it just hit a nearby tree, it could shower you with a rain of deadly splinters. Anyway, they sent in troops for a direct assault. Amidst a roar of gunfire from our line and theirs, they charged ready for hand-to-hand combat. I see one guy racing for my position blasting away with a semi-automatic rifle. He got pretty close as I took cover behind a tree, but I was able to get off a couple of shots of my own. The second one hit him in the shoulder and dropped him. But he got back up and charged again. I fired off the last two rounds in my magazine, got him in the leg. He was at this point maybe ten yards away. He was still able to point his gun at me, and was looking to do so after recovering from the initial shock of being shot. I was afraid I couldn't reload a new magazine in time, so I felt I had to rush him, and I took him out with my bayonet to his gut. It was mostly reaction, as if I didn't even think about it. That was a whole lot worse than shooting someone. He looked so young, I thought not more than seventeen, like he didn't need to shave everyday, much like myself. Luckily for me, the battle was a short one. We held our position. Then we had air cover which pounded the German artillery support, and that sent them into a running retreat. That was about the extent of my fighting, fortunately."

My dad looked drained after recalling those experiences, and I felt drained of my life-giving sap after hearing them. For a moment I felt as if I were in the woods with him, viewing the scene, but as I realized where we really were, I refocused my thoughts.

"Wow, Dad. I can hardly believe it's true. You never told me that before."

"I thought I was good at putting it behind me, but I still remember it so clearly. Now you see why I don't blame you that you don't want to be like your old man."

"I'm not ashamed of you, Dad. I don't think that what you did was wrong necessarily, if you felt it was what you had to do. I'll probably never fully know what your circumstances were, although I think I understand some of them. Some wars are inevitable. If we're attacked, then we need to defend ourselves. And I might have felt exactly as you did during that time. I even may have volunteered as you did. But I don't know. That was then. This is something different."

"How different? All I know is that if your country calls, you have to answer."

"After what you've been through, I would think that you would be the last one to want me to go off to war. Why does it sound like you want me to go?"

"But I don't want you to go." My father fought back the tears again. "You're right. I don't want you to do what I've done, see what I've seen. That's why I wanted you to stay in school! Why didn't you just stay in school?" He lost this battle as the rivulets wetted his cheeks.

"I told you!" I said with exasperation. "If I just go along feeling safe and cozy back on the home front, while others are forced to fight, kill, and die, then I'm a hypocrite. Some people might say that that's not much different than being a coward. I don't know if I can live with that either. If the war was being fought with only volunteers, I probably would still be against our involvement. But at least the people there would be there by choice. Instead, they're forcing people to fight for a cause they don't believe in. We've got regular servicemen stationed all around the country and other parts of the world. They're not the ones going to Vietnam for the most part. They're sending all the draftees to Vietnam, though. Why is that?"

"Please go back to school, Tom," he pleaded with me. "I don't want to see you get arrested, either."

"It's probably too late to get my deferment back even if I wanted to. And I don't want to. I want all this to stop. And I've got to protest the best way I can so that I can convince as many other people as I can to do the same, and maybe it will stop. There already are a lot of people who think like I do. And I think we can make it stop. We'll do what we think is necessary, even if that means getting arrested. With enough people, we can clog the jails, clog the court system."

"You're not going to do something drastic, are you? I'm not going to bail you out of jail if you do."

"I don't want you to. But, no. I'm talking about non-violent civil protest, is all. Fighting violence with violence is not the answer, just as Dr. King preached."

"But look what happened to him. Please, Tommy, please think about what you're doing."

I couldn't go any further with this argument, so I stood to leave. "I have, Dad. I have. I can't think of what else to say to make you understand where I'm coming from. And I can't understand where you're coming from, so where does that leave us? Bye, Dad. See you later."

I walked out of the bar feeling strong and resolved, leaving the Selective Service letter on the table. As I glimpsed my father over my shoulder while opening the door, he looked sad and broken. I had no way of knowing how my relationship with him was going to change after that day, or how much later it would be before I would see him again.

CHORUS 3:

As I went back to the Pink House after the confrontation with my father, I felt strangely exhilarated by the heavy scene and wanted to relate it to Lorelei as soon as possible, and as I neared the house, my pace quickened as I stepped with strident purpose. I felt bolder than I ever had before, as I wanted—and was ready—to take full charge of my life as never before. My mind was made up. I was going to evade the draft, I was going to move out on my own, and I was going to ask Lorelei to join me in the struggle, come what may. I fully expected the struggle, but we would love each other and give each other strength to face it head on and conquer it in the end and be happy in our triumph.

As I charged through the door, however, my grand-illusion train was sidetracked for a moment when I came upon Lorelei engaged in what looked like a heated discussion with Augie, one of the residents whom I construed to be the "leaders" of the house, despite the casual openness of the place. I mean, I didn't pay rent there, and I couldn't be certain that any of the other "residents" paid rent or not. It had the reputation as a communal "crash pad." If you felt like staying over, you could stay over. And many different people would spend the night on any given night, or a few nights, if the mood struck, while the high lasted—which could have lasted a few days for some of the people I met there. But for those who had a permanent room, like Lorelei, I wasn't sure what the arrangement was. I never broached the subject, in respect for her mysterious ways about herself, particularly. I would sometimes offer her money to buy food for us, or for the group, whoever was in attendance at any particular mealtime. So much was shared. I ate what was freely served many times, and others ate what Lorelei and I contributed. It was all very casual. I took Augie for a leader because of his energetic contributions to the group conversations, not oddly enough, most times involving Marxism. I never got to know him that well because, of all the residents, I spent the least amount of time at the house. I was so often working at the restaurant. But Augie would be the main organizer for group projects when things needed to be done around the house, cooking, cleaning, or fixing a few things. He never bossed people around, telling them to do this or that, but he had a subtle way of cajoling people into pitching in to do this or that, so that the place didn't end up looking like a sty most of the time. It did look like a sty some of the time because of the lack of any rules, and the lack of any vested interest from most of the users of the house. From the main group of residents who had some kind of stake in the place, however, Augie was the main initiator of action, when action seemed necessary.

I kept back a bit when I first spied them in a nook across the main room, and so, I couldn't hear what they were discussing. They weren't shouting at each other, but they both seemed a bit animated with animus from the gesturing I witnessed and, also, the exasperated looks on their faces. It was the first real sign of any kind of rancor that I had experienced there that it struck me as immediately out of place and curious. I let the scene play out, as if I weren't interested, and I picked up a book that was lying around that I wasn't much interested in and slowly leafed through a few pages to feign interest in reading it.

When she finished talking with Augie, Lorelei spotted me, ambled over and sat down on the sofa beside me. She simply said, "Hey, Tom," without her usual sparkling energy.

"Oh, hey, Lorelei. What's up?" I said, offering up an invitation to unburden herself of what was clearly preoccupying her. Her only reply was, however, "Oh, nothing much. What's up with you?"

Maybe she would discuss it later, so I went back to what was occupying my mind. "Well, I got a big surprise today when my father came to see me. We had this super serious talk today that just kind of blew my mind. I could see it coming eventually, but this is where we had to lay it all on the line about what I'm doing with my life. Some heavy stuff, but exciting, too. I'd love to tell you all about it because there are some things I think we need to discuss as well."

"Certainly. Please do."

"Well, you know my old man couldn't understand why I quit school, right? He was worried about me giving up my draft deferment. Well, the reason he came to see me was he had gotten a Selective Service letter for me in the mail, and he made the special trip up here to deliver it because, I guess, he was very concerned about what I might do with it."

"Really? Do tell! What was in the letter exactly?" Lorelei's eyes brightened now and leaned forward as if to listen more intently.

"It was a letter ordering me to report for a reclassification physical, since my deferment was revoked when I quit school. He was afraid I wouldn't go, or I would burn the letter at some demonstration. Well, he was right that I'm not going to go, but I don't feel the need to put on a show about it. I don't want to go take a physical because I have no plans of stepping forward if they do draft me. I don't want to be sent to Vietnam to fight a war I don't believe in. So, I'm not going to go. I told my old man, I'm not going to blow up government buildings or anything just because I decided this. It's just that my decision was based on legitimate personal reasons, and I'm making a stand for what I believe in, and I'm not going to go, no matter what."

"Excellent. I fully support your decision one-hundred percent. Although, maybe you could speak out and use your story to embolden others to do the same thing."

"I don't know if I'm ready for that. I just feel that what I'm doing is right for me. I don't know if I feel comfortable enough urging people to do something that might not be as right for them."

"Well, it's something to consider. What's right for you *is* 'what's right.' No harm in spreading the word."

"I just don't know. I feel as if I'm only now being educated. I'm still learning, and it takes a while. I don't think I'm ready to be a teacher just yet. But all this kind of happened on top of something else that has been on my mind lately—something that I've wanted to discuss with you."

"Lay it on me," Lorelei said.

"You know that I only asked to stay here temporarily, to help me get on my feet. Well, I've been working a lot now, and I feel as if I am ready to stand on my own in that regard as well. I've saved up enough that I'm pretty sure I can get my own place."

"If you feel you are ready, then you *are* ready."

"I'm quite grateful for your hospitality, but it's so much more than that. I feel as if we've gotten very close over the past few months, and I would feel incomplete without you coming with me. I mean, I don't know how you feel. Maybe you're very comfortable the way things are for you, here. Maybe it's not that big of a deal. As long as I'm welcomed to stay here, I could stay here with you, but I've gotten a taste of independence now, and I crave more of it. I feel as if we could go anywhere. I was thinking we could get our own little apartment at first here in Cambridge, or Boston. Or maybe we could go someplace completely different and explore the unknown. You know, we could be like Jack Kerouac and go 'on the road' and see this country from coast to coast. Go West. Maybe San Francisco." Truthfully, before I uttered it, I hadn't considered going anywhere like San Francisco. My plan was the little cozy apartment for two in Boston, but as I was trying to convince her to join me, it suddenly occurred to me to play up the romantic possibilities of joining me. I even came up with the outlaw angle, somehow. I continued, "I mean, I don't know how the system works. I don't know if or when they'll come looking for me if I don't report, but maybe it would be best to go somewhere else for now."

I think that struck the right nerve. Lorelei's eyes seemed to twinkle as she replied, "It's amazing that this has come up with you just now. I've been entertaining similar thoughts myself recently, but I've got a different direction in mind: north."

"North? What's north?" I asked.

"Why, Canada, you silly goose. As a matter of fact, I have some friends who have a farm up there that they are running as a commune. Recently I've been considering their offer to join them. Just practically, there's only so much you can do living communally in the city. But on a farm, we could live off the land, reconnect with nature, and work in a spirit of true proletarian cooperation. Now with your issue with U.S. law, it could be perfect for both of us."

"Wow, Canada. I know people are starting to move up there to evade the draft, but it's not something that occurred to me." And it hadn't. I didn't realize it, but my whole identity was forged as being an American, that I never thought that I could actually choose to not be an American. My brain had to turn 180 degrees to see things from this different perspective.

"You should consider it. I mean, I've been bummed out lately at the state of anti-war efforts in this country. Sure, they are growing, but what real effect has it had. The war still goes on day after day, people dying day after day. Maybe we can't change the system. Maybe it would be best to just opt out of the system, to drop out, forget it as a lost cause, go someplace where you're wanted and respected, to live your life in peace and harmony like you're supposed to."

I was a little taken aback by her sudden defeatist attitude. She always seemed like a fighter. "I'll consider it," I told her. "But give me some time to mull over all the ramifications first."

"Certainly. But especially consider it for your own sake. For my own sake, it may be purely philosophical, but for you it's an issue of practicality. You can decide all you want to drop out of the system here, but then if they come and arrest you, put you in jail, they take away your freedom. And without your freedom, what have you got? Nothing. You won't be out of the system in jail. You'll be so far in the system that you may never be able to get out. Better to leave it all behind, and say, 'Fight your silly, cruel, evil war if you must. But fight it without me.' As long as they leave you alone, who cares what they do. Better to live a life that will serve as a shining example to all on how to lead a better life."

"You may be right. That's all I want, to lead a good life. I don't want to fight. I certainly don't want to kill."

"No one should force you. I'm sure you'll be more than welcomed by my friends in Canada. They all have similar thoughts. Some are Americans who just figured it out sooner. So please, give it some more thought, and let me know your decision. Okay?"

"I will."

Over the next three weeks, I could hardly think of anything else. It seemed like such a huge decision, to leave one's country. America was so massive in size and breadth that someone could start a brand new life by simply picking up and moving. And, in fact, so many have done so. Some may have gone so far as to adopt a new identity, but even that didn't seem completely necessary. Just go to a new state where you didn't know anybody, and you could start out being anybody you wanted to be. I mean, pick a new state, and there are forty-nine more to choose from. But even within states, some of them are so large you could go to a different city in a different section of the state, and you would be completely unknown, a virtual foreigner. You could blend in in any big city, or you could be the new guy in any small town. Maybe you're looked upon askance by a few suspicious minds, but you go about your business, don't bother anyone, don't cause trouble, and before you know it, you're one of them. Anywhere you go in America, they speak the same language. That would eliminate most foreign countries as a place to go and blend in because I didn't know any other language besides English. I guess that's what had made Canada such an alluring, ready-made destination for American expatriates. Most of Canada speaks English, and even in the French-speaking Quebec, it is spoken as well. Going to Mexico would be a lot harder for someone like me, having to learn Spanish as well as a different culture. Canada and America share a similar history and culture, and Canada was showing itself very sympathetic to people in my particular predicament, those who oppose the Vietnam War and the draft. Going to Canada might solve that one problem, however, but what new problems might it cause? My father was the only close family I had left in all of America, and by leaving, I probably would have difficulties ever traveling back. Perhaps I'd be barred from ever re-entering the country. I wouldn't be able to see him again unless he traveled to Canada. I suppose that wouldn't be a huge issue for his travel, but would he even want to see me again after what he might term 'deserting' him and this country? I really didn't want to do that to him. I don't know if I could leave if it meant destroying our relationship. I mean, Muhammad Ali didn't leave the country when he refused to go in the army, and he didn't go to jail. But he was a celebrity. Maybe the government *would* go after a nobody like me. Maybe going to jail would also destroy the relationship with my father. I certainly would have travel restrictions placed on me there. I couldn't go out of the jail to see him. He could visit me. But again the question arises:

would he wish to see me in jail? Perhaps I would become a *persona non grata* in his eyes. I didn't feel as if I could consult him to get his input into this decision, but I felt I knew which way he leaned with both of the options that I weighed. There was a possibility if I stayed that I would never go to jail. As I said, Ali wasn't in jail, but he was stripped of his livelihood. He couldn't box anymore. Not that I would be disappointed if I was barred from washing dishes again, but if that somehow happened, what would I do then? Could I ever hope for a better job? Perhaps I wouldn't be barred from gainful employment such as dishwashing, but could my decision right now bar me from ever advancing to any other worthwhile job? Wouldn't going to college be effectively barred from me? I most likely couldn't afford it on my own. And without college, what was I even suited for where I could make a decent living in the future?

My thoughts did turn to my own family's history of immigrating to a new country. My own great-grandmother, a woman I was able to meet in a brief overlapping of our two lives—I was four years old, she was one hundred and seven when she died—was born in Ireland. Her family left due to the potato famine when she was a mere infant and came across the Atlantic Ocean to resettle in Boston. No one today knows what happened to the cousins of the MacGillacuddy family. Maybe no one stayed behind. Maybe they all left too. But that was such a trauma visited upon a whole nation. It was leave or die. It seemingly made the decision easy for them, but without the famine, would they have wanted to leave their native soil? My great-grandmother married an Irish man named Moore in America, and who knows, maybe he left Ireland to simply look for adventure? The motivations of our ancestors to immigrate are mostly lost now, but there was one thing in common they had: America was their destination. America for so long was the Promised Land for so many. What happened in the three succeeding generations where I would even contemplate leaving for someplace else? The Vietnam War was the first instance where I'd heard of people's desire to leave this country for good. So many people were still trying to get in to this country. I didn't want to leave, and I didn't exactly think that my American dream was broken beyond repair. Mostly, I was hoping for a settlement and a withdrawal so that we could put this nonsense behind us and get back to living our dreams and pursuing our happiness. As time continued to pass, however, I was growing more and more anxious for that to happen, while seeing no signs of a break in the continually darkening skies. Suffice to say that I was very confused in my thinking, but I was leaning more toward staying, to give peace a chance of happening, so that I wouldn't have any regrets of making haste. I was in a period of working six straight twelve-hour days, when I didn't have much opportunity for discussing my feelings with Lorelei. I was waiting for my next off day to try to persuade her to move out of the house, but stay with me in America.

The night before, I had worked late, and as usual, I had slept in a bit later than the other residents, including Lorelei. She tended to wake early and get started with her day quite independently of me. While we shared the same bed, it was absent her presence when I awoke. I went downstairs to see what I could find for breakfast and what I could find of Lorelei.

While descending the stairs, I spied Augie having another curious tête-á-tête, with Jim, another regular resident. I passed them by on the way to the kitchen and causally asked Augie, "Have you seen Lorelei around somewhere?"

"Earlier. She left a while ago. I don't know where she was going, though," he responded in a somewhat curt tone.

"Okay, thanks." I moved on to the kitchen, while the two of them moved on to continue their discussion on the front porch. In the pantry I found some granola for breakfast, and in the fridge I found some milk that passed the sniff test. On the counter were several books, and I plucked out a well-worn, dog-eared and underlined paperback of Kerouac's *Dharma Bums* to read while I enjoyed my breakfast. After the meal, I plopped myself on one of the sofas and continued to read while waiting for Lorelei to show. I had no other plans that day than to talk to her about our plans. I was well into the book when she finally came in around one o'clock.

"Tom, I'm so glad you're here," she said with a beaming smile. "I wanted to ask you about what we discussed earlier. Have you decided about coming to Canada with me?"

From the framing of the question, it sounded as if she had already decided to go, with or without me. "Well, I've given it a lot of thought," I said. "But I haven't decided one way or another yet. I wanted to hear more of what your thoughts were first."

"My thoughts are that I want to go. The timing, the situation, the circumstances all seem just right, right now. I trust that my friend Ziggy will provide us with a wonderful environment to plant our little seedling of love and peace and harmony. The fertile soil and the community spirit will nurture that crop to sustain us metaphysically as well as the crops we'll grow to sustain us physically. I'm starting to feel as if I'm withering here. I'm looking forward to a fresh start."

"That does sound wonderful, but I guess I was leaning toward staying here because of the unknowns. I don't know the people you know; I don't know the place. A fresh start is what I'm looking for as well, but I was only wondering how far do I really have to go? America is still a familiar element for me, and maybe I'm afraid to get into something I don't know enough about. I've been thinking that I haven't been drafted yet. Perhaps I never will be. So as of now, I'm not feeling an immediacy of need. While the offer is still tempting, I don't know if I could go yet without an imperative reason to go."

We had never discussed love, and I felt as though I was just about to learn that she didn't love me. She may have liked me well enough, and I was invited to join her, but if I had reservations to the contrary, she was just as quick to say, 'Fine, I'll go my way, you go yours and no hard feelings.' I felt a growing love for her, but I didn't feel I was ready to jump headlong into something that I wasn't very familiar with. I was no farmer. I had no prior thoughts of being one, and yet I should consider it because Lorelei had that calling? And maybe it was only a whim. I didn't know. It came on all of a sudden as far as I could tell.

"Well, it was a thought, just another option to consider for me, until recently, when I did get my own rather imperative reason to leave."

I was curious. "And what was that?"

"I'm pregnant." The word shocked and stunned me for a moment. It was the furthest thing from my mind. Pregnant? But why was I that surprised? We had sex freely and it was quite in the realm of possibilities. Before I could gather any thoughts to respond, she continued. "So, you see, it does change things quite a bit. First there was only myself to consider, and being female, it is true that I am not subject to the draft like you are. While it was desirable for me to leave, I must admit, it was not imperative for me to do so. I thought you'd be more concerned, but I guess it's an individual's choice how to face such a situation. But you see, now, if there is any possibility— and of course there is a 50 percent probability—of having a male child, I would not want to, nor would I let him be subject to such a barbaric, evil system. I know it wouldn't be an issue for eighteen more years, but if I had a son who was born in Canada, he would never have to worry about the decision that you are now faced with. And who knows what the future has in store? Maybe girls will be eventually drafted as well. And philosophically, in terms of equality, we should be subject to the same rules as men. I have no right to expect any special treatment, or for my daughter, just on the basis of our sex. So I would rather protect my child from ever fighting America's imperial wars. So it *is* imperative that I leave the country now."

"Pregnant? You're pregnant with my child?" I was flabbergasted and wanted to make sure I was not taking something for granted.

"Yes, your child, silly. Our child."

"B-but I thought you were taking care of things. Weren't you taking the pill? 'Cause I thought I saw the pills before. And I guess I thought that you wouldn't let me—you know—unless you had the birth control covered. Or that you would ask me to cover it."

"I was taking it for a while. But one time, a few months ago, I ran out and never got them refilled. It wasn't a totally conscious decision. I wasn't laying a trap for you. But I did start to think, let whatever happens happen naturally. It's usually the best way. I understood the consequences and was ready for them. Are you disappointed?"

"W-well, no. I mean, I guess I'm just caught a little off guard." I admit that I was pretty naïve then. I knew where babies came from, but I thought that at that particular time, with the advent of the birth control pill, that girls would control their own fate when having sex, and it was something that they could do without bothering the guy—who is usually lacking full reasoning capacities at those moments—about it. It does seem to be the last thing on a guy's mind. The ones who had it on their minds, used their own protection. But myself, not being a worldly guy at that age, and being rather awkward and bashful in that area, I was too embarrassed to go into a drug store and ask for prophylactics, as you had to do in those days. They were kept behind counters instead of on a shelf to pick up casually. I never used one with Allison, and never with Lorelei. It was totally a matter of chance with Ally because I knew she didn't use anything either. We took a couple of calculated gambles using the rhythm method. I simply assumed the more-worldly Lorelei would use something. Either that or tell me she wasn't so that I could be prepared. But now this new revelation had me thinking in many new directions. Having a baby rely on me to raise him or her, suddenly took the decisions I was contemplating out of the context of only affecting me. Absolutely my decision to stay would affect the baby if I were drafted and jailed for failing to report. Or, if facing that, I decide to now join the military if called, I would not only be risking my life, but be risking the chance of my child to grow up with a father. Even in surviving a war, I wouldn't wish to miss out on years of watching my child grow and develop so that I could be a positive influence on his or her life, as my parents were for me. I was lucky, I suppose, to have had my mother around for the first twelve years of my life, but her absence in my youth was extremely painful and traumatic. If I had a choice in the matter, obviously, I couldn't consciously do anything to traumatize my child. And I did have a choice.

"I'm not going to force you into anything you don't want. I'm a modern woman. I can take care of myself. I'm not going to rely on you to take care of me or my baby. I consider myself responsible for getting pregnant, so you don't have to feel responsible for taking care of us. Perhaps it's something you didn't want to happen. I'm two months along now. I had suspicions earlier but didn't find out for sure until today. I just got back from the doctor's office. I didn't want to tell you my suspicions. I wanted to wait until I was sure. I was already considering joining Ziggy's commune, but as my suspicions grew, I considered it more thoroughly. And I've concluded that it is something I have to do. You may join us if you'd like, and I wish you would for your own sake, to help your own situation, irrespective of my situation. Or you may stay here, if that suits you better. Live *your* life as *you* choose, not as anyone has chosen for you. I wouldn't want you to come with me and feel as if I have chosen for you. You are free from any obligations toward me. You have no responsibilities but to yourself."

Despite Lorelei's pleas for detachment, I was sensing that she did love me after all. She had a hard time expressing her love in words. Perhaps romantic love was too bourgeois or pedestrian a concept for her to deal with. But I had a difficult time imagining that she would allow herself to get pregnant with my child if she didn't love me. She wasn't inside the sentimental, idyllic *you-and-me-and-baby-makes-three* world that I found myself inhabiting with her. But she was encouraging me to be with her, just in her own way. She wasn't the type to ask, nor definitely to beg, for someone to be with her. Perhaps she was afraid of being rejected.

"Of course I have responsibilities. Can't I choose to be a responsible father?"

"Certainly, if that is strictly your choice."

"It is." I was getting a bit choked up now, trying to put my newly gushing feelings into words. "I can't let you walk out of my life and have no connection when I feel the way I do. If I have a choice, I choose to be with you, and our baby. I'll follow you wherever you wish to go because I wish to be with you. I had reservations of leaving before I found out about this, but I still may have gone because I wanted to be with you. What you laid out does make a lot of sense for us right now. It's big, it's huge, but as long as I'm with you, I think I'll be able to handle whatever I've got to face better than if I had to face it all without you. Is that okay?"

"Of course it's okay." Lorelei wiped away a tear that had trickled down my cheek. "Does that mean we're going to Canada?"

"I think it does."

"That's so fantastic. It's going to be wonderful." Lorelei let her guard down and showed me how excited she was at our new covenant, as she nearly leapt into my arms and kissed me. Then we ran up the stairs to the bedroom to make love for a couple of passionate, karmic hours that afternoon. It was funny to me that for all the planning Allison and I did for our future family, it didn't happen that way, and with a complete lack of planning with Lorelei, it was happening in spite of it. I didn't see it coming, but there it was.

I was afraid at first, but now that I was in the proverbial free-fall of my headlong leap, I felt exhilarated, and amazingly free. The decision was made, and thus ended all the fretful debates. But if I delved any deeper, there was still a nagging question left unanswered. Was I doing the responsible thing (I thought I was), or was I in actuality acting highly irresponsible? I knew what my father would think, and I could not bear to face him now that the wheels were set in motion.

VERSE 6:

"Life is what happens to you when you're busy making other plans."
Lennon

"A working-class hero is something to be."
Lennon

Much like Dorothy being scooped up by the twister and deposited in the strange Land of Oz, I felt caught in a whirlwind once Lorelei dropped her pregnancy news on me. It hit me all of a sudden, and I was being sucked up in the vortex to be abruptly dropped into the strange land of Canada. A mere three weeks later after we talked, I wrapped up my life in the United States as best as I could and was on the road to Ziggy's farm, the commune in Ontario. We had to hurry off to be able to help with the planting season soon arriving.

A good deal like when I moved into the Pink House, I didn't have much in material possessions to pack and take along with me, just a suitcase and duffel of clothes. Likewise, for Lorelei. There wasn't much choice anyway. We were to pretend we were a couple of tourists on a vacation trip to avoid any hassle at the border. There was, of course, a huge satchel of emotional baggage that I had to leave behind—telling my father what I was doing. I couldn't face him or talk to him on the phone. I spent most of the three weeks trying to compose a letter explaining myself to him. I revised and re-worked it so many times to try to come up with the right words to soften the blow, and, perhaps, to justify my own actions to myself. I couldn't finish be-fore I left. I would complete the letter and mail it from Canada. I knew what I was doing was going to hurt him deeply. So how do you explain why you're hurting that person? But adult children have to be able to live their own lives as they see fit and hope the parents will understand. The future seemed so fuzzy then, more than usual, I guess. I had no idea if or when I would ever see my father again. And he was going to be a grandfather now. I told him that I hoped he could see his grandchild when the time was right, even if he might not be too keen on ever seeing me again.

Saying goodbye to my friends was more like saying goodbye to Lorelei's friends, which we did when the Pink House threw a big *bon voyage* bash for us. I quit my job at the restaurant without a hint of remorse. No one there cared a whit that I was leaving, and I didn't volunteer any informa-tion about why I was leaving. So all that was left was to get into the car and hit the road.

At times, while still tooling through the city streets, nothing really seemed out of the ordinary. It could have been any other time when we took our little day trips—Walden, Lowell, Andover, Cape Cod or Cape Ann—and night time would again find us in the comfort of our familiar bed at home. The immensity of our actions didn't start taking effect until we got onto the Massachusetts Turnpike and headed west. I had never even been as far west of the city as Framingham, and the unfamiliar names on the road signs were now beginning to make it sink in. Worcester, Amherst, Pittsfield as we inched closer to leaving the state completely. Physically it wasn't impossible to still turn around, but as the distance grew, I did feel that the emotional gravity was losing its pull. I don't know exactly where it occurred, but our Saturn-V-like Karmann Ghia rocket did reach escape velocity, and I realized I wasn't coming back until I completed my mission, to my new home, which I was anticipating to be quite nearly as alien to me as the astronauts would soon find the moon.

Lorelei did most of the driving, and sitting in the passenger seat watching the landscapes roll by gave me plenty of time to think. Something had been on my mind nearly as soon as Lorelei gave me the pregnancy news, but I resisted my natural impulse, knowing that she had a slightly different outlook on the world than I. As I gazed at her in profile, her concentration predominantly fixed on the traffic ahead, I let my thoughts wander back, with each passing mile seemingly compelling me to broach the subject that I had let lay dormant. I was at the point of speaking several times when the fear gripped me and stopped me cold. Then my mind would offer new arguments for, and I would alter and edit what I had planned to say to have the best impact. Then I would hear her arguments against in my mind, and I would back down once more. Once or twice she would sense that I was looking at her, perhaps wanting to say something, so she smiled at me and asked me what was on my mind.

"Nothing," I said the first time.

Later down the road, I spied her again, her eyes intently gazing forward, her long mane of hair wildly whipping in the wind that was created by her open window. Lorelei brushed a few strands out of her eyes with her right hand, caught me looking at her again, and said as she lowered her hand to pat my left thigh, "How's it going, Tom? How are you feeling about everything right now? I know it's a huge deal. Are you okay with everything? Let me know what's on your mind right now."

Instead of answering her questions, which were dealing with my thoughts on the big transition, I finally felt the urge strong enough to unburden my mind, and I blurted it out.

"Let's get married!"

"What?" Lorelei was taken aback for a moment, but when she quickly turned her head to see if I was serious or joking, she had a smile on her face as if she were amused by the proposal. Although, it could have been the look you give someone to tell them, "You're crazy."

"I think we should get married. You're having my baby; I love you; and I think you love me. We should be a family. I know it's more famous as a honeymoon destination than someplace you actually get married, but since we're going to Niagara Falls to cross the border, I was thinking that maybe we should get married before we cross because it might be a lot harder when we get to the other side."

"Man, you are bourgeois to the bone, aren't you?" Lorelei chuckled.

"You always use that term, but what do you mean exactly? Is there anything wrong with that?" I wasn't offended by the term, but in her lexicon it was nearly the ultimate insult, maybe just below "capitalist pig."

"Yes, in a way there is. Your thinking is so commonplace, so entrenched that you really aren't thinking for yourself."

"I'm thinking for myself. I don't know what you mean. I want to marry you, so I'm asking you to marry me."

"If that were really the case, then maybe you are thinking for yourself. But let me guess, your parents got married, and their parents, and so on. So you think you should get married. Your peers all get married, raise their kids in quaint houses on safe streets behind white picket fences. So that's what you want too. You think it's expected of you as well. You probably call it the 'American Dream.' I call it a form of brainwashing."

It didn't feel as if we were arguing in anger, but I was getting annoyed by the way she tended to belittle my opinion, especially about something I felt strongly and naturally, so I felt as if I had to defend my view. "You can call it whatever you like. But I don't see anything wrong with that picture you just painted. I don't see anything wrong with the American Dream. It's a form of happiness, and isn't it part of man's natural desires to find levels of happiness? And yes, my parents got married before they had me, and just about everyone I know, if they haven't already fallen in love, they seek to fall in love and get married. Didn't your parents get married?"

"Yes, they did. Bourgeois as they come. They got married most likely because they were expected to. Society puts a lot of pressure on people to do so. It's rife in our literature. But they also got divorced because they were sold the bill of goods that the 'marriage' was happiness itself, but when they saw what was really there, they found the truth behind the lie. More and more people are waking up to that fact, and the ones who aren't, are waking up every day in loveless marriages they feel compelled to sustain because society shames them into it. Forgive me if I want something else."

I was a little surprised when she revealed that first glimpse into her upbringing, and was hoping she would be more forthcoming. "But my parents loved each other when they got married. If you asked my father if he found happiness in his relationship with my mother, I'm betting that he would say yes. Do you not love me, is that it? Is that why you don't want to marry me? You can just say so if it is so."

"I love you. And you should know that. That's not what I'm saying at all. It's the whole concept."

I took some consolation in her profession of love, but wanted to get to the crux of what she was saying so that I could understand. "I don't know exactly what your concept is, but mine is that I see marriage as a simple declaration of love for each other, a declaration of the level of commitment two people have for each other. You know, 'til death do us part' and such."

"But if it's as simple as you say, why would a society-sanctioned declaration be necessary? Can't we just declare to each other and be done with it? Whom else does it really concern? I say no one else. Don't you realize the genesis of the institution of matrimony? It was created by the ruling classes as a way of transferring property, including the woman. I'm sorry, but I don't want to be considered your property or anyone else's, for that matter."

"I'm not asking you to be my property. That's not my intention at all.

And that maybe how it used to be, but I don't think anybody thinks of it like that anymore."

"But don't you see in the eyes of the law of this land that I am still viewed that way. I wouldn't have the same rights as my husband, and it is solely based on my gender. A man can make many decisions independently of his wife's wishes, but the wife can only make certain decisions with the permission of her husband. It may not be slavery in the truest sense of the word, but it is a step above it and not something I want to be a party to. We need a new line of thinking, thinking outside the confines of the simple perpetuation of the past. 'Let's keep doing it because it is the way it has always been done.' You're not afraid to think outside the confines of your comfortable little box, are you? You're not afraid to try something new that might be an improvement over the past, are you?"

"No, not exactly," I said reluctantly.

"That's the only way that progress is made: new thinking. I thought that's what you were searching for when we first met. I took you for a seeker of truth. Was I wrong?"

"No, I suppose not. I'm not saying that I have all the answers, and that my ways are the only ways. I don't want to be stodgy and stuck in my ways. I am open to new experience. But I thought it was something for both of us and our child. I don't want him or her to miss what I thought was an important element in life, a solid family. And I think my child should carry my name."

"Whoa, see right there. There you go. You say that you don't want to be stuck in your ways, but then you say something like that. What importance is that name really? It was just passed down to you. You had no say in it. True, it is a way to identify you, but why be stuck on a name that has no real attachment to your true identity, the most important aspect of your identity, which is how you define yourself?"

"So we're not going to name our child at all, then?"

"We can provide a name temporarily, but it is then up to him or her to define himself or herself, including an identifying label such as a name. I see that as the paramount role for a parent, to provide the child the freedom to define oneself and form one's own identity. Everything you say that you want us to give this child—a solid family, a name, a safe home—we can provide without marriage. If you truly are open to new experiences, and I think that you are—that's why I asked you to come with me—the best thing to do is to drop all preconceived notions, all traditions, all old ways of thinking and free your mind to new possibilities. That's what we're heading into. Please let me know now that is what you want as well."

I couldn't argue. What she was saying made some sense to me. I didn't want my fears of the unknown future (and who could really know the future?) to stop me from challenging it.

"Yes, that's what I want as well. You'll have to forgive me if my *bourgeois* thinking rears its head every now and then. I guess it was just the way I was raised."

"That's okay. I understand that. Most people don't see the box they're in because it's all they've ever seen. They don't know there is something beyond, until someone shows them. I hope that I can do that for you."

We smiled at each other, and Lorelei reached out, patted my head and tousled my hair briefly before turning back her attention to the road.

After I at least got my proposal off my chest, I tried not to think about what was happening, the unknown we were headed for, the places and people we were leaving behind, and enjoyed the new scenery of the trip. I relieved Lorelei in the driver's seat after we crossed into New York State, heading toward Albany and then Buffalo to the big border crossing at Niagara Falls. I convinced Lorelei to stop over in Niagara Falls for the night, to rest up, do the tourist sightseeing, since neither one of us had seen the natural wonder of the falls in person, and there was no real hurry to get to the farm, no deadline to meet. While not getting married as I had hoped, we did sort of have our 'honeymoon' there in Niagara, although I wouldn't call it that in front of her to avoid further philosophical discussions. I was simply trying to enjoy the moment. We weren't going very far into Canada. Our destination was a small farm about thirty miles north of London, Ontario, which was about eighty miles west of the border. So we found a motel on the American side, spent the night, and then in the morning took the boat tour to the falls. After lunch, we headed to the border crossing site.

Passports weren't needed to cross the border. We simply handed over our driver's licenses to the Canadian border guard, who asked us the purpose and length of our visit. Lorelei, back in the driver's seat, answered that we were going for a two-week visit to a friend's farm in Ontario. The guard did a cursory inspection of the vehicle, and then waved us along, wishing us an enjoyable stay in Canada.

While being a little nervous at the idea of lying, I thought, "That was simple enough." Little did I know that our attempt to avoid complications actually made things a bit more problematical in the end.

We felt a bit giddy once we were in Canada, a feeling I must admit I wasn't expecting. But after all the anticipation, I felt much more relaxed as we traveled down the Ontario highway. Although a foreign land, the countryside was much like upstate New York in appearance, and the only differences that I detected were very small ones, such as the different look to the road signs and license plates of the fellow automobiles we passed or passed us by. Lorelei tried to see what she could pick up on Canadian radio and came across a station playing "Hey Jude" by the Beatles and commenced singing at the top of her lungs and then prodded me to join her. I look back on that moment now and see us being caught in between our past and future worlds, completely carefree and happy. But it was a short trip.

After navigating our way through the maze of unfamiliar side roads, we located Ziggy's farm. It was a ten-acre plot, which was fairly small for farming, but with me being a city boy, it looked quite expansive and daunting.

Upon arrival we were greeted by the inhabitants of this communal experiment, including the aforementioned Ziggy, or Sigmund Leominster, who was its founder and the owner (although he would have never used that capitalistic term) of the land it occupied. As our parked car was being surrounded by the residents, Lorelei bolted out of her door and ran up to a tall, bearded fellow standing on the porch steps, and she practically leapt into his embrace.

"You made it, finally, I see," I overheard Ziggy say as he hugged Lorelei. "Did you have any trouble finding us?"

"No, not at all," Lorelei replied. "It's been a long time. It's wonderful to see you again, and to be here."

I stepped out of the car and was greeted by strangers, who patted me on the back and welcomed me home, even though I had never been there before. Lorelei led Ziggy over to me for a formal introduction.

"Tom, over here. Tom, this is Ziggy. Ziggy this is Tom Moore."

"Hello, Tom. So nice to finally meet you." Ziggy extended his hand for me to shake, and once he grasped it, pulled me into a hug as well. "So this is the moon cat you told me so much about."

He evidently had heard about my interest in the space program and astronomy, and that stuck in his mind. He was using the term "moon cat" as a descriptive term the first time, using the "beat" lingo, calling a person a "cat," as in "cool cat" or "hep cat," but it soon became the name I was known by. I didn't particularly like it, but with our group of hippies eschewing all things bourgeois, such as given names, I was not Tom anymore. I was initially called "*the* moon cat," and then it was my moniker, "Moon Cat." But I suppose it fit in better with the group, as I was introduced to Saffron (no doubt inspired by the Donovan song, "Mello Yellow"), Lotus (as in the flower), Juniper (ditto), Michelle-my-belle (all run together, inspired by the Beatles song "Michelle"), North Star (or occasionally "Polaris"), Ganymede (or Gany for short, but another celestial inspiration, after the moon of Jupiter), Mountain (inspired by the classic hippie chronicle *The Electric Kool-Aid Acid Test* by Tom

Wolfe), and several nicknames inspired by Kerouac characters: pals Paradise and Moriarty, Tristessa and Maggie Cassidy. The Kerouac names were given by Ziggy, I later found out, when their real names sounded too mundane. His real name Sal, he became Sal Paradise, or later, simply Paradise, and Moriarty got his name because he was close buddies with Sal, though his real name was Bill. Patricia or Trish was too plain, so she was soon Tristessa to sound more exotic (although she didn't seem to mind being named after a prostitute's character), and Margaret Wilson became Maggie Cassidy after the title character.

Ziggy was the only one of the crew whom Lorelei had met previously, and they seemed to have known each other pretty well, although I couldn't venture to say if they had been anything more than friends. At least I tried to size him up as he introduced us around the group. Ziggy seemed a bit of a Jesus figure, which I would say came from my initial impression of his appearance. He was tall and slender with long, flowing brown hair like many a speculative portrait of Christ that I've seen from artists throughout history. While Ziggy's facial features differed somewhat from the iconic images of Him—his nose was rounder and shorter than His and his forehead more pronounced—but his beard bore close resemblance in that it was full but relatively short and somewhat wispy in spots. He also came across as the leader of the group, or the others came across as his followers. Ziggy was often the preacher of the hippie philosophy, and the others were disciple-like.

"Why don't you and Tom, the moon cat, settle into your room for now," Ziggy said to Lorelei. "There's some work that needs to be done this afternoon, but don't you fret about that stuff just yet. Saffron, my lady. Would you be so kind as to show our two newest family members their lodging? Then, Lorelei, my dear, we'll have a welcome supper for you and your beau and we'll be able to go over the whys, the whats and the wherefores so that you know what to expect coming up. We'll get you acclimated as soon as possible so that you can help out. We can use all the help we can get. You've come at an auspicious time, my friends. We're just ready to plant the crops and set our grand experiment in motion. 'Til this evening, then."

Ziggy bowed to her with a flourish and left with most of the others to parts unknown. He did have a penchant for grandiosity that made me question his sincerity, but it was his style of manner, and I grew more used to it as time passed. Saffron led us into the house as we toted our belongings.

While relaxing a bit after we settled into our new room, Lorelei prodded me with a few, "Isn't this exciting?" questions and "This is the dawn of a whole new life for us," comments. I didn't let on that I was actually a little overwhelmed, but instead "Mmm-hmm"-ed in agreement. I likened the feeling to the first day of the school year at the new junior high or high school. I maybe knew one or two people in the class, as I only knew Lorelei, and the new people I was sizing up, whether or not this or that person would become a friend or an enemy, or even one of those people you share significant parcels of your life with, but never get to know beyond a name and subsequently pass on by without much of an acknowledgement.

Saffron gave us a tour of the farmhouse and barnyard while we awaited the First Supper. When the others returned from the day's work, we gathered for the feast of "greens and beans." The "greens" were salad fixings (mostly different from the kind of salads of lettuce, cucumbers, and tomatoes I was used to) including my first introduction to bean sprouts, bean curds and arugula. The "beans" were the products from the farm—dried and stored from last year's crop. While I had grown accustomed to more vegetables in my diet while staying at the Pink House, my diet wasn't strictly vegetarian as it was about to become on the farm. Cost-savings was a big reason meat wasn't plentiful back in Cambridge, and I always could get a burger or a steak at the restaurant if I was really feeling meat withdrawal pangs. But Ziggy's farm was strictly vegetarian in keeping with the hippie philosophy of loving your fellow creatures enough not to eat them. The only farm animals were goats, for milk, and a couple of mules for labor. The economic system of

the farm was set up to raise what food we needed to subsist, and sell the sur-
plus at the market for cash to purchase whatever supplies and tools were
needed, Ziggy explained during the supper. We were to raise several varieties
of beans, which were high in protein and thus an ample substitute for the
lack of meat, and the goats—because they were a bit easier to handle on a
small farm—would provide milk for us and a local goat cheese factory. Alfalfa
was grown on a couple of acres for goat and mule food, and a couple of
fields were fallow this year to allow for crop rotation.

The very next day I got down to the very hard and dirty work of farm
labor. Now, I had worked some pretty long, arduous days before in the restaurant's steamy kitchen, and at my father's supply warehouse (inventory days
were always dreaded by every employee, especially in the summer in the un-
air-conditioned warehouse, having to climb around the dusty steel shelving
structures trying to count pipes, fixtures and whatnots that were too heavy
to even move), but nothing had prepared me for the strenuous nature of
farm work. This was absolutely where the bourgeoisie met the proletariat.
For that first day, and seemingly endless several days after that, we planted
the seeds of the bean crops. Ziggy's farm in 1969 was not fully mechanized.
He did own a tractor, but that was nearly the extent of machinery on the
farm. I didn't know the state of Ziggy's wealth, but even if he had money to
buy more farm machinery, it wouldn't fit the image of "back-to-the-earth"
hippie he was trying to cultivate. With mules carrying sacks of seeds, we hand-
sowed the countless plowed rows. (I say "we," as in all the available
farmhands: Lorelei by tacit agreement on her pregnant condition was assigned house duties with Saffron, who really was like a delicate flower and
thusly designated as "house-mouse," along with Juniper, cleaning, laundering
and cooking for the crew. The four other women at the commune worked
right alongside the men in the fields.) There was the mid-day sun to contend
with, and the endless stooping to cover the seeds with soil after they'd been
dropped in a group. It wasn't a couple of hours, with complaints from my

aching back, before I wondered what I had committed myself to. But also eager to find out of just what "stuff" I was made, I persevered with the rest of our herd. Tristessa, Maggie and North Star were newcomers to farm work as well, and we encouraged each other along. Ziggy pitched in as well, but he also was a leader. All the while he kept talking about the glorious things to look forward to: the sight in a few weeks of sprouting plants, the visible "fruits" of our labor, and ultimately the joy of feeding yourself directly from your own labor. He even talked about the "joy" of hard-earned work exhaustion at the end of the day, as if that were a goal in and of itself, a prize justly won.

It wasn't just the planting that was back-breaking. After that was finally done, the constant weeding commenced, and I became intimate with the phrase, "a hard row to hoe," though I confess I have yet to find an easy row to hoe, and that was partly due to the fact that there were countless rows to hoe. I didn't come to "love my rows," as Thoreau had. He wrote, "What shall I learn of beans or beans of me? I cherish them, I hoe them, early and late I have an eye to them; and this is my day's work." This was my day's work, also; but at the time it didn't seem quite as poetic as Thoreau had made it sound. "But why should I raise them? Only Heaven knows." Indeed! Lorelei complimented me on my blistered and soon to be calloused hands, as they were transitioning from bourgeois hands into proletarian hands. I had to grow accustomed to seeing the appearance of my hands change, as the constant contact with the soil made it harder to look clean with the dirt under my nails even after washing up with soap. After a long day's work, dirt pervaded my body as I would wipe the sweat from my face and neck with my stained hands, and I used my clothing to wipe my hands so that I looked like either a bourgeois slob or a regular working man. Let's don't forget milking the goats and cleaning the pens of their droppings, and the mule's dung as well, collecting it for composting into manure fertilizer, and what that did to my appearance and new bodily scent. We got a chance to bathe at the end of the day, but it was just something I was getting used to. I was now part of a group of very pungently odoriferous people.

I was also learning, however, so much more than I ever had imagined, about growing plants, and fixing engines when the tractor broke down, or irrigation pumps when they went bad, or animal husbandry when goats got sick or pregnant and gave birth, or a myriad of other simple things, such as how to handle a mule who had become very stubborn (which is how I became intimate with the phrase "stubborn as a mule" as well). I never became an expert by any means, but even through all the complaining I was doing on the inside (as I tried to put my best face forward for Lorelei because I knew how much this communal experiment meant to her), I did feel richer for the experience I was gaining in life. I realized how sheltered I had been in my life. I never had much appreciation for how my food had reached my plate, or for the significance of weather. I had mostly thought of rain as a nuisance instead of the life-giving gift that it was—and the welcomed respite from a day's field work. I considered a sunny day as a mere pleasantry until working on the farm, where it was an essential element to our miracle-of-life growing cycle. After a few weeks, the burgeoning plants that were sprouting up did fill me with a sense of pride as Ziggy and Lorelei suggested they would. I was now their caretaker, and how well I did my job helped determined their fate.

In the first few weeks, as I was getting accustomed to my new work life, I also was getting accustomed to my new leisure life, whatever down time I had after the work day. There wasn't much television watching to relax as I had done habitually in my former life. I was most often too tired to read. Lorelei and I didn't have sex, partly because of her condition and partly due to my exhaustion. I mostly was ready to go to sleep an hour or two after sundown so that I would be ready to start the next day before sunup. But what non-working waking hours I had, I told Lorelei that I had to work on a letter to my father.

The letter took me weeks to finish, as I was looking for exactly the right words to explain my actions. I revised it a few times before ending up with a twenty-two page tome, where I said "I'm sorry" maybe forty different times. I had to tell him why I decided to leave the country, and I knew he wouldn't understand. The hardest part was trying to tell him about his future grandchild and how it wasn't certain that I could ever travel back home so that he could eventually see him or her. I told him he could come to Canada to visit if he ever felt the desire to see me again. I doubted that he ever would, at least in the immediate future. Maybe time would soften things, but as I was struggling to write, I easily imagined that I may have seen my dad for the last time in that Copley Square hotel in Boston when we fought, all because of my actions. When I finally felt I had said enough, I sealed the letter up, and shook the weight of it off my back when I drove Lorelei's car to the town post office by myself on a rainy June day. It was mid-July when I got a reply. Perhaps he had to choose his words carefully as well, not to say something he might regret, and it was a subdued and somber letter that came to me. He absolutely didn't understand my decision, and said perhaps I wasn't the same boy he raised, but a different adult who was part of a whole new generation that he was finding difficult to understand. He wasn't planning to come to Canada any time soon, and said, as I was an adult, he respected my decision to live my life as I pleased. He also said, "But I'm sorry that it has come to this." He signed it "Dad," not "Love, Dad," as he always did in cards or letters he sent my first year in college.

Nineteen Sixty-Nine was full of historical events worthy of remembering, and, for me, the memories became closely associated with my life on Ziggy's farm. With our fields full of beans on July 20th, the Apollo 11 mission landed on the moon. There was one small black-and-white television set that was not much watched, due mainly to poor reception in the area; but just as at the Pink House, my roommates got into the spirit of the occasion and gathered around to watch the coverage. We were able to bring in a Canadian

Broadcasting Company telecast with some difficulty. It took quite a lot of adjusting the rabbit-ears antenna on top of the set to get a clear enough picture to see what has going on—Ganymede having to keep touching the metal antenna and standing completely still to become an extension of the antenna itself. I regretfully missed Walter Cronkite's take on the event. My fellow residents, knowing my acute interest in the goings-on, made a party of the two days of the landing, Neil Armstrong's first step, his and Buzz Aldrin's frolicking on the surface, the planting of the flag and the eventual lift off the next day. Ziggy *proclaimed* a work holiday for the two days of coverage, and it did make me feel a little more at home than I had my first couple of months there, which tends to happen with sharing certain experiences, moments and events.

As Lorelei and I were about to retire for the night—and the astronauts prepared for the first snooze on the moon—I suggested that we take a walk outside. The night air was still warm, and the gentlest of breezes made it completely pleasurable. I took Lorelei's hand as we strolled across the barnyard to the bean-fields to gaze up at our newly tenanted moon. I stood behind her and wrapped my arms around her belly, which was quite pronounced now, and tried waxing eloquent on the waxing moon, nearly at its first quarter.

"Can you believe that there are people up there right now?" I said, even though we just finished watching the live television pictures.

"It is amazing," she said. "From here, where are they exactly?"

"They're on the far side, so you can't see it from the Earth. But their base is in one of the dark spots, like you can see on this side, a big flat area called the Sea of Tranquility."

"I like that—Sea of Tranquility."

Taking the time to really look at the sky in my new neighborhood for the first time, I realized how many more stars were visible while being away from the city lights I was used to, and I regretted not having my telescope.

"I'm not that religious, you know, though I was raised a Catholic," I told her, "but I often feel a bit more spiritual when looking up at the sky and that big rock up there."

"Yeah?"

"I mean, I was thinking the other day about how some people have been saying that, with all the new advancements in science these days, people might be moving away from God and religion as a result. You know, because the more we discover, it seems like the universe has a natural random order to it, that it seems to lack any indications of intent or design."

"What do you mean, exactly?"

"Like in primitive times, man thought he was the reason for the existence of the universe, that the Earth was its center because it was created by God to be the home of mankind, and everything revolved around it. But because of views from people like Copernicus, Galileo, Darwin and Einstein, and all the great scientists we have today, we can view life as a kind of chance occurrence, where instead of the conditions for life being just right because it was created to support it, life itself simply developed because the random arrangement of conditions needed to sustain life already existed here on Earth: the right amount of heat from the sun, the right amount of gravity to stick to the planet's surface, the right amount of atmosphere, and so on. We see the Earth, Moon and Sun as part of a solar system, which is part of a galaxy, one of countless galaxies. There are so many worlds out there that the chance of there being at least one other that has just the right conditions for the formation of life is pretty good. We may not even be unique. But we can look up to the sky now and see other planets, other bodies like the moon, where variances occurred in the conditions that obviously made life impossible to be sustained. Mars doesn't have life as we know it because it is too far from the sun and thus too cold. Likewise, Venus is too close to the sun and too hot. Did you know that if the Earth didn't revolve daily as it does, if one side of it constantly faced the Sun like one side of the Moon faces us, that it would be too hot for us to live, and consequently that the other side would be too cold?"

"Yeah, so what does it all mean, then?"

"Exactly. What it means to some people is that they think we are just cosmically lucky to have had this prime piece of real estate to call home. It just happened to be in the right temperature zone for life to develop. Pure chance. No cosmic significance to the human race at all. We're just animals after all, just like the other animals and life forms of this planet, seemingly destined to live out their existence on this planet because it supports them. But the more science discovers, I still see some kind of divine influence, and thus, some kind of cosmic significance to mankind."

"Do you now?" Lorelei looked back at my face, which peered over her right shoulder, and smirked a bit.

"I do. And I know it sounds humorous, and I'm not claiming to be the smartest person who finally figured out man's reason for being. I know there are religious types that still believe in a divine creation but scoff at the scientific endeavors that seem to reiterate the randomness of it all. But I embrace science and still see the strong possibility of a divine purpose to our lives. I'm not trying to be too heavy-handed here, but take a look at that Moon up there, and what do you see?"

"I see a big rock. Human beings have been curious about it for centuries and finally have the technology to go to it and investigate."

"Yes. And people used to think it was made out of cheese. But now they know it isn't. People used to think the Moon was a ball of fire like the Sun, but now they know it is reflected light it's giving off, and now they know we aren't the center of the universe because we revolve around the Sun like the Moon revolves around us. But think of this. Take the two biggest objects in our sky: the moon and the sun—completely different in nature, and in size. You look at the Sun and the Moon side by side, and the Sun totally dwarfs the Moon, as it does the Earth. But by its relative distances to the

Earth, the Sun and Moon appear to be exactly the same size in the sky. The sun is four hundred times larger than the moon, yet somehow it is precisely four hundred times further from the Earth than the moon is. You can take any two objects of differing sizes and by changing the relative distance to the observer, you can make either the larger to appear smaller by increasing its distance or the smaller to appear larger by decreasing its distance. Other planets have moons—some several, like Jupiter and Saturn—and I don't know if there is a similar phenomenon, but our Moon and our Sun have *one and only one* position where an observer can stand and the two objects appear to be exactly the same size, and that is on the surface of the Earth, where we happen to be. You can see it more clearly in a total solar eclipse—a perfect match. There are minor variations that would make it less than perfect. Yes, a tiny bit of sun peeks around the moon during some eclipses, but I'm talking about a human observer, not a robot observer. What are the odds that the only place this could be observed is the surface of the planet, where I might add, there is a certain species of animal which has the cognitive power to recognize it?"

"I don't know."

"Well, the odds are astronomical, pardon the pun. The three astronauts up there just changed that perspective. They obviously don't view the Sun and Moon as the same size anymore. But it is unique to our position on Earth."

"I guess I never thought about it like that before. So you think it is some kind of *heavenly* sign?"

"I do. I mean it could be. It's not proof of the existence of God or anything, but it is one of the things that makes me think there is something of a plan going on here. It amazes me that we've advanced this far to send men to the moon, and it sets to mind what other discoveries and enlightenment are possible."

"It is amazing that there are people up there," she said pointing to the populated moon, "but I have to think what a waste of money it is. There are so many problems here on Earth that need to be addressed, like poverty, ending the war, saving the environment from damage. What's it all going to do for us, besides just saying that we went and then came back?"

"Well, that's part of it, to go, to explore, to see what they can find."

"I hear they're supposed to bring back some rocks. I wouldn't be surprised to find out that they were looking to mine the moon. They're probably looking for gold in the rocks. Or with the United States involved, they're probably looking to build some kind of military base there."

"I don't know about that. It's more the spirit of exploration. Better to know what's really there than not to know."

"That doesn't seem so worth it to me then. I certainly hope that they don't discover any new life forms while they are up there. They'll probably conquer them just as the European *explorers* did when they *discovered* the Indians. They even misnamed them because they didn't truly know where they were."

So she didn't exactly share my enthusiasm for the event. I gazed up at the night sky a little longer, wistfully thinking to myself that I would never work for NASA as I had dreamed. I was fairly certain that a U.S. governmental agency would have no need for Canadian engineers, particularly one that evaded the draft. I wasn't even training to be an aerospace engineer anymore. I didn't know what I was doing. It was okay to attempt this experiment, but without thinking it through, I suddenly thought, "Am I to be a bean farmer the rest of my life?" I was pretty sure it was not what I wanted, but I didn't express myself to Lorelei because I wanted her to feel as if I were happy with my life here with her. We took a last look at the heavens and turned in for the night.

Next up in August was the Woodstock music festival. The gang started hearing about it on the radio, and because it was in neighboring New York State, discussions began about possibly going to the concert. At first, the group talked about how fun a festival would be, a gathering of our generation and for our generation, and how nice it would be to "groove," or hang out, with so many people who thought alike—the biggest "be-in" of the decade. Oftentimes, society marginalized our age group, particularly of this era because we were so rebelliously different from previous generations, and so it almost was casually thought of as a nice opportunity for a little diversion from the farm work, a bit of a summer vacation for us. But when they started promoting who would be performing—the really big acts—such as Jimi Hendrix; Janis Joplin; The Who; Crosby, Stills, Nash and Young; and Jefferson Airplane, some of our group started to realize that this could be *the* cultural event of our generation and became extremely excited about it, like Ziggy and Lorelei.

I, on the other hand, while being interested in any diversion from farm work at the moment and in seeing some of my favorite performers, added my reservations about going back across the border, and then having to re-cross it to get back to the farm. It felt too risky for an American citizen without a visa, particularly if one wanted to stay in Canada. Lorelei didn't seem to have any qualms about it, though, because she thought it was going to be easy to cross, like last time. Some of the other Americans in our group—the ones like me, the males evading the draft—did express the same reservations. What tipped the scales for Lorelei not going was her extremely pregnant condition. She was in her third trimester, and I pointed out how hard it was going to be for her. She was already beginning to feel the discomforts of pregnancy.

"It's going to be *four* solid days spent outdoors," I said, pleading my case. "Who knows what the weather is going to be like? It could be very hot during the day, probably cold at night. I'm having a hard time imaging how you guys are going to have any decent meals during the show. I don't know what they're going to do to have enough lavatories for all these people. It probably won't be very sanitary. I'm just too worried about your condition right now. I don't think you should go with them."

"I don't know. Maybe you're right," she said. "It would be hard on me. They are bringing tents with them, but if it was a different time and I wasn't in this condition, I sure would like to go."

After further deliberations, Lorelei decided to stay with the other Americans in Canada, and Ziggy led the Canadian contingent to the historic festival. While they were gone, we who stayed had a vacation on the farm for the four days, at least—excepting a few chores that couldn't be postponed, such as milking the darn goats.

Upon the return of our band of merry pranksters, being regaled with their stories of this new-found hippie heaven, we earthbound souls regretted not attending this seminal event, or—in Lorelei's case—outright rued the day. During the weeks of the aftermath, Lorelei expressed sadness in saying, "I wish I would have gone," or more adamantly, "I should have gone to Woodstock." She mentioned it less as time passed, seemingly resigning herself that it was *fait accompli*.

After the summer faded, in between harvesting the crops at the end of one growing season and the end of Lorelei's growing season as well, on October 21st, we found out that Jack Kerouac had died in St. Petersburg, Florida, where he had moved with his mother. He'd had a massive internal hemorrhage brought about by his years of heavy drinking. Everyone at the commune, being fans of his, was greatly saddened by the news. He was only forty-seven years old. Ziggy and Lorelei were such big devotees of his, and they set up an impromptu tribute that evening by having everyone take turns reading favorite passages from his different books.

Funny thing was that for as big fans hippie-types were of his work because it embodied the free-spirit nature that they were beginning to express, Jack Kerouac was not a big fan of hippies. Personally he was somewhat conservative, and at times ridiculed what the hippie generation was doing. Yes, he coined the term "Beat Generation," which begat the "beatniks" of the fifties, which begat the "hippies" of the sixties, and he wrote the iconic novel of the bohemian lifestyle with *On the Road*; but he was of our parents' generation, who fought World War II, and whom we were mostly rebelling against for their stodgy thinking. Obviously Kerouac didn't quite fit that image either, but for the generation who coined the phrase, "Don't trust anyone over thirty," he was one of the few exceptions to that rule in being someone older that they looked up to. He was like Bob Dylan in that he was identified with a movement but didn't necessarily fully participate in it. Dylan wrote great protest songs like, "Blowing in the Wind," "Times They are a-Changing," and "Masters of War," but he wasn't an activist, like his one-time girlfriend Joan Baez was. My thoughts were that he knew what he was, which was a poet and musician, and that's all he wanted to be. He left it to others to interpret what they wanted from his music. Kerouac did the same with his books.

I was a fan of Kerouac as well, but I didn't look to his depictions of the unfettered, carefree and rebellious lifestyle as inspirations. I found him enjoyable to read because he was poetic in his prose, very descriptive; but also as a young person searching for my identity, I connected with his thinly disguised main character's quest for elusive things. In *On the Road*, it was his quest for Dean's father and the spirit of America. In *The Dharma Bums*, it was his quest for dharma, or eternal truth. In *Big Sur*, it was his quest for inner peace. Most of his work was highly autobiographical (more straight autobiography with names changed than actual fiction), but I identified with his depictions of his formative years even more—his stories from his youth in *Vanity of Duluoz*, *Visions of Gerard* and *Maggie Cassidy*. Kerouac was perhaps more working class than my middle-class upbringing, but I closely identified with his stories of childhood and adolescence because mine were similar. Maybe because where he grew up in Lowell, Massachusetts was so close to Warwick that it seemed as if it could be the same, or that he was French-Canadian like my mother's side of the family, or that he was raised Roman

Catholic as well as I. So that's more of why I read my passage from *Maggie Cassidy* than from his more famous books. But like the end of the Sixties and the forthcoming break-up of the Beatles, Kerouac's death signified the end of something else, other than just one man's life. It was the passing of a legend and an era.

CHORUS 4:

"Beautiful, beautiful, beautiful boy."
Lennon

About a week after Kerouac's passing, we celebrated the arrival of a new life to this world when Lorelei delivered our son—on Halloween Day, October 31. The farm had wrapped up the harvest a few weeks prior, and we had our fallow period of labor as the autumn temperatures tumbled. Most of us caught up on much needed rest after the long summer. Lorelei still had a bit of labor to finish up with, though.

As her due date approached that September and October, we began debating names for the baby. I offered Thomas Jr., Paul, Michael, Steven, James or Jack for a boy; or Mary, Darlene, Laura or Lucille for a girl. Predictably, Lorelei denounced them as too bourgeois. Like our comrades' names, she delved into the exotic, with her main themes being the hippie-ish flowers, astronomy or Indian. She thought with my interest in the moon missions that I would like our child's name to be moon-related. But when she brought up Luna, I immediately thought *tic*—as in *lunatic*. So I vehemently vetoed that one. I had already heard about Frank Zappa naming his daughter Moon Unit, and when Lorelei said, "How about *Moon*?" I immediately thought *pie*—as in *moon-pie*. That was also a no. Then she started on flowers. She liked Daffodil, but I only thought of *daffy*; or Dahlia, Larkspur, or Marigold—not bad I told her, but only for a girl. She said that flowers didn't have genders and that it shouldn't matter. I said that there is a reality out there, that no matter what we think, other children will find it funny and laugh at it, particularly if a boy were named after a flower. She responded by saying that we should always keep him in a positive nurturing environment anyway where names aren't made sport of. I wouldn't mind several flower names for girls, such as Rose or Rosemary, Lily, Violet, and Holly, but they were too prosaic for Lorelei. She ticked off some American Indian-type names, like Spirit-in-the-Water or Wind-in-the-Grass. I didn't like the idea of a child of the Sixties to be associated with *grass* his whole life, for one thing. She liked Andromeda and Alpha Centauri in the astronomic realm. She also like peaceful sounding names like Placid, Harmony or Serenity. What eventually got her most excited was Tranquility because she remembered the association with the moon landing. The astronauts landed in the Sea of Tranquility. I wasn't that comfortable with it because it was a bit cumbersome, but we were bound to be locked in a stalemate if I didn't give in on something, so Tranquility is what we agreed on. It sounded nice as a word itself, but not for a person's name exactly, I thought. I sought a bit of a compromise, however, after the delivery.

"You know, you have to admit it is kind of a mouthful," I said. "It doesn't lend itself to shortening to a nickname either. 'Tranq' is a bit awkward, even though it rhymes with Frank. How about if I called him 'Jack' for short, as his nickname, you know, like in Jack Kerouac?"

"I suppose that's not too bad. If you feel you must," she relented. "Okay. Tranquility Jack, then." I threw in the Kerouac thing to make her more amenable. I don't think I ever mentioned that Jack was my father's name, and the real reason I suggested it.

Lorelei had other new-fangled ideas about giving birth, which were really from a re-birth, if you will, of old-fangled ideas. While it was not very widespread at the time, Lorelei wanted to experience a natural childbirth, just like in days of yore when hospitals were not the primary place to deliver babies. She wanted to deliver at home and didn't want to be drugged numb with pain medication.

"It's the most natural thing in the world," she said. "And it's a shame to mask the beauty of it all with that artificial, sterile atmosphere of a hospital, the only ones with you to share the greatest experience of your life doctors and nurses you don't even know. I want to be surrounded by people I know and love. And if there's pain involved, then at least it will make me feel more alive."

I was thinking that the hospital's atmosphere was sterile for a reason, so that there aren't any germs. No infections—at least that will keep you alive if not make you feel alive. I mean, if they improved on things over time—increase cleanliness in a delivery room, have qualified medical personnel on hand if things go wrong—what's wrong with that? Man-made, synthetic or plastic were all curse words in hippie culture. I didn't bring it up to Lorelei, but maybe it was the science enthusiast in me. I had an appreciation for plastic, which, yes, man invented, to do a myriad of wondrous and fascinating things. But I digress.

What else wasn't that common for the day was the father being present at the delivery. When I offered that I had no clue that I was expected to be there to at least *bear* witness, Lorelei forcefully invited me.

"You have to be there, if just to witness the biggest miracle of your life!" she implored.

"I have no doubt that it's miraculous, but I can also take your word for it," I said.

"You're missing the point. I want this to be a shared experience. You and me, and baby makes three. Nobody gets to be absent. I certainly can't be, nor the baby, so *you* can't be either. Besides, I need you for support. This is the *deal*, man, the biggest deal in all our lives besides our own births that we can't even remember. We're going to remember this forever."

Not only was she inviting me in the room, but as she considered our comrades as her new family, she invited the whole commune to be with her, if they wished—the men as well as the women. I had reservations over exactly what the men might see, but I let it pass. Again, it was outside the realm of my thinking, or at least my modern thinking. I knew it wasn't that long ago where American pioneer women didn't have the luxury or the option to have hospital births, or even doctors present. It was more of a village or community event to give birth.

Lorelei contacted a local midwife to assist with the delivery. As I said, I was a science enthusiast, but I was mostly oblivious to what happens at the time of labor. I did witness a kid goat being born, but it kind of disgusted me as well as amazed me all at the same time.

I was helping Lorelei with washing dishes on Halloween Eve when her water broke. I was drying plates and from over my shoulder I heard a big splash on the floor, and I thought she just slipped and maybe brought her hand down in the water-filled sink and it got on the floor. When I turned around to find her doubled over, I asked her if she were all right. When she said, "My water broke," I thought she meant she broke some dish, and she had to explain exactly what happened, and then she had to calm *me* down because I didn't know it was basically supposed to happen. I got all agitated and worried that something wrong happened with the baby. But it was just the first sign that the time was drawing nigh. Luckily, we didn't have to rush her to a hospital. Saffron helped me walk her to the bedroom, as Lorelei gingerly stepped with her arms draped on each of our shoulders for support. The midwife knew the due date was imminent and was on alert for our call after the water broke and contractions began. The woman arrived only an hour or so after we called.

The rest of it pretty much went by in a blur for me. In the room, I did my best to make Lorelei feel comfortable, yet it was next to impossible. I fluffed the pillows, held her hand, stroked her forehead, rubbed her temples, fed her water, and helped her breathe with a method the midwife taught her to mitigate the pain. As her labor was not progressing rapidly and time was drawing into the night and morning, I felt sleepy and nearly dozed off several times, but of course, Lorelei couldn't sleep while contractions clenched her like a fist every few minutes. A wave of guilt washed over me as I felt I was the cause for all her suffering. That the act of conception was conceived as a hedonistic indulgence of sensual gratification was pure irony, if not a cruel, malicious trick, considering all the pain it ultimately caused. Who would pro-create knowing the pain it would produce if the act were not disguised by pleasure? "Be fruitful and multiply," was not exactly a necessary command-ment after the creation of the orgasm, was it? Surprising how far removed sex was from giving birth, however, during labor.

As the contractions grew stronger, as well as my guilt, I excused my-self to take a brief walk outside. I needed to do something physical to alleviate the nervousness of anticipation, and so I, the expectant father, paced back and forth in the barnyard like the proverbial expectant father. I saw my breath cloud in the chill of the night air, which did an amazing job of clearing my senses. As I gazed up into the starry, starry night, I said an "Our Father" and a "Hail, Mary" to the heavens. I gave up church services after my mother died, and I didn't do much formal praying, but it seemed appropriate if not formulaic and habitual in this time of distress. Also, while searching the heav-ens for guidance, I prayed to my saintly mother to be the patron saint of this birth that everything would turn out okay. I told her, "I wish you could have been here for this. And I'm sorry I screwed things up with Dad so bad that he's not a part of my life right now." Tears welled up until they dripped down my cheeks. I quickly dried them, somewhat embarrassed even in my solitary moment of grief, or at least I hoped I wasn't observed. Quickly, I glanced around me, saw no one, and headed back inside.

Lorelei had been crying, too, but that was physical pain. Amazingly to me, that's what she asked for. Here she was *hoo-hooing* and *hee-heeing*, and she could have been feeling more at ease with an epidural shot. Sweat was pouring down her face, and Saffron helped out by mopping her forehead with a washcloth, while I went back to her bedside to hold her hand. I suppose she was squeezing my hand about equally as hard as her contractions squeezed her abdomen that she nearly broke some of my bones. I had such a hard time watching her suffer, but I did my best to comfort her through it saying, "You're almost there, now. You're almost there," and "You're about to be a mom. You're about to be a mom. Breathe, breathe," and then when the midwife directed her, I repeated, "Push, push, push."

Ziggy was the only other man in the room, and things were kept discreet by having everyone on the headboard side of the room, with a sheet draped over Lorelei's splayed legs. The baby's head finally started to crown, and the midwife guided him out amidst cheering and congratulating from the group in the room. Immediately, Lotus ran out of the room announcing to the "waiting room" of the remaining men of the farm, "It's a boy! It's a boy! It's a beautiful baby boy!"

I was dumbfounded and flabbergasted when I saw him for the first time, all covered in placental goo, umbilical cord still attached. I started shedding tears of joy as he took his first breath and almost immediately began crying, too. The midwife did an expert job tying off and cutting the umbilical cord, and, with the help of Juniper, cleaned and wrapped him up, then placed him on Lorelei's chest to bond with her. She kept repeating his name softly, "Tranquility. Tranquility." It sounded more like a mantra than a name, though. The women commended Lorelei, who now tried to relax and grasp that it was finally a done deed, and they shortly after filed out to get some air or relieve themselves of the intensity of the room. Ziggy grasped my hand to shake it and clapped me on the back and just said, "Outstanding, man. Outstanding," and then left our new nuclear family to be alone finally.

I couldn't stop looking at our newborn son. His skin was a bit darker at the start and sort of mottled in appearance, but that gradually faded to a more normal color. He kept his eyes closed those first few moments, maybe because the lights were too bright in this new world. His features were incredibly delicate, and I was amazed. I hadn't been around too many babies, particularly not at zero hour like this before, and I was astounded how fragile and insubstantial he was. His nose wasn't so much of a nose yet, more like a bump with two nostril holes at the bottom. While he was nearly completely hairless, my attention was caught by the wisps of eyelashes that he had. And I didn't know exactly what I did expect, but I was surprised by the sight of his primitive, dainty fingernails and toenails when I counted his digits, as I imagine all parents do; although, I don't know how often they fail to find the correct amount. I was just happy everything was there and appeared normal. Actually, I was ecstatic simply to see this doll-like creation exhibit signs of life: a gentle intake of breath here, a muscle twitch there, a lip-purse here, and an eyelid blink there. Having no recollection of it obviously, though, I could imagine my baby self looking up at my father and mother in the first few minutes of my life. I suppose my imagination substituted the faces I had seen in an old photo of my parents around the time I was born, or right before, because they were my parents' *young* faces in *black and white* that I was seeing. They cooed and baby talked to introduce themselves to me, and so I did the same to introduce myself to my own son.

My son! My God, I couldn't believe it. At different times in one's life, there is a certain feeling of what age one is, regardless of the actual chronological age. I was a couple years into what they call adulthood, but somehow I still felt as if I were a fifteen year old kid. How could someone my age have a kid of his own, even though it was actually pretty commonplace at twenty? I was still *Son* to my dad, but now I was *Dad* to my own little *Son*. That kind of frightened me, because I only had experience being a son. I had no experience of being a dad. And now I had estranged myself from the man who could give me advice on being a dad, calling on his many years of *dad* experience. So while this was the happiest moment of my life, there was a hint of sadness to diminish it all. Still, as the midwife helped Lorelei deliver the afterbirth and everything was cleaned up, as the *event* of a lifetime drew to a close, this was *the* happiest moment of my life. There is a natural tendency for a comedown after such a highlight as this, but for the moment, without knowing how precipitous the come-down would be, I reveled simply in being the happiest I had ever been.

VERSE 7:

"Why she had to go, I don't know, she wouldn't say,
I said something wrong, now I long for yesterday."
                                    Lennon-McCartney

"Try to see it my way, only time will tell if I am right or I am wrong,
While you see it your way, there's chance that we might fall apart before too long."
                                    Lennon-McCartney

For the remainder of 1969, I exulted in my new job as father. With less farm work to do during the winter months, I could spend as much time as possible with Lorelei and Tranquility Jack. He slept a lot those first few months, so the interaction was rather minimal, but when he was awake, I did what I could to bond with him. Obviously, Lorelei handled the feeding as she insisted on breastfeeding, but when he was finished, I would take him to hold on my shoulder to burp him. I shared equally in diaper changing duties, which I enjoyed because I was taking him while he was cranky with the dirty diaper and changing him back into a happy baby most times when he was all fresh and clean. He had a little wooden rocking cradle, fashioned by the tacit, grizzled-looking, but tender, Mountain; but sometimes Lorelei and I would lie awake in bed with our little TJ asleep on one or the other's chest. Many moments like that I simply thought, "This is what it's all about." I now had a family of my own. This was the start of everything I wanted out of life. I had a wife now—though not technically—instead of just a girlfriend in Lorelei, and I had a son. We started off the perfect picture of a happy family. The only thing that would have made me feel even better, though, would to be back home. I couldn't quite get over the feeling of being out of my element here. But I tried my best for my family's sake.

The world outside the farm seemed to be going by in a blur as the Sixties drew to its close. There was another Apollo moon mission to track in November. We had also heard the name Charles Manson for the first time when the news of his capture for the Tate-LaBianca murders in Los Angeles back in the summer was broadcast. The murders of Sharon Tate and the others didn't register with our group, even if someone may have heard about it in the news at the time, but, then again, Hollywood was pretty much out of our realm, and she wasn't as well known as some other celebrities who might have better captured our attention. However, when the details of Manson and his "Family" started to be reported that November, it definitely did register with our crowd because Manson was head of a commune-like ranch where he and his followers indulged in the hippie lifestyle in a big way. There were major amounts of drug and sexual experimentation going on in his group; but as hippies were peace-loving, Manson definitely didn't live by that code. While not directly participating in the slayings, he manipulated his cohorts to do the dirty deeds to facilitate the "Helter Skelter" gospel that he had been preaching to them. Later details revealed that Manson thought the Beatles were somehow communicating with him through their songs, particularly on the White Album, with backward-masking recording techniques. He somehow equated the avant-garde "Revolution 9" with Revelation 9.

My commune comrades may have been insulted by this guy who co-opted their look, style and phraseology, but I also found the similarities unsettling beneath the surface as well. I was witnessing the draw of a charismatic leader who could manipulate weaker-minded people who were seeking guidance of some sort. While Ziggy was not maniacal, he did portray himself as a father-figure, guru-type who did his share of preaching his own brand of salvation. Once you give yourself over to his type of guidance, I could see that your mind would become highly suggestible, even to malicious suggestions. Fortunately, however, our group was primarily concentrated on work as a means to our salvation. But I understood the influential dynamic that ol' Charlie had on the young women in his group because I saw the same kind of idealization of Ziggy as a leader from the female members in our group. And while Lorelei definitely had a mind of her own, I still wasn't quite sure if she weren't falling under his spell, too. I knew that she did look up to him as an ideal of her own philosophy. Once you allow someone else to lead, then you follow, and you can't be too surprised if you happen to get led astray.

The next event that riveted our attention was the draft lottery on December 1, 1969. Even though it was an American story, Canadian broadcasters probably understood the interest from the growing number of American expatriates in the country, and put it on live television as the United States did for all its concerned citizens. Some Americans in Canada were draft-dodgers; they were already drafted. Some were actual deserters from the military. And then some, like me, were here in anticipation of getting drafted.

Besides the out-and-out war protests, there had been calls for a more fair draft system, which included many deferments, including the one I used in going to college. But college was still an upper-class and upper-middle-class enclave so that the lower socioeconomic classes were getting drafted disproportionately. The lottery was the answer to this call. They assigned each day of the year for 1970 a random number one through three hundred sixty six (one to cover leap day), and if a male born before 1950—as I was—had his birthday assigned a number *one*, he would be drafted first, and so forth. Low drafted numbers were definitely bad news. Pundits were speculating that high numbers, anything from 180 on up, were relatively safe from not being drafted because the needs of the military would be met before they reached that point.

The draft made some sense on an intellectual level, that it was a fair way to do things. If you were a "fortunate son," like John Fogerty sang about, you didn't have to go to Vietnam and possibly die prior to 1970. In terms of serving the military needs of the country, the country of the Declaration of Independence where "all men are created equal," it shouldn't matter who your parents are. But it did. The lottery idea, though, reinforced the idea that your fate was beyond your control. And who should be deciding for you that you be sent to a foreign land to possibly die? Obviously, it would be the most momentous decision in your life, and yet, have no input in making it? It was a tough pill to swallow.

So the group again gathered around the small black-and-white television set with rapt attention. Even though we were technically safe from the repercussions of the drawing, the Americans, such as I, had no mere passing interest in the results. So as the first big snowstorm of my first Canadian winter loomed, I watched as each *pill* was drawn and revealed. There was calm when the first few days came out because nobody in the room had them. When a high number was revealed, a comment came from the peanut gallery, "You lucky bastards," or "They're all probably calling their mommas and daddies to thank them for having sex on the right night all those years ago." When a low number was revealed, there were some snickers, and the comment, "I guess you should be packing your bags for Vee-eht-naam right about now," to the abstract crowd of men born on that day. "Maybe those poor slobs should slap their mommies and daddies right about now," I heard Moriarty say to Paradise. When my birthday finally came up attached to the number forty-two, it hit me like a ton of bricks.

"That's mine; that's mine," I repeated, in shock.

Good-naturedly, Moriarty said to me, "Well, it was nice knowing you, Moon Cat. Say hello to the Viet Cong and Brother Ho for me."

"Well, aren't you glad that you're right here with us?" Ziggy said to cheer me up. "We're glad to have you. Screw them and their war machine, huh, Moon Cat?"

I just sat in stunned silence as more numbers were drawn. When the birthdates of my comrades were read, they continued with the jocularity, but I wonder if any of them secretly felt the conflicting relief and still remaining horror that I felt, and apparently outwardly showed. I didn't have to go, but before, it was more abstract. It was just an idea that I could be sent to fight in Vietnam. Now it was reality. If I would have stayed, if I would have submitted to the system, I would likely be heading to Vietnam before my next birthday even arrived. I was going to be twenty-one years old the next year. Having taking the action of leaving, I wasn't going, but I couldn't help wondering if it didn't just reinforce my cowardice. I didn't want to die that young, but more than simply being afraid to die, I never had any confidence that I would make a good soldier. I could only be tested under the extreme conditions of warfare, but I sensed that I wouldn't be able to function well enough under the stress of being under fire, that I just wouldn't be able to protect myself or my mates in the state of chaos of battle. I didn't understand how anyone could withstand the onslaught to the senses—the explosions and the yelling attacking your hearing, the blood and maiming and death assaulting your vision, the fatigue and pain gnawing your nerve-endings. Could my aim be true under those conditions when I wasn't even sure that my aim could be true under the best conditions on a rifle range? Could I be of any use to anybody as a soldier? More mundane thoughts arose of when I was on the high school basketball team. At crunch time, I hit a few shots from the field or some free throws, but honestly, I missed more than I hit. I felt those *yips* that bite you when the game is on the line as opposed to practice being able to sink them the majority of the time. Our coach knew who the gamers were and went to them in the pressure spots. I wasn't one of the *gamers*. I tried my best, but didn't perform as consistently as some others. I knew that I had the type of conscience that would be bothered by failing the team when it counted most. And what bigger team is there to play for than your country in a game of real war? And if I failed in a mission but somehow survived, while my buddies had died because of my failure, I would find it extremely hard to live with myself. But what did I know? The answer that kept troubling me at the time was *nothing*. I knew *nothing*.

Lorelei also tried to console me after the events of that day. "You see, this is what I wanted to protect you and Tranquility from," she said. "You shouldn't be subjected to this kind of madness. You did the right thing for yourself coming here with me. I don't have to worry any more about you or our son about that. Maybe there won't be a war when Tranquility is your age, but with all the wars America has been involved in for successive generations in the twentieth century, or in its existence for that matter, I don't doubt that there will be another one just like this one. It's over for us. It's done."

I did try to put it behind me. I was where I was, and I didn't have to worry about the draft anymore. But while it was easier being out of the country and thousands of miles from the war zone, I still couldn't erase the image, unclear though it was, of the guy that would have to go in my place. The draft board would come across my name, see that I wasn't anywhere to be found, so they would have to move on to the next guy. Although the next guy on the list would have been going along side of me, it was really the guy on the end of the list who wouldn't have been called if I had gone. Because it would be someone from Rhode Island, and it being the smallest state, I wondered if it could be someone I knew, perhaps someone else from my high school. He'll probably be someone a lot like me where we could have easily been friends. Perhaps he had the same reservations about going, but didn't take that drastic step as I did. I simply went on with my new life, safe and sound.

While my relationship with my new son was continuing to grow day by day as he grew, there were some signs of strain with my relationship with Lorelei. We argued about her plans to not celebrate our first Christmas with

T.J. She didn't believe in God, and obviously didn't want to be teaching any religious belief system to her son. But she said to me that even if I did believe in God as a Christian, she didn't understand my need to celebrate the mythology of Christmas—the part with the tree, the presents and Santa Claus—that it had nothing to do with a religious holiday. I countered that it was just supposed to be fun, especially for the children, and it taught them early on about the joy of giving. She countered that it did the total opposite, that it taught children the joy of getting. If children didn't get what they wanted, then all they would get is disappointment. And who would want to initiate that feeling in his or her children? Or if you gave in to your children's every wants, you'd end up spoiling them for certain. I told her I grew up with it, and I turned out fine. She only said, "Why take the risk?" I just knew that Jack wouldn't have memories from his first Christmas anyway, so I didn't put up my toughest fight. But I had in the back of my mind that I should fight for it in upcoming years so that he could have similar happy childhood memories of Christmas that I enjoyed. And I couldn't see myself completely hiding my Christian upbringing from him. Even though I wasn't a churchgoer, I did feel that it was a part of who I was. It was hard for me to imagine totally disassociating myself from it.

Then some time after the New Year, Lorelei brought up a new complaint. She had been showing signs of more and more moodiness since TJ's birth. I didn't know if her irritability that day was part of post-partum depression or if it was related to the baby teething on her breast during feeding. She handed him off to me pretty much as usual to burp, but her remark was a bit biting as well.

"Here, you take him. Do *something* for a change."

"What does that mean?" I said. "You know I'm here to help you out all the time."

"But not without complaining about it constantly."

"I do not. When have I ever complained about doing any work or helping you out with Jack?"

"You've been complaining about the workload ever since we got here."

"I have not." I couldn't remember doing a lot of complaining anyway. "The farm work was a lot harder than I expected, but I don't recall ever complaining about it. And I think I've done my share. I've worked very hard since coming here."

"I've heard your grumbles, and even if you don't say a lot, you always look like you are so unhappy about it all."

"Well, being happy about the work is another story. It's been a hard transition for me, but I think I've done my part. Have there been complaints from the others that they don't think I'm doing my share?"

"Nobody has said anything, but I'm just talking about your attitude mostly."

"My attitude? What's wrong with my attitude?"

"You don't seem to want to *join in* like everyone else. When the others pass around some grass or mushrooms or even some wine when we're all hanging out, you always say, 'No thanks.' It makes them uncomfortable if you don't partake. Some have asked if you were a *narc* or something."

"Yeah, right, I'm a narc," I said with all the sarcasm I could muster. "Just because I don't want to get drunk or high doesn't make me a narc. They can all do what they want. I'm not even judging them. I just don't particularly enjoy losing control of my faculties like I see them do. I've tried different stuff, but I don't think it's for me. Your crowd is always talking about being *hassled by the man* for being different and doing what they want to do. Well, don't I deserve the same freedom from hassle? Shouldn't I be able to do what I want to do, even if it means the opposite of the expectations of the group majority? They're not saying that I should do drugs just because of peer pressure, are they?"

"No, of course not. I think they'd respect your decision if you articulated it to them. But I just want to see that you want to fit in here, that you want to be a part of this. So does everyone else. You are so uptight. That's another thing some have said about you, and that's all they intend by offering you something, to relax you."

"Oh, I'm uptight? How so?"

"Oh, I don't know. But I've been observing you here, and it seems as if you're isolating yourself from the others by hanging around me so much. I feel like your mother sometimes with you always tugging at my apron strings. Every time that we are with the group, you're always gravitating towards me as if you're afraid to face the group on your own. You did the same thing at the Pink House. I'm not your only friend here, you know."

"But you are the only person here that I know. I don't know, maybe I do that a little, but it's only because I want to be with you. I don't know the others well enough to want to hang around with them. But I do interact with them now and again—whenever—all the time."

"Don't you want to get to know the others? Maybe you'll find that you can be close friends with them as well."

"If that's so, I'll find that out. But from my initial impressions, I'm not sure that anyone else here would become a *close* friend. This is a contrived organization of people, and not by me. Not everyone is going to necessarily become friends. All I know are you and Jack. You are my family now. Why wouldn't I want to spend most of my time with my family?"

"We're all your family now. You should want to fit in as a family member with *everyone*." I cringed a little at her definition of family because of the association with the Manson family.

"But I didn't choose them to be my family, and I didn't really choose to be here. I chose to be with you and Jack." I could see the frustration and anger growing on her face.

"But that's the whole point; you should *want* to be here." She ranted her tirade. "We want you here. We want you to be an equal part of the whole deal. That's the way it's supposed work. If you're not fully on board, then you'll be forever complaining about the work or eventually trying to avoid the work. It's what I was afraid of, but you've been *so kind* to at least finally admit it," she said sarcastically. Then she snapped, "And his name is Tranquility, not Jack!" and stormed out of the room.

I shouted after her, "And my name is Tom, not Moon Cat!" I tried to comfort the baby as he started to cry on my shoulder.

I let Lorelei wander away to cool off. Later, she admitted that she was a bit emotional that day for reasons unknown to her, so she attributed it to hormones. But she did reiterate her point more calmly that she thought I should interact with the others more. They would like it, and I would find that I would like it too. Admittedly to pacify her, I said that I would. And I consciously tried in the coming weeks to not gravitate toward Lorelei in group situations so I could demonstrate my commitment, and to see if she had a point. She did have a point, but it didn't make me want to spend more time with the others, as opposed to her. I just couldn't have the same level of affection for them as for my de facto wife. I didn't think I should have to apologize for it. But I didn't want to seem intractable either.

A couple of weeks after that little conversation, we were hanging out as she described, and as marijuana was being passed around, I still declined because I didn't like it that much, and philosophically I didn't agree with mindaltering substances. Some claimed they were mind-expanding, but I simply found them to be ways of detaching from the real world, or pure escapism. No one asked me to articulate my philosophy upon my rejection this time. So I was just sitting back, on the opposite side of the room as Lorelei, relaxing, when I saw Lorelei do something shocking to me. When a joint was passed around to her, she took a hit. Obviously, she was no stranger to the drug scene, but out of respect for the baby she had carried for nine months, she had abstained from drug use during that period. For the period since the birth, I hoped she was still refraining because she was breast feeding. I also felt that parents, with weighty obligations that accompany raising a child, should always strive towards mental acuity to accomplish this tremendous feat. But there were parents throughout history who drank alcohol, and this new generation was going to have recreational drug users among their ranks when they became parents, so I shouldn't be surprised. But I was amazed at Lorelei doing it now because she was still breastfeeding. I suppose I already imagined that at some point after she stopped that she would again pick up her old habits. But now?

"What do you think you're doing?" I said directly to her from across the room.

"What?" Lorelei said, oblivious. "I'm just taking the edge off, just like everyone else."

"But you shouldn't be. You're still breastfeeding our baby. You'll be exposing him to—to those hallucinogens, whatever's in that stuff."

"A little grass isn't going to affect the baby. It's been a long time. I put it away while I was pregnant, and now I'm not pregnant anymore. Did you think I was going to be like you and never do anything anymore?"

"No. But you know for certain that it won't affect the baby, who is still getting his nutrition from your body? I remember you saying not too long ago how dangerous cow's milk was becoming because all the drugs and artificial hormones they were using now. Doesn't that work the same way for humans, whatever you ingest the baby ingests indirectly?"

"Now you're comparing me to a cow? Listen, me having a couple of drags of one joint is not going to contaminate my milk and harm the baby."

"Like I said, you know that for certain? You're the one always harping on being *all natural*. I don't think this is *natural* for the baby."

"Marijuana is a very natural herb, not man-made, earth-made. It's not harmful."

I had only my logical thinking to back me up, no medical facts, and this was in a time when the term *secondhand smoke* wasn't even in use yet. Nor was *contact high*, but I think the others in our group probably experienced it at one time or another. I certainly did while hanging around this group and not participating myself. When I felt a little buzzed—which was actually a headache—from being around them, I would usually find an excuse to seek fresh air. Even though the baby was sleeping now and in no danger of a contact high, I had no doubts that if Lorelei used drugs, it would get into her breast milk and do something to the baby. I felt I had to put my foot down here. "Please, be reasonable, for the baby's sake! I'm going to have to insist on his behalf that you keep abstaining from drug use until the point where you stop breastfeeding. Okay?" Silence. "Okay?"

"Okay, *Dad*. If you say so, *Dad*." Lorelei passed the joint on after one last drag for spite. "You're so square, you know that?" Silence from me. "You are so righteously square. But I'll do it so you don't get all bent out of shape and bring everyone down. It was just one joint, man."

I certainly didn't feel a part of the crowd then. I guess they really got to see me uptight this time, but I felt I couldn't back down. I just got up to go to my bedroom to do something else on my own. I picked up a book and started to read while Jack slept in his crib. A little while later, when I went to go to the bathroom, I heard the party still going on. Lorelei could have been doing whatever she wanted, I supposed. I wasn't going to check up on her. But I ran into Saffron on my way, and she stopped to say something to me.

"I just wanted to tell you that you weren't bringing everybody down. And I don't think you're square at all. You're a very beautiful soul," she said in her little, meek voice. "You're just a good father, that's all." Saffron looked up at me and smiled with all her wide-eyed innocence and her youthful naïveté, comfortingly touching my arm. She was strikingly beautiful, and it was perhaps the first time I truly noticed that in her. I was surprised that she wasn't attached. She wasn't what I would call my *type*, and it was the furthest thing from my mind, but she was the type of girl who imbued the strong desire to protect her because she seemed so delicate, not just in physicality, but in spirit as well. I simply thanked her.

So, in the next few weeks and months leading up to the next planting, while Lorelei and I took to parenting our son, we took turns trying to parent each other. I kept my eyes open for further attempts at drug use, while she kept prodding for me to fit in with the crowd. Come April, when work was picking up with the preparations for plowing, we at least fell into a comfortable pattern, which I wouldn't exactly call back to normal, but more like a truce, and we both tried to not fight. Like the spring thaw, I sensed some of her iciness toward me start to melt. Because of everything that goes with giving birth—the abdominal soreness early on, the breastfeeding soreness, the waning of sexual desire when you see firsthand what that desire all leads to, and possibly post-partum depression—and because of our disagreements, I hadn't been intimate with Lorelei in quite a long time. But I was sensing that she was perhaps ready to wake up from her winter of sexual hibernation. I saw her smile more often, particularly at me. I made it a point to smile back to let her know I was pleased if she were happy again. She was a little more playful with the baby, and in general the playfulness in her that I fell in love with was beginning to blossom again.

On a relatively warm spring day for Canada, I felt the need to shake off my cabin fever, and I took Jack for a long walk on the farm, he in a little papoose that one of the girls made for us. I was reveling in the fresh, warm air, as it was one of the first days of the season where I didn't need my coat. I wore a long-sleeved flannel shirt still, but I rolled up the cuffs to loosen some of the shackles of the prolonged winter. I walked the barren field to the edge of the property and back with Jack snuggled in the sling across my chest. He was rather oblivious to the sights, but he seemed happy to have the sun shining on his little face. I tried pointing out the returning wildlife, the birds and rabbits and such, and stopped at the goat pen on the way in to introduce him to the farm's animals. He seemed to enjoy the little tour, and I was happy because of him. As I was tiring and it approached his feeding time, we went back in the house.

Inside, most of the gang was enjoying a leisurely day, talking in the main living room. Saffron had come into the room from the kitchen and was looking for something in and around the others, didn't find whatever it was and headed back to the kitchen. It was near lunch time, and so I imagined that Lorelei might be with her preparing the noonday meal, since I hadn't seen her yet. I followed into the kitchen a few moments after her, but I only found Saffron there.

"Have you seen Lorelei?" I asked her.

"Oh, hmm, I think I saw her going upstairs a while ago." She paused in her food preparations and cooed at the baby, playfully touched his nose and smiled big for him. "Is somebody hungry in there? Is somebody hungry in there? I think so. Yes, I think so, little one. Maybe someday I can feed you too." She meant with her cooking. I smiled at her and put my hand on her shoulder to thank her for her kindness as I walked off to find Lorelei.

Finding her was the worst thing I'd ever experienced. Not knowing to expect anything untoward, I blindly climbed the stairs to my doom. I expected to find Lorelei doing something mundane in our bedroom, or perhaps just relaxing. But I didn't find her there. Back out in the hallway looking with growing curiosity, I heard the faint but unmistakable sound of two people having sex. It wasn't unheard of by me there in the house before. The group coupled up in various combinations during our stay, and I didn't pay too much attention to who was doing whom because Lorelei and I were the only, what I would call, *real* couple of the bunch. And in close quarters as we were sharing with this many people, you heard *things*, and at various times of the day. At the far end of the hall, from Ziggy's master bedroom the noises seemed to be emanating. I stepped forward to verify my suspicions, and they were confirmed. I almost stepped back for guiltily eavesdropping; I almost even smirked at the secret I was privy to. I correctly guessed Ziggy was involved, but for the girl, I didn't take close enough scrutiny of those I saw downstairs to know who was with him. As I started running through the inventory of possibilities, I gagged in horror at recognizing the sound of the woman. They were sounds of which I had intimate knowledge. They were Lorelei's sex sounds.

I froze, not knowing what to do. I wanted doubt to creep into my mind, but the same sure answer kept doubt at bay. I thought, should I bust in right now on them to break it up, removing all deniability? Or should I back off and wait for her to either tell me on her own, or wait for her to lie to cover it up? Should I confront her with the evidence when we were alone, or should I peck away at her cover story, not letting on that I knew, just to see how long it took and how deep she would go with her lies?

I had my hand forced a bit. While standing in front of that door, Tranquility Jack, feeling some discomfort of his own—although obviously, thankfully, still ignorant to what was causing my discomfort—whimpered and was about to cry. I may have been holding him a little too tight in my anger with Lorelei, unawares. The baby's noise was very likely heard through the door, and I think it caused the action to cease, for I stopped hearing the sex noises, heard nothing for a second or two, then heard some scampering around like thieves caught by surprise in the middle of a burglary. Instead of bursting in on them to remove all doubt about what was going on, I still felt bold, and wanting to be smarter than the two of them, I played it coy to start. I held my ground, waiting for them to come out of the room, as they would eventually have to. I also tried to use the baby's presence to play on Lorelei's conscience even more heavily.

As if in response to Jack's cries, I said, trying to project my voice through the door, "Where's momma? Where's momma? I know, I know, sweetheart, but we'll find her. She's got to be around here somewhere." I kept repeating something to that effect trying to let them know that I was right in front of the door, not moving away, possibly allowing them to slip out un-noticed. "Where's momma?"

After a few more moments, Lorelei came out of our host's bedroom, girded I supposed to finally face me, and closed the door quickly behind her so that I wouldn't see him in there.

"Look, honey, there she is," I said to Jack. "I was looking all over for you," I said to Lorelei, the stern look on my face belying the sing-song, happy tone of voice I used for the baby's sake. "It's feeding time for our little man, and that's your department. What were you doing in there?" I nodded to the bedroom which was absolutely not ours, my tone of voice quickly changing to accusatory.

"I—I, uh—I was just looking for—uh—"

"Stop right there. I'll spare you the need to think up a good enough lie. I know what you were doing, and I'm patently shocked at your audacity."

Lorelei knew the jig was up and that she was busted. "I—I wasn't trying to hurt you. I guess I had a moment of weakness."

"Not trying to hurt me? Is that some kind of joke? You couldn't hurt me more right now if you were to stab me in the heart with a kitchen knife."

I thought I had her on the defensive, but she balked at that.

"Please spare me your bourgeois melodramatic scene. I knew it. I knew it from the start. I should have trusted my instinct that you couldn't shed your middle-class frame of reference. It's people like you and their puritanical views on sex that's got this whole world hung up."

"Hung up? Hung up on what, the idea that two people should be able to trust each other not to screw around on each other?"

"Did I ever promise that to you?" she asked.

"No, I guess not. You conveniently side-stepped that when you refused to marry me."

"Marriage is just a form of slavery. Husbands treat wives like possessions, as you're trying to treat me now. You don't own me."

"Where do you get this nonsense? I'm not trying to own you. We have a family going. Is it wrong for me to expect you to be faithful for our family's sake?"

"Faithful to what? Faithful to caring for and loving one another? That hasn't changed. Or simply faithful to you as my sexual partner? Why should having sex with another person change anything when it is so completely meaningless?"

"Meaningless! Meaningless!" I was trying not to raise my voice in front of the baby, but my frustration was boiling over. "It's not meaningless to me! I don't want you sleeping with other men. Maybe that makes me some kind of unenlightened, pre-historic caveman, but that's the way it is. That's the way it ought to be. Who knows where *lover boy*'s been? Where is he anyway? Why won't the coward face me like a man?" I started banging on his door. "Come on out! I know you're in there."

I was amped up for a fistfight, to defend my woman's honor. I realized that I had never been in one my whole life. Had a few close calls as a child on the playground, but they were always defused in the nick of time. When Ziggy finally slinked out of the door to his room, he likely expected I would challenge him, but he did face me, and he tried his best to defuse me.

"Moon Cat, listen, man, I'm sorry. You probably want to bash my brains in, but let's be more rational. Give me a chance to explain." Given my lack of pugilistic endeavors, my sudden thoughts about my first encounter with Lorelei and how I wasn't free of guilt myself because of the understanding I had with Allison at the time, and the fact that I was still holding Jack, all kept me from pouncing on him with blind rage.

"It wasn't your lady's fault," Ziggy continued. "It was mine, and I'm sorry about it now. I know you've got a tight thing going on between you and Lorelei. I maybe didn't realize how tight. It's just that we had our own thing in the past before she met you, and we kind of gave in to old feelings."

"I knew it!" I turned to Lorelei. "Is that why you wanted to come here, to be with your old boyfriend? See if you could rekindle things?"

"That's not why I came here," insisted Lorelei. "You know why we came here. Ziggy is an old *friend*, but I came here to help you out and our son, to help you both escape the clutches of the American military. *We* came here for your sake."

"Well, don't think me rude to not thank you," I said snidely. "You conveniently left out that tidbit of information from your past, among other things. It certainly became important information today that had I known, I wouldn't have wanted to come in the first place. What are we supposed to do now, fight over you? Am I supposed to challenge my rival here to a fistfight outside, and the winner gets you?"

"Let's be a little more mature than that, please," Lorelei answered.

"Mature? Forgive me if I'm not some Left Bank, laissez faire, beret-wearing, chain-smoking French snot who thinks affairs are *mature* behavior, or even downright fashionable."

"Listen, man," Ziggy chimed in, "I know my word doesn't mean a lot at a moment like this, but I'm not going to fight you over Lorelei here. I don't want to fight you. I'm out of this scene, man. Guaranteed. She's yours. You have my word—I swear."

"Well, you're absolutely right about your word not meaning anything. And so gallant of you to give her up two minutes after you fucked her. Why don't you just—" I was about to release another tirade at him, but Lorelei jumped in over my words.

"Whoa! Wait just a minute. Who do you think you are? What do you think I am? You don't own me! You don't own me," she said pointing at me, "and you don't own me," she said pointing at Ziggy, and continued to light into him. "I'm not your chattel. You can't pass me off to somebody else when you're done with me like some old clothes or old furniture. I'm my own woman. You can't make decisions for me whom I'm going to be with. This is not what I wanted! This is not what I wanted at all. Why don't you leave us alone right now, Zig. This is between Tom and me at the moment."

"You're right," said Ziggy. "I should leave you alone."

"You should have thought about that before you fucked her," I said, trying to get the last word, trying to establish some atavistic dominance that I always felt I lacked in the past.

"Tom, please!" Lorelei implored me to stop. After Ziggy walked away, she continued to chastise me. "Please, you need to stop your little caveman routine right now and use some reason. You can't go around beating back all contenders to the prize you thought you won, or something, because I'm not that girl. You're a man I love, and you'll have to trust me to not go off and leave you. I know—I know that I broke that trust today, and for that I'm truly sorry."

"You're only sorry you got caught in the act, literally."

"No, I'm truly sorry, that I broke your trust. I shouldn't have. But also, what is in the past is in the past. I can't change whatever happened in my past, recent or far distant, and neither can you. What we can do is try to repair that gap in trust that I broke, if you want to."

I looked at her for a while, and then said, "I don't know if I want to. I don't know how. I'm pretty devastated right now." I looked at her with disgust, and I was pretty sure she read it clearly.

"I understand. You think about it for a while. But, you know, we can still have all the big dreams we had before this. This doesn't have to change that. It's up to you."

I was silent for a moment more. I looked at Tranquility Jack. He was quieter now, but his face still looked cranky. "Here," I said holding out the baby to Lorelei. "Take him. It's still his feeding time. I'll think about it." As Lorelei took him from my arms, I had one more comment I said to the baby but was absolutely directed at her instead.

"Hey, little guy, just think, you might be getting a little brother soon," I said in bubbly baby talk. I added in adult tones, "Or a *half-brother*, anyway," and I walked away.

I went downstairs for the midday meal. I doubted seriously that Ziggy would broadcast what had just transpired, but I couldn't know for certain what may have been heard by the other inmates. There were some loud voices at times in our heated exchange. Nothing seemed amiss that I could detect at any rate. I spied Ziggy out of the corner of my eye. He noted my entrance, then glanced away quickly. I ignored him and went about the business of eating lunch.

Even though I thought the dirty little secret was safe for now, my mood was dark. I didn't speak with anyone, and just focused on my plate of grubby beans. As Saffron had served it up to me, I faked a brief smile, and then went back to sulking. But I was beginning to hatch a plot.

Lorelei never made an appearance as she was busy taking care of feeding the baby, which was all the better. My anger might have spilled out again at the sight of her, and we'd probably argue some more. At the conclusion of the meal, the group scattered to do whatever. Michelle-my-belle filled in for the absent Lorelei in helping Saffron clean up the kitchen, but I volunteered to take her place myself.

"Thank you so much. That's very kind of you," Saffron said affectionately.

"Yeah, thanks, Moon Cat," Michelle-my-belle said perfunctorily as she exited the kitchen.

After I got the sink prepared for washing dishes, I chit-chatted with Saffron, first about the nice, warm weather we were having that day. She responded by saying it was truly a beautiful day.

"Do you like it here?" I asked.

"Do I like it here? Of course I like it here. I suppose I wouldn't be here if I didn't like it here."

"I mean there's quite a lot of hard work involved and all."

"Oh, I don't mind," she said brushing it off.

"Sometimes, though, you must feel like everybody's servant, cooking and cleaning for all the others."

"Like I said, I don't mind. I'm just doing my part."

"I'm just not sure that everybody fully appreciates you."

"I don't know. I think they appreciate me. I don't feel unappreciated, if that's what you mean. I do my little part, like you and the others do yours. I appreciated what you do, and all the others who do the jobs I don't."

"What I guess I wanted to say is, and I can't speak for anybody else, but I appreciate you very much. I notice what you do."

"Well, thank you, Moon Cat."

"I prefer Tom, but that's okay."

"Oh, no. I'm sorry, Tom. Tom it is."

After scrubbing the plates and glasses and handing them to her to rinse for a few silent moments, I tried to formulate my words. "So what's your story? I mean, you're such an attractive girl. How come you're not with someone? Like you don't have an *old man*, yet."

Saffron blushed a bit. "Oh, I don't know. I haven't met the right guy, I suppose. Maybe I'm not so attractive."

"Stop. You're kidding me, right? Any guy would be lucky to be with you. You're a very happening chick. You've definitely got beauty on the outside, but I've gotten a strong sense that you're even more beautiful on the inside. You're sweet and caring and selfless. Who wouldn't love that?"

"You're just being nice, but you're so sweet for saying that. I wanted to say that you have a very beautiful soul, too. I know some people make fun when I say that I see people's *auras*—and I mean visibly see—but I saw your aura right off and knew that you had a gentle, sensitive soul. Lorelei too. You are lucky to have found each other."

"Yes," I said simply. After more washing and drying silently, I said, "I hope you're not lonely though, by yourself."

"Oh, I'm not lonely. I've got my whole new family here with me."

"That's not what I mean exactly. You've at least had boyfriends before, haven't you? Or are you still a virgin?"

Saffron blushed again. "No," she said meekly, "I'm not. And yes I've had boyfriends before, but not the type to stay with, I guess."

"That's what I mean; sometimes it's lonely if you don't have that."

"I'm okay with that right now."

My mouth was going a little dry, and if my hands weren't drenched in dishwater, she may have noticed that they were sweating. "Do you believe in *free love* like everyone's talking about these days?"

"Well, I suppose I do believe that two people who are connected spiritually shouldn't feel afraid or ashamed to connect physically—sexually. It's all part of the universe we share. Good connections seem so rare and difficult to find, that when we do, we should nurture those connections in any way that seems appropriate."

"So you think it's okay for people who aren't married, for example, to have sex to express their love?"

"Sure, I'm certainly not a prude. Anything that adds or expresses love in the universe has got to be okay."

"I'm glad you feel that way because, you see, I have this immense attraction for the beauty of your soul right now, and I was afraid that you'd be offended if I expressed it to you."

"I'm not offended," she said after a moment of thought. "I'm—I'm flattered and grateful."

"It's just that I've never felt this strong a connection with very many girls before. It's more than just physical attraction. I know I don't know you that well, but I care very deeply about you. I'm not sure why, and I don't know what to do. All I know is that I want to hold you, comfort you and do something to reach out across this divide of space between us and make sure you don't feel lonely, even if it's just for a brief moment, if that's all that I can do for you."

I never thought of myself as a good liar, but I was pouring it on thick. I guess it was a little easier that I did find her physically attractive, but I didn't feel the same connection that I did for Allison or Lorelei. I didn't love her the same way. And I was trying to woo her out of spite. I knew that I could never erase the image of Lorelei and Ziggy from my mind. The pain was very great at that moment, and the only way I thought of easing that pain was to at least be on an even playing field. If she had an affair, then I would have one, too—if I could—and then maybe we could go on. At least that's what my brain came up with at the time.

Saffron actually embraced me to comfort me. "It's okay. Don't be ashamed of your feelings. Many men are."

"I want to make love to you."

"What about Lorelei?"

"She and I have a very open relationship. We love each other and are secure in that knowledge, and we're confident that sex outside the relationship isn't going to threaten it. It's happened before already."

"It has?"

"Yes. She was the one, but I knew that it didn't mean she stopped loving me. I mean, we're human creatures; we can't just turn off the part of us that gets attracted to the opposite sex. So straying now and again outside the relationship is natural, if not inevitable. But I'm not trying to justify anything. I'm not concerned about her because I know she understands. I'm concerned about what you're concerned with. Do you wish to make love to me, too?"

Still in our embrace, she whispered, "Yes. I do."

I was a bit shocked at the ease of my success. Thank you to the guy who invented *free love*. I know it had to be a guy, anyway, whoever he is. I told Saffron that I had a fantasy about making love to her in the hay loft, and she was game. So after we finished cleaning up the kitchen, we snuck off to the barn to explore our animal instincts. Lying naked in hay was not as comfortable or as romantic as I thought. But overall, the experience of making love to virtually a complete stranger was wildly erotic, so creature comfort be damned. The nude Saffron was heartbreakingly beautiful, like a little wood nymph enticing the horny satyr. Her slender torso and limbs, her pert, A-cup-sized breasts made her seem like a still fragile little fledgling that I wanted to take under my wing for warmth and protection.

Still, I rate the act as the worst thing I've ever done in my life. Afterward, we engaged in a little pillow talk. Or should I say hay-bale talk? I learned that she had a sexual relationship with Ziggy when she arrived about a year before I did. She was just out of school when she met him in Toronto, and I could imagine him charming the delicate flower of a girl with his phony act of a visionary ready to plant a new Utopia on the farm, as only he could build and lead it. I don't know if he promised anything in terms of a relationship, but eventually he strayed, seemingly trying to sample the rest of the henhouse. So Lorelei wasn't an exception. It looked as if she were part of the rule: sleep with Ziggy at some point. At first, I wasn't too happy that Ziggy got Saffron too, but in a way, I had one of his girls as he had had mine. But it wasn't that satisfying a triumph because I wasn't exactly getting back at Ziggy. Even though I was avenged, I wanted to keep my dalliance a secret so that I could have that little edge over Lorelei. I wanted to be truly vindictive.

I was still too angry for me to face her or speak to her that day. I didn't seek her out, or she me. As she was likely busy caring for the baby, I didn't run across her later that day. I wasn't too concerned because I kept tabs on Ziggy's whereabouts. At least she wasn't with him again. Whenever I crossed his path, however, I scowled and glowered at him, while he quickly looked away to avoid another confrontation; or it could have been shame, I supposed. At the end of the day when the others retired to their rooms, I didn't have the desire to go to mine, and I simple crashed on one of the sofas for the night.

The next morning, with Saffron usually being the first one up to prepare breakfast, she noticed me sleeping and gently woke me up concerned.

"You're not sleeping separately from Lorelei because of what we did yesterday, are you? Because you said—"

"Oh, no, no, no," I reassured her. "The baby was quite cranky with colic or something and keeping us awake too. Lorelei actually suggested I try sleeping out here, that there was no reason for both of us to lose sleep." The lying started to come so easily after a little practice. I don't know if she fully bought it. Maybe she noticed the lack of an all-night crying baby, but she didn't say anything like that.

"Oh, okay. Go back to sleep then if you can." She kissed the top of my forehead and went into the kitchen to begin her day. After shaking off the slumber, I followed to help too. I didn't want to ignore her and make her feel bad about what we did.

She was preparing a typical oatmeal breakfast with wheat toast. While I had a chance to speak to her without any witnesses around, I sidled up to her, put my arm around her waist and said, "I just wanted you to know how much I appreciated yesterday. You have such a beautiful soul, and I felt our souls truly connected. It's a rare thing, and I'm truly grateful that it could happen."

"I feel the same way. A tender moment shared between two people is a treasure in and of itself, more valuable than any amount of gold. I cherish it." With a heart like that, it was a shame things couldn't have worked out differently.

"Now, despite my understanding with Lorelei, there's no need to throw it in her face. You probably appreciate the sensibilities of women, so it can be our little secret. Okay?"

"Sure, I understand. We had an understanding from the start. It was what it was. I know my place, and I won't let it affect your family in a negative way."

Saffron was such a gem in so many ways, but I felt a little sad for her when she said she knew her place. She let things end satisfactorily, however. But I had to be careful of what her future expectations might be.

When the others started coming in for the meal, I was nearly finished mine. I said a simple hello in reply to their greetings to be somewhat polite. I snubbed Ziggy completely. When Lorelei came in with the baby, I felt I should say something to her, but my anger kept returning whenever I saw her; and if I said anything, it would be to lash out again, so I bit my tongue, rising from the table when I knew I wouldn't be able to contain myself any longer, leaving my dishes as they were instead of clearing them. It wasn't my turn to milk the goats, but I went to the barn to keep busy and put my mind on something else for the time being. Lotus, who came in to milk, was surprised that I had beaten her to it, and I just said I was a little restless and figured I'd pitch in.

When that task was done, I sort of kicked around outside the barnyard, keeping away from people. I slowly paced here and there, occasionally picking up a stone to throw off into the distance. Ziggy, Paradise and Moriarty took the truck to deliver the goat's milk to the cheese factory and to buy some seed and other supplies. So I was left to my own devices for the day. When I had my thoughts more organized, I went in to talk to Lorelei.

"We need to talk," I announced to her when I found her in the living room.

"Okay. I think that would be good start," she replied. We went to our room. She left the baby in the care of Saffron, Juniper and Tristessa.

"You know I'm still having a hard time getting over what you did," I began.

"Yes, I see. You're making yourself quite obvious."

"Well, I don't know what else to do. Every time I look at you or look at Ziggy, it's all I can think about, and this anger—no, rage—is just boiling inside of me. I mean, I don't know if I can ever forgive you. Or if it takes more time, I don't know, maybe I can, but I don't think this place is conducive to do that. I'm going to have that little *incident* shoved in my face every time I see *him*, that swine of a host we have, even if never says a word to remind me. I'll certainly never forgive him. And he runs that whole damn show around here. That's why I think we need to leave this place, post haste, and start fresh someplace else."

"You're just being a little rash. Your emotions are talking for you, and I understand that right now. You just need a little time to cool off, and perhaps you'll feel differently afterward. I made a horrible mistake, and I hope it can be forgiven. I'm sorry, and I promised to not let it happen again, but the place isn't to blame. This is our home where we can make really good things happen."

"This doesn't feel like home to me, definitely not now. And how do you know for sure? You gave into temptation once, and you'll still have the same temptation staring you in the face day after day."

"You'll have to accept my word."

"I would if I could, but you broke my trust. I just don't see how that can be put back together in this environment. Leave the temptation behind, and maybe I can see things in a different light. Is it the place, or is it *him* you want?"

"It's the place. It's a commune where we all share in the toil and reward. It's our attempt to do things the right way once and for all. It's what I'm committed to doing, instead of simply continuing on the selfish path that the whole world is on."

"That's all well and good, but I can't separate the place from the man as long as he's here."

"Ziggy owns the land. He can't be separated from it."

"Of course he does. That makes him the master, whether you want to believe it or not. You can try to trust that his soul is still selfless, but I seriously have my doubts. And you're right; he can't be separated from it, but we can. That's why we have to be the ones who leave. We don't need this place. We can build our utopian future anywhere. You, me and Tranquility, that's what I'm committed to."

"Where do want us to go? What are we supposed to do?"

"Right now, any place other than here is better. We can figure things out in detail later. But for the time being, we can move to one of the cities around here, and I can get a job. Maybe I'll have to go back to washing dishes again until I can find something better, but I don't mind. We just need to start fresh, someplace else."

"How can you just toss away my dream like that? I knew you might not be as committed as I was from the start, but once you saw it too, you'd be just as committed."

"Well, it was never my dream. I'm not committed to it. I'm only committed to you and our child. You wasted several opportunities to commit to me, particularly when you refused to marry me."

"There you go again. You won't let go of your commitment to a piece of paper, but your chance to commit to something real, tangible, something truly noble, you can't do it. Maybe we should have gotten a piece of paper to marry you to the commune: a binding contract. Would that have worked?"

"That would be the day that I'd sign that."

"If you can't be committed to it, then how can you be committed to me? If it's not what you desire, why don't you leave on your own? You don't need to stay for my sake. I told you from the beginning that I wanted to come here, and that you could follow me if you wished. And you did. I don't remember dragging you. But if you hate it so, then go."

"I don't want to leave you. And I certainly can't leave you here to stay with that freak with the Jesus complex, who really is a Judas. And needless to say, you wouldn't allow me to take Jack with me."

"Absolutely not."

"And so I can't leave him here, maybe have my place taken by that smarmy, slimy rat-bastard, having *him* raise my child. Is that what you want? I'm not the perfect mate, so you want to replace me with this prince of '*the cause*?' I think he's a pure fraud and an imposter. But he definitely speaks your language better than I do. Is that what you're looking for? Some better version of me?"

"No. But if you're not happy here, why suffer in silence, or maybe not so silently? Why torture yourself to fit in if you don't?"

"But I don't want to fit in. I want to leave with you and the baby and start over. What's wrong with that?"

"If you can't see it, I don't know how to explain it." Lorelei turned away from me quickly with a lot of exasperation. She continued, saying to me or to herself out loud, "This is not how this is supposed to be! This is not how I envisioned all this! We were supposed to be building a paradise here—a new Eden!"

I didn't articulate it at the time, but she could have answered herself by seeing her own resemblance to Eve who picked and ate the forbidden fruit which got her and Adam cast out of Eden. And if that farm was Eden, I was eager to leave it voluntarily, without delay.

After airing it out with Lorelei, my anger remained, but it was beginning to be replaced with a kind of depression and sadness. I couldn't get over it because she was opposing my expectations, which I thought were completely reasonable. How could I be expected to forgive and, more importantly, forget when we were living with the man with whom she had an affair, and was the person whom we relied on for our food and shelter? Everyday there would be a constant reminder to me, unless I could somehow become near saint-like in my ability to forgive her sin. And though Lorelei wasn't aware of it, I made the same mistake with Saffron and regretted it deeply. I also would have to be faced with the daily reminder of my own sin. I couldn't fathom her response of wanting to stay, which made me think all the more that she didn't regret her mistake. She was making me feel as if I were the mistake by suggesting that I leave on my own, leaving her behind to be completely free to pick up her relationship with Ziggy. How could I not feel as if she were choosing him over me?

I tried, however, to give her a chance to change her mind. I didn't really have a choice either. I felt imprisoned there, caught between the proverbial rock and hard place. I couldn't be happy with either choice Lorelei was giving me. So, I tried to contain my anger and to not talk about the incident by focusing on taking care of Tranquility Jack when we were together. I tried sleeping with Lorelei again in the same bed, but there was not the same affection as before. Sex, in my mind, was completely out of the question for the time being. I couldn't help but look at her and feel as though she were now dirty, tainted. I didn't think of the likelihood of her being literally contaminated by a venereal disease, but it was in the realm of possibilities. I thought more about the grossest aspects of her tryst—the bodily fluids exchanged, the stench of another man being on her body. I didn't know how long it took on a chemical level to be clean of those things—simply one bath, perhaps—but it was still there in my eyes. I know now that it was a complete double standard, but that is how I felt about her. It is likely how I *made* her feel, as well. We maintained our distance—physical and emotional—in and out of bed. A constant state of tension existed between us and around us. No doubt, the others in the commune felt it, even though we were attempting to not display our dirty laundry. For my part, I always felt it was me against them when the whole group was together, excepting Saffron, but I couldn't ever again look to her for comfort. After a couple of days of sleeping in the same room with Lorelei, I again went to one of the living room sofas to spend the night, telling her I was having trouble sleeping and not wanting to disturb her. This was a moment when the most intense sadness took over me, and I really escaped to weep alone. I was utterly unhappy with the life I was leading, and I had no clues on how to fix it. I loved Lorelei and wanted to stay with her. But I didn't know how much longer I could stay in that environment. Apparently, Lorelei felt the same way about the environment.

When waking up from one of my nights on the couch, dawn was breaking, and I walked around to loosen up my stiff neck and back. I grabbed a coat and stepped outside to brace myself with the still cool morning air. I noticed that the Karmann Ghia—Lorelei's car—which was used every now and then for trips into town for essentials but was mostly a fixture of the barnyard, was gone. I couldn't imagine that this would be a time to run errands, but the initial explanation I came up with was what I wished to do many times—go for a drive alone for a moment of escapism, to change the scenery beyond the all-too-familiar walls and farmland we looked upon daily without variation. I doubted that it would be anyone else besides Lorelei who took the car. And if she took it, she must have taken the baby with her. She wouldn't have left him by himself, even if he were just sleeping. But I went to our room to verify what exactly was happening. Neither Lorelei nor the baby was there.

As I looked around at the scene (of the crime, perhaps), I noticed that things seemed to be missing. Without taking an inventory, I noticed that the baby's things were gone, and then Lorelei's clothes as well. It began to look like more than a joy ride. I found a brief note on the dresser. It read:

"Tom: You've finally poisoned this place for me with your overreactions and lack of forgiveness toward me, so I can no longer stay. I don't want you with me anymore because I can't see you raising our child like that. You're free from any and all responsibilities in that regard, and so I'm gone. Lorelei."

I looked at the note incredulously. I was dumbfounded. First of all, she was blaming me, as if it were really I who *poisoned* the place. Secondly, she was calling me a bad father when I was the one who was expecting for us to be faithful to each other so that we could raise our child the right way. And of course, I couldn't believe the abruptness of her last sentence, *"—and so I'm gone."* Where did she go? Was she just blowing off steam somewhere and would soon return? It didn't sound like it saying that I was "—free from any and all responsibilities—" She didn't want me anymore, but she also didn't want me raising our child in any way. I was starting to become scared.

I decided to go to the remaining source of my problems. I loudly banged on Ziggy's bedroom door. When he immediately came out of his room with alarm, he said, "What's going on? What's wrong?"

"Lorelei has taken off somewhere with the baby," I said urgently, pushing the note toward him. He took it and read it.

"I don't understand."

"It's not that hard to figure out. She's gone because of you."

"I—I—I don't know what—"

Our roommate neighbors poked their heads out of bedroom doors or came into the hall asking what was going on.

"Moon Cat here says Lorelei has split, with the baby, too," Ziggy explained.

"Are you sure? Are you sure?" came the replies.

"She left a note, and her car, her stuff and the baby are gone," I said.

"Why would she?" came from Ganymede.

I didn't feel like explaining the whole deal and just said, "She's just gone." Someone made the move to look outside for traces of her or the car or something, and the group was seemingly pulled along to investigate this bizarre mystery. All anyone found was the vacant spot where her car used to be parked, the weeds growing up around the blank spots where the tires used to sit. Everyone looked on in amazement when I challenged Ziggy.

"Where is she, man? Where is she?"

"I don't know. I don't know where she went," Ziggy said defensively.

"She must have gone somewhere," I said. "Does she somehow have any other friends around here?"

"I don't know of any. She never mentioned any to me. I'd figure you would know her best."

"Now, I'm beginning to see, I barely knew her at all," I said dejectedly. Thoughts rushed at me such as where she might go. Would she have gone someplace else in Canada? Did she know other people here? Just as Ziggy said, she never mentioned any to me. Does that mean she would go back to the U.S.? If she didn't want me to track her down, maybe she thought with my legal issues I couldn't or wouldn't follow her back to America. She would have been wrong. Had I a lead to go on or knowledge of her whereabouts, I would have followed anywhere. She had my son. I wasn't about to abandon him to her, despite her apparent desire for me to do so. But I was desperately lacking any leads. The realization came to me that I still didn't know her last name. One idea that occurred to me was that she went back to family, but I didn't know where her parents were from or what their names were. I quickly quizzed everyone in the group.

"She never told us," was the common response, as well as, "We never bothered to ask. We didn't think it was important."

I challenged Ziggy again. "You knew her from the past, before I even met her, and you don't know?"

"No, I don't. It was no big deal to know."

"I asked her directly, and she would always playfully brush it off, saying it wasn't important," I said. "I played along, but it's the most important thing in the world to me right now. I don't even know if I can go to the police without a name for them."

"You don't want to call the fuzz on her, do you?" Ziggy asked. "Maybe she'll change her mind and come back soon, in a day or two, after she thinks about things for a while on her own."

"Her note seemed pretty final." But what else was there to do without a single lead than to wait to see if she did come back? So, I reluctantly waited, despite wanting to run from that place and never look back. I thought of the only other connection I had left to her, which was where we met. I tried to call someone at the Pink House, hoping that someone would have better information about where she came from, but the line was disconnected. I desperately reached out to my old college roommate Rolf to see if he could work some angles with any acquaintances or former acquaintances of hers. When I finally got hold of Rolf by telephone, he explained that the Pink House was no longer as it was. It was sold to a more traditional homeowner, and the people who had hung out there scattered to wherever else they could find. Rolf said he would get back to me after he attempted to find anyone connected to the place. When he called back, he had been somewhat successful in finding a few people, but not in getting any further clues. Most importantly, he tracked down Augie, the leader of the Pink House, and Henry Riefenstahl, aka Reefer, who introduced me to Lorelei. She was unfortunately just as mysterious with them about her past, her name or anything that would provide a clue to her current whereabouts. They hadn't heard from her or about her since the day she left with me. They both promised to let me know if they did. I thanked Rolf for his good work and said goodbye.

I never understood Lorelei's reasons for such mystery, but I only had to wonder that it was planned for a moment like this. She never wanted to be tied to her past, and now, suddenly, it was beginning to dawn on me, I was part of her past she didn't want to be tied to anymore.

I waited patiently more than a week after Lorelei left, with no return or even a word from her. Coincidently, I heard on the radio news that the Beatles officially broke up the previous day. Now, I'm not one to put any cosmic significance to both events as if they were somehow related, but it does provide me with a landmark of the time in my life when this tragedy struck. The Beatles broke up; Lorelei broke up with me a week earlier.

The commune went on with its business as plowing time was drawing near. I don't know what kind of talk was going on among the group; they basically left me alone, not wanting—or afraid—to anger or sadden me further. But from time to time, when I ventured out of my room, Ziggy asked me to help him, or help somebody else do some work, as I was strictly planted supine on the sofa, wallowing.

"Get lost," was one response I had for him. "Not likely," was a response to him asking me if I was going to do anything that day. "Pffft," was another response, dismissing him with a wave of my hand, derisively. The group indulged my self-pity for awhile, but I didn't know for how long they would. If I could have laughed, I would have chuckled at the irony of my situation. I was now on this farm which was factually the last place I wanted to be on earth. My whole goal was to get Lorelei to leave. She did, but she left me behind, as a sort of punishment, I supposed. If she had left with me, I imagined that we could have worked things out.

Saffron intently wanted to comfort my aching heart, but I couldn't in good conscience let her. I didn't love her. I was in love with the woman who abandoned me, and absconded with our baby. Go figure. But she did pass on one tidbit of information about Lorelei. The day before she disappeared, she had brief cryptic words with Saffron. Saffron told me Lorelei had walked up to her and said, "He's all yours," and walked away. Saffron was convinced that someone must have spied the two of us that day we went to the hay loft together, told Lorelei about us, and that's the reason that she left. Saffron apologized profusely about breaking up my family. I tried to ease her mind on that. I told her that given Lorelei's past and her feelings about free love, she wouldn't have reacted so drastically. I told her I didn't know what she meant by those words, but it must be something else. I imagined that it could have referred to me, but also to Ziggy. I didn't say anything about that, however. If Saffron had known the real reason that Lorelei left, that it was Ziggy who broke up my family, the tenderhearted, peace-loving Saffron might have wanted to do violence unto me, especially knowing the timing of their affair and our affair was a mere two hours apart.

At my wits end, I had to leave this place to retain my sanity. I couldn't look at Ziggy anymore without wanting to do him harm. I couldn't look at the doe-eyed Saffron anymore without wanting to harm myself. If Lorelei returned, then so be it. At least I would know where she was. I could keep in contact with the farm to see if she did return. The realization hit me that I wasn't trapped there anymore. I was free to escape, to reform my life somewhere else—likely still in Canada for the time being—and take stock after I got my head straight. I had had it with Ziggy's farm. I didn't want or need any farewell, so I pulled off what Lorelei did. Under the cover of darkness, slightly before dawn, I packed my bagful of meager belongings and hiked down the road, not knowing where it would lead—and as long as it took me away from there, not caring.

CHORUS 5:

"Obla-di, obla-da, life goes on, bra,
La-la how the life goes on."

Lennon-McCartney

I walked down the road knowing next to nothing about where it led, physically or metaphysically. My vaguely formed plan was to walk or hitch to the closest town with a bus station and head to Toronto, about the only city in Ontario that I knew of, at least by reputation. It was a fairly big city much like Boston, I imagined, where I would be comfortable in its surroundings. I felt as if I could blend in better than in a small town. My initial plan, other than needing to find a hotel for shelter before the night was upon me, was to get a job—most likely washing dishes in a restaurant—until I could figure out something better or form some other plan. I could have just made for the border and headed back home, but I still faced the legal issues of the draft and the extreme likelihood of being sent to Vietnam. While I still had the savings I collected from my first job, I could take some time to think things over.

I knew nothing about my immediate whereabouts, and simply looked up in the sky for guidance and found the road that would take me east, toward the rising sun, toward Toronto. My disposition was one of defeat. I had nothing left. I had no family anymore. I had no wife or son anymore, and I couldn't comprehend how it all came to this. All I had were my duffel, a pair of walking shoes and the legs to carry me; so I walked on.

I wanted to be alone so much so that I didn't even attempt to hitchhike. There were only a few vehicles on the road in the early morn, and without me sticking out my thumb, the cars and trucks passed me by without much notice. Only briefly did I think about the scene I left behind, how the others would be discovering my absence at the time. It might have generated some discussion, some gossip, but I imagined thoughts of me would quickly die as they went on with their chosen lives as bean farmers. Meanwhile, I walked for hours and began to tire. All around me I saw more farmland, no town or city in sight. The sign for the closest town read 21 kilometers farther. I hadn't heard the name before, and I had no idea if it had a bus station there.

The day started very cool—not freezing, but downright cold while I was exposed to the elements—but warmed considerably with bright sunshine and a scarcity of clouds. I was beginning to question the soundness of my plan, feeling the growing discomfort of walking and carrying the awkward duffel, as well as a growing hunger caused by skipping breakfast for a secretive getaway, when a pickup truck rolled to a stop next to me.

"Where you headed, man?" the guy who was driving asked me.

"I don't know," I answered with reticence. "I mean I don't know the area around here at all. Wherever the nearest town with a bus station is. I'm heading Toronto way."

"Well, I'm not going there. I'm heading to Hamilton. They've got a station there, and it's not much farther to Toronto. But I can also take you into Kitchener, which is closer and right on my way, if you're looking for a ride?"

"Not really," I said. "Thanks anyway, but I can walk, I suppose. You say Kitchener is my best bet?"

"Yeah, but why don't you hop in. It's no trouble really. You've still got quite a ways to go."

I looked at the man's friendly face and at the generous offer. I considered my aching feet, back and hands, thought for a moment and reconsidered. "If it's no trouble. I'd be grateful for a lift. I've been walking for a while now."

"It's no trouble. Like I said, it's on my way. Hop in."

After I tossed my duffel in the back of the truck and got in the passenger side, the man offered his hand and introduced himself. "The name's John MacArthur."

"Tom Moore. Thanks again."

He motored down the road once again with me along for the ride. The man was mid-thirties with a bushy mustache, no beard, and unkempt hair under his ball cap with a John Deere logo on the front. He wore a light cloth coat over a checkered shirt, faded dungarees and boots of a farmer, I surmised. My plan was to remain silent, if possible for the entire ride, as I was in no mood to talk, even small talk. He was obviously in a different mood.

"What brings you out to this neck of the woods? Touring Canada or something?"

"Something like that, I guess."

"Hey, are you American?"

I looked at him with curiosity, not sure if I should answer him. Maybe it was easier than I thought to spot a foreigner around there. "Is it obvious?"

"It's no big deal if you are, but I did figure it since you said you weren't from around here. And you've got an accent." It never occurred to me that I had an accent, growing up in the same relatively small geographical area. But years later, after meeting more people from all over, I knew I did have an identifiable, typical Rhode Island accent, which is possibly an offshoot of a Boston accent.

"Yes, I am." I figured there shouldn't be any harm in confessing that fact. But I was in fact an illegal alien at the time, so I was still a little guarded.

"You here because of the war?"

"Ah, no. I'm just visiting. Like you said, touring Canada."

John continued as if he were unconvinced. "You don't have to worry about me. It's no big deal if you are dodging the draft or something. There have been a lot of guys like you around lately—your age, your long hair. Listen, I don't support that war at all, and you may be surprised, but you'll find plenty of people around here who don't either who will understand your reasons for coming here."

"I suppose I stick out like a sore thumb." He sounded very sympathetic, so I relented in my denial.

"So what are your plans? Are you looking to immigrate permanently?"

"I don't know," I said.

"You looking for work, then?"

"Yeah, I suppose I'll be needing something sometime soon."

"You ever do any farm work? I own a farm back in the direction where I came, and I'm looking for a few farm hands with the plowing and planting season approaching. You'd be doing me a favor. Workers are hard to come by these days."

I chuckled at the irony. "It's funny. Actually, I've been working on a farm the past year. But I think I'm pretty much all done with farm work at the moment. Thanks anyway. I'm a city boy, born and raised. That's why I was headed to Toronto, to be in more familiar territory, so to speak, and find some job there."

"You know, I still might be able to help you out. Hamilton is where I'm heading right now, to see my sister Kathy and her husband Neal, and as it turns out Neal is even more fervently anti-war than I am. He likes to help out Americans who've come here to get out of going over there, almost like he runs a program. He helps them with legal status, helps them find jobs and places to live. He owns a newspaper there. Many times he's given jobs to American draft dodgers at his printing plant, entry-level, manual labor stuff to get them started. He's sent some guys my way to work on the farm if they're interested. As a matter of fact, that's why I'm going to see him. I'm picking up a couple of guys he's helped out to work for me for a while. Neil's a very cool guy. I'm sure he'd help you too."

"I don't know." I looked at him askance, not knowing how to take this offer. He was a complete stranger whom I just met. No level of trust had a chance to build, but he seemed sincere at any rate. At the moment, I wanted to stick to my plan, which was to just go it alone and see what happened. I didn't like the thought of depending on anyone else's generosity anymore, my ability to trust being completely shot to hell. But he gently pressed his case.

"Are you a landed immigrant?" he asked.

"What's that?

"Do you have legal status to be here? Did you announce your intention to immigrate here when you crossed the border?"

Again, I was reticent to discuss with a stranger my legal status—make that obviously *illegal* status. "No. But does that make a difference? I just said I was visiting the country for a couple of weeks when I crossed the border."

"It does make some difference. If you announced your intentions at the border, they would have granted you *landed* immigrant status. But most of the Americans like you don't know, so they cross illegally. It just takes much longer to get legal status and citizenship. Neal actually published a pamphlet that gives advice to potential draft dodgers who are thinking of coming here, and he distributed them on big city college campuses like New York, Boston, Philadelphia and Washington, D.C. He's really a great guy. You'd really like him."

With the ride it wasn't long before we were in Kitchener. John asked for directions for the bus station and took me there.

"Thanks for the ride and your offer," I said. I thought I should just stick with my original plan. Neal sounded a bit like another guru-type crusader, and I think I had my fill with guys like that.

"Are you sure you're going to go it alone, by yourself? You've got money to get you by for a while, right?"

"Ah, yeah, some. Although it's American money. I brought some with me when I came. I should be all right for a while." A thought just occurred to me. "I don't even know if you guys accept American up here, or do I have to exchange it for Canadian?"

"You might find better luck changing it to Canadian. But do it in small doses because that's another thing. You probably didn't declare it at the border, did you?"

"No, I didn't. I didn't know if that would make them more suspicious or not, like it would contradict our story of a two-week visit."

"Of course. But if you want to reconsider, Neal can smooth out things like that. He does it all the time."

I thought about it. Toronto was still a complete unknown. I had no clue to what awaited me there. Maybe someone wouldn't be so nice, notice that I was a draft-dodging American and have a completely different opinion than John did and want to turn me in. Or maybe someone would mug me. I was carrying my savings in cash. Thoughts of all the bad things which could happen started popping up. The idea of having something more definite was drawing me back to John's truck.

"On second thought, I am pretty much out on a limb here, dangling in the breeze, so to speak. I have to admit I'm a bit naïve about a lot of things. I would greatly appreciate any help I can get right now because, truthfully, I'm feeling a little lost right now. If it's no trouble."

"Not a bit. It's where I'm headed, eh. Neal will be glad to help, guaranteed. Funny, I'm usually picking up people *from* him. He'll damned sure be surprised to have me deliver one." John let out a laugh.

"Just one thing though. Can we make a pit stop for lunch here? I'm famished, and you just don't know the craving I have for a nice, juicy hamburger right about now."

"Sure thing."

I hadn't eaten meat in a year on the vegetarian farm, and the thought of sinking my teeth in some tender cow flesh again overwhelmed me when we passed by a diner. I had lost about fifteen pounds on a rather light frame as it was during my stay on the farm, due to all the unappetizing food they offered. I was a little anemic, I think, and it felt nearly like a protein injection when I downed my burger, with the tasty animal fat reinvigorating my diminished body. I chased the burger with a malt and some French fries. John paid because he had Canadian dollars, but I paid him ten American for the meal that was less than two Canadian.

After the satisfying meal, we got to Hamilton shortly and he introduced me to his brother-in-law, Neal Howe. It was as John had described. After I related my situation, including extra details about how my girlfriend abandoned me and took our baby with her, Neal was eager to help. John left me in his hands as he took *his* two new charges back with him.

Neal offered me a job as a helper in his paper's printing plant, as well as all the good advice I needed and could stand. I exchanged my money, and he guided me to a nearby boarding house where I could get a room for the time being. Fortunately for me, I was set up to completely start over. All I was concerned about for the first couple of months was working hard for this man who helped me get back on my feet. Neal was a very busy man, but he checked up on my progress now and again to see if I was doing okay, or if I needed anything. I told him I was fine and that I didn't need much. I settled into a very basic routine with the job. It was manual labor, lifting and stacking bundles as they came off the press, or sweeping up, or loading the trucks for delivery. Truth be told, the work was about as dirty, monotonous and backbreaking as hoeing rows, but I didn't mind it as much because I had wages to look forward to at the end of the week. With communal living we were supposed to share in the benefits of our labor, but beyond not having to pay rent or for food, we didn't see much in terms of benefits. I don't know what the profit/loss statement looked like for Ziggy's farm, but if he did realize any profit, it didn't reach us proletarian workers. I felt like slave labor at the farm. Had I done the same work, but for wages, I would have felt a lot more freedom. I could make individual choices about my own circumstance. If I wanted to save to build toward something for the future, I could have, had I been paid. But without being paid wages, the only fruits of my labor that I received were the fruits of the farm, i.e. beans. There's nothing quite like being paid *beans* for your hard work, *literal* beans.

I kept making periodic calls to the farm to check on Lorelei. I always spoke to Saffron, but she always had the same bad news for me, which was no news about Lorelei. She hadn't come back, and she hadn't left any word about her whereabouts. Lorelei vanished into thin air.

After about a year of checking in with Saffron, I heard from Juniper that Saffron had also left the farm. No reason was given, just that she went back to Toronto. Other people had left here and there. Another year and the grand experiment of the commune collapsed, everyone scattered and Ziggy eventually sold the farm. (No surprise to me, and it couldn't have happened to a nicer guy.) Ziggy's farm was like many communes of the era which failed, not because of lack of commitment to the cause ideally, or selfishness trumping sharing. More basically, I believe that they failed because the sharing people didn't wish to share poverty ultimately. Working the land was not lucrative and didn't provide beyond basic needs. It is human nature to want to improve one's condition in life. That's why people moved out of caves and built more comfortable houses. That's why people invent labor-saving devices. That's why people pave roads, build cities and go to the moon. On the farm communes, people were nearly reversing their standard of living by a hundred years.

Once Ziggy's was gone, I let go any hope that I would hear from Lorelei again. I was stunned and bitter. I couldn't quite grasp exactly what had gone so wrong. The reason I was there totally escaped my grasp to comprehend. As 1970, turned into 1971, and into 1972 and finally 1973, fervor about the war had gradually died away. The United States, partly because of the backlash on the home front and the lack of military victory, began to negotiate a withdrawal of troops, which was completed by 1973. Even by 1975, the war was over for the Vietnamese when the North overran the South. I was in Canada to get out of going to that war, so when it was over, my reason for being there was over. But I still had issues with U.S. law for evading the draft, which I was still afraid to face. It was hard to see myself as a criminal, yet I was facing possible jail time if I went back. So it was easy to just continue doing what I was doing, even though my *raison d'etre* vanished.

Because I wasn't a landed immigrant, it took years longer to process my application for citizenship. I didn't have a strong desire to become a citizen, so it was just as well. I was nearly indifferent to Canada. I had no strong desire to come, I had no strong desire to stay, but there I was. Neal helped me with the legal process. I worked in the plant as a basic laborer for about a year and a half. He seemed more concerned with my well-being than I was, noticing that I worked hard, but that I didn't seem happy about my job. I told him I wasn't, but I didn't have any ideas about what I'd rather do, so I kept on as I was. He knew that I had some college, and asked me if I wanted to try to learn other jobs there. I said I'd be willing to learn just about anything else.

"Have you ever done any typing?" Neal asked.

"I took a class in high school." It was a business class that I took with Allison, to help me type my papers in college.

"How fast?"

"I got up to about sixty words per minute. But I haven't practiced in a long time."

"That's not bad. I'm thinking you might be a decent candidate to train for the linotype machine. It takes manual dexterity, and some English basics, like how to hyphenate words at the end of a line. It's basically typing, but it has a different keyboard layout. Is that something you might want to give a try? I know being a helper has its limitations."

"I'll give it a try."

"We've got a linotype keyboard you can practice on after hours, so there's no harm in trying. I'll let the foreman know. He'll keep his eye on things and let me know how you progress."

So, I practiced retyping stories from the paper until I got fast enough to be switched to working the linotype. The machine was used to set type for printing. It actually made metal casts of letters in a line. After finishing a line, I pushed a lever which completed the cast, which then could be combined with other casts to form a column of type. It involved a lot of pressure with the speed required and in spacing everything properly, but it kept my mind more active, and I enjoyed it so much more than pitching bundles. I felt skilled, and I settled into my life a bit more, where the job was now a good enough reason for getting up every day. And Neal continued to look out for me. He offered more suggestions about different training.

After two years of working the linotype, he suggested going to the newsroom, saying that he could find a good replacement for me in the shop, but that educated workers were hard to come by as his paper was growing. Even with the limited college I had, Neal said that he thought there wasn't any reason that I couldn't handle a few things in the newsroom. I could start writing obituaries, which was formulaic writing. It also didn't take a whole lot of time each day, and that I could fill in as needed with other things. The paper ran a news brief column from the wire services. It didn't require a lot of writing, as sentences could be used verbatim from the wire, but they had to be edited down to size and occasionally reworded to retain clarity. After the editor got to know me, he would have me fill in for small stories that didn't require a lot of experience to handle. But doing this for a couple years, talking to the other reporters and seeing how it all came together, led me to be assigned bigger stories. The editor liked my work, and again, I found something that I really enjoyed doing. I had been so fixated on becoming an aerospace engineer that I hadn't thought of any alternatives. And when that dream collapsed, I didn't have anything else to look forward to, so I stagnated for a while. With the opportunity I was given, however, I found something else that I could excel in, and I had the luxury of learning on the fly instead of being required to go back to school.

Because I was progressing in my new career, it was hard to just leave Canada, despite not having to avoid the war anymore. I had nothing certain to go back to in America. I wrote to my father a few times to tell him how I was doing, still afraid of his disappointment in me. He wrote back and said he'd be willing to accept anything I decided, but he didn't understand why I stayed. Partly, I was attaining my first level of self-sufficiency in my life, and it felt pretty good. I mostly concentrated on work and managed to save most of the money that I earned. My biggest purchase was a used runabout Honda Z600 to get to and from assignments. At the time, I had little interest in women and stayed single during my time in country. I felt I messed up my previous relationships so badly that I was completely gun shy about starting another one.

Then in 1977, a momentous event south of the border changed my whole Canadian perspective. With the election of Jimmy Carter in November 1976, he decided to keep at least one campaign promise, and he did it on his first day. January 21, 1977, Carter granted amnesty to all Vietnam War draft dodgers. I was completely free to return to my home country without fear of prosecution.

With my career path being established by then, at least, I felt I did have something to pursue in America and was comfortable leaving the paper in Hamilton. I was so grateful for the experience that I was given, and I thanked Mr. Howe personally for rehabilitating me. He said he was sorry to see me leave, but that he also understood and was willing to give me a good reference as well. After I made my final decision, I called my father and asked him if I could come home. He unhesitatingly said yes, removing the final obstacle.

VERSE 8:

"Get back, Get back, Get back to where you once belonged."
                                                    Lennon-McCartney

"You and I have memories,
Longer than the road that stretches out ahead."
                                                    Lennon-McCartney

I knew where I was going this time—home—but I didn't know exactly what awaited me there. I felt that my relationship with my father was certainly changed, but I didn't know to what extent, or if it had been damaged permanently. Even though he was saying it was okay for me to come back home, I think we both looked forward to our reunion with more than a little trepidation.

I decided to take my first airplane flight from Toronto to Boston, as there was no direct flight to the state airport right in Warwick where my father lived. I would take a bus from Boston into the Providence station where my father would pick me up. The flight was uneventful, but I enjoyed looking out the window for that unique bird's-eye perspective. I half-expected to be able to tell when I crossed back over U.S. territory—or even see this great dotted-dashed line such as they use on globes to mark international boundaries—but as Canada didn't feel as much like a foreign country as some could, I couldn't tell one bit of difference looking at the ground below. Only when we landed, and I saw the familiar sites of old Boston, did I feel that I was back home. I was an American again, just as I was born to be.

The Vietnam War was a huge shadow cast over my life, and a large reason I was stepping off that plane, but as I looked around at the bustling crowd at the airport, hustling off to a myriad of destinations, unawares, I thought if I explained the reason I was there that day and mentioned the war, people would look at me strangely and only wonder why I was talking about ancient history. Only four years after our pullout, the Vietnam War was history, like Korea or World War II. People knew about it, maybe even knew someone involved in it, but now it was completely out of everyday consciousness, such as I had almost never experienced. Only in my youngest school days did I have no connection to the war. I grew up with the war looming on the horizon of my life, and every decision I made about my life up to that point had some kind of direct or indirect connection to it. Even though I was nothing like a returning veteran of the war, I too was so very glad that it was over, behind me. I could look forward again and not see its dominating presence.

The bus ride was another hour and forty-five minutes with a couple of stops along the way, which gave me time to practice what I was going to say. It was bitter cold that day before Valentine's Day, 1977, when I came home, remnants of snow from previous storms of a long winter decorating the landscape outside my bus window. Bright sunshine, though, made the whole scene sparkle with freshness and hope. Providence was a bit different than the countryside, however, as too many smoke stacks from the factories marred an otherwise idyllic day.

As the bus pulled into the station, I looked through the small crowd of people for my father. I wanted to spot him first. I looked around for his white 1967 Mercury Cougar, but couldn't find it. I wondered if he even had it anymore. I was gone a long time, and that's the last car I knew that he had. It wasn't until I was descending the steps of the bus when I caught a glimpse of him.

I recognized him right away, of course, but the absence of almost eight years made him appear slightly different. He soon recognized me as well, and came over to stand next to me as I awaited the driver to open the baggage compartment beneath the bus.

"Tommy!" he called out to me. He walked over to me in no great hurry and extended his hand to shake. At first, I thought this was going to be our greeting, slightly formal, but he did a sort of combination maneuver, after a second or two of shaking my hand, his left hand clapped me on the shoulder for a little more intimacy, then he clutched my shoulder and drew me into a half-hug while we were still shaking hands.

"Hi, Dad," was all I could say at the moment. He stepped back as I turned to get my bag and he looked me up and down.

"My, how you've matured. You look good. You've really grown into manhood."

I was twenty-seven years old, and while I thought I looked pretty much the same, I had to realize that he hadn't seen me since I was nineteen. I might have seen what he saw in me had I a picture of myself from back then. I noted the change in his appearance as well.

"You look good, too—not too much different." My father was in his early fifties then, and I did see some obvious changes: graying hair around the temples, thinning hair at the back, wrinkling around the eyes and throat.

"Well, you ready?" he asked when I had my bag.

"Yes, sir." He led me to a car I didn't recognize, a blue 1975 Cadillac Seville. "What happened to your Cougar?"

"Oh, you know, it was getting older. I traded it in for this one. Do you like it?"

"Yeah, it's very nice," I said climbing into the passenger seat. "But you really loved that Cougar."

"Well, it was eight years old when I traded it. By that time it doesn't seem as nice anymore. And I'm getting older. I can't be driving sporty cars my whole life. I don't think I want to be one of those guys like in their sixties and driving fast cars to hold on to their youth or something. This seemed more my style at this point in my life."

"Business must be good."

"It's not bad, considering the current economy, rising inflation and all." We continued small talk during the drive home. It seemed safer to stick to topics like this for the time being. My father kept pointing out things that had changed since I left. Providence looked about the same. The cars on the road were the big difference to me. I somehow expected the peripherals, such as the cars and how people dressed to be the same as when I left. I had seen newer cars in Canada, of course, but in coming back to a familiar scene years later, I half expected things to be exactly the same, as if I were stepping back into a photograph. Instead of the almost complete saturation of American cars during the Sixties—Fords, Chevy's, Chryslers—I saw more Japanese cars on the road that day—Toyotas, Datsuns and Hondas. There was a lot of construction on Interstate-95 as well that made me feel out of place.

"So, were you still able to keep up with the Red Sox in the '75 World Series?" my dad asked.

"Yeah, it wasn't as easy as around here, but I did. They're getting more into baseball there, especially with a new major league team starting in Toronto this year."

"I caught a few Pawtucket Red Sox games in '74, and saw Rice and Lynn play there. I knew that they'd both be in the bigs soon after. Rice won the triple-A triple crown that year."

Just in simple diversions like sports, I realized how much I missed during my absence. The Boston Bruins two Stanley Cups, and two more NBA championships for the Celtics. Biggest of all, of course, was the World Series in 1975 with the Red Sox against Cincinnati, even though they lost. My father and I being fans of the New England teams, it was an easy connection for us to share and make conversation. With him, I totally missed the Nixon and Ford administrations, for that matter, and I started feeling as if that void was now a chasm that would be difficult to bridge.

As I thought about the things that had changed, we pulled onto the old familiar tree-lined street of my childhood and up to our house. Those things did seem exactly the same. After we parked the car in the driveway, I got out and looked around in amazement at the old place and felt an enveloping comfort return. As we settled down in the living room, our homecoming took on a more serious and intimate track.

"You can stay in your old room," my father said to me. "It just has the bed and furniture in it now. I hope you don't mind that I packed your things in boxes and put them in the attic. I didn't know how long you'd be gone, or if you were going to ask me to send some things to you."

"That's fine, Dad. I guess I should look through that stuff to see if there is anything I want to keep. It has been a long time." I suddenly pictured him packing my things, just like he packed up my mother's things after she died, the sad and lonely project that must have been. I couldn't expect that he would keep everything the same, especially after I abandoned him as I did. "Dad, I just want to tell you how sorry I am for everything, and for how and why I left. I didn't mean to hurt you." Emotion welled up inside of me, and it came bursting out suddenly as I wept in front of him.

He sat down beside me on the couch to comfort me. "It's all right, Tom. It's all in the past. You're here now. That's all that matters."

"But I made such a mess of things. I screwed up my life beyond belief. I have a son out there somewhere—your grandson—and I have no idea how to find him. He doesn't even know me. He probably believes that I abandoned him, too."

"There, there. I don't know what went on exactly between you and his mother, but maybe someday she'll come to her senses and realize that the boy needs to know his father."

"She's trying to punish me for something, but I don't even know what I did to deserve this. All I ever tried to do was be good to her and our son. By her actions, she's treating me like I'm some kind of evil monster. I tried to be a good person."

"You are a good person, Tom."

"How can you say that after what I did to you? I left you all alone. Your only *son*, and I walked out on you. Over what? Over some disagreement that doesn't even make any sense right now? How can you ever forgive me?"

"Of course, I can forgive you. You came back." I just wallowed in more of my self pity at the depth of his kindness, which made my actions seem all the more deplorable. "You know the story of the prodigal son, don't you, Tom?"

"Yes."

"It's just like that. It doesn't matter what you did, or why you left. It only matters is that you returned to me safe and sound. You *are* my only son, and I'm glad to be looking at his face this day."

"But don't you think that I'm a coward for running off to Canada to dodge the draft?"

"I didn't agree with it at the time. But with a little perspective of time, I can't say that it was necessarily wrong. It meant you survived the war. It means that you're here with me now. A lot of fathers with sons your age can't say that today. When I saw that your birthday was such a low number and that you'd likely be called to go to Vietnam, I was secretly glad to know that you were safe instead. It was hard to admit to myself at first. But I don't look at you as a coward. Now that the war's been over a few years, I don't know if it was worth it to be over there in the first place. Where did it get us? Where would it have gotten us even if we had won? When you make the ultimate sacrifice, you want to be sure that a life is worth it. And I have to seriously doubt it. I don't think you were worth sacrificing. I never could. Only the *man upstairs* could have made that sacrifice."

I put my arm around my dad and hugged him. "I still wish things could have turned out better than they did. You do things for reasons that you believe are right, but even still, they turn out so horribly wrong. I guess you have to forgive my arrogance of youth. I thought I knew what I was doing. But I don't know anything I thought I did."

"That happens to us all, son. It's nothing to be ashamed of."

"But you seemed to do things the right way. You went off to war honorably. You came back, married the girl you loved, started your own business. You must have known what you were doing?"

"You would think so. Yeah, I went off to war, volunteered even though I knew I would have been drafted if I didn't. So I don't look at is as making the brave choice. I had no choice basically. I didn't want to go. But it seemed pretty clear cut at the time who and what the enemy was. That's the only difference between you and me. I didn't know what I was doing. By volunteering, I basically jumped into the deep end without knowing if I could swim or not. Luckily I could. But I also didn't know what fate awaited me. You don't go to war planning to survive. I was one of the lucky ones who did. And I did get to go home and marry my sweetheart. But did I know she was the right girl for me? She felt like she was, but how could I know? I probably felt just like you did with your girl. Again, I jumped in the deep end and found I could swim. Lucky me. And I don't know if you know the story about how I started in the business. Grandpa Moore was a cobbler and owned a little shoe store. When he died not too long after the war was over, he left me a business I didn't really want. I was able to sell it for what I expected would be a nice down payment on a house for your mother and me. I had gotten into a trade as a plumber. But an opportunity came along at the right time, and someone was selling a small supply store. With my down payment and a G.I. bill loan, I took another plunge. I bought the store thinking I could run it, and be a businessman like my father, only in a business that I liked better. I was scared, but I wanted to give it a try. Lucky me, it worked out well in the long run. Most times it takes a simple leap of faith. You believe in yourself so you do it. But even failing is not the worst thing. It's not trying. I trust you gave it your best, and it didn't work as you'd hoped. The only thing left is to try something else."

"That's really good advice, Dad."

"And you know that I'm here to support your decisions and whatever it is you choose to do." The phone rang, and my father got up to get it.

"Thanks, Dad," I called after him.

"—Yes, he's here now—" he said into the phone. "Yes, I think you should come over now. I think you should meet as soon as possible. No time like the present—"

"Who was that?" I inquired.

"Someone who I can't wait for you to meet, so she's coming over right away. It's a woman I've been seeing for the last year or so."

"Seeing?" I asked in wonderment.

"Yeah, you know, dating. We met at the American Legion. I would go there for the suppers on Friday nights, to be around people, you know. Occasionally, I would help in the kitchen and cook spaghetti dinners or fish fry's or some such. Well, there's this attractive lady that I get to talking with, and she was really wonderful. Ann is her name. She's a widow, too; so we had something in common we could talk about and get to know each other."

At first I was amazed because I had this image of my father as the devoted widower who would never stop loving his departed wife. I was somewhat shocked at the thought of another woman, even now, some sixteen years later. But I had to appreciate the loneliness of my father, what his loss meant, all the years alone, and me leaving him for the past eight, as well. Of course he had every right to carry on with his life, with certainly no disrespect toward the memory of my mother. My father waited much longer than he probably was expected.

"That's wonderful, dad. That's great news. I'd be happy to meet her."

So, Ann arrived shortly thereafter. I wasn't in my best mood to meet anybody new, never mind my father's new girlfriend, but I put on my best face I could. I greeted her with a polite handshake.

"Hello, Tom. Jack has told me so much about you that I feel I know you already." I was starting to think I barely knew myself anymore, but I let it pass. I couldn't help comparing her physically to my mother to see if Dad was looking for a Mom substitute. Obviously, she was much older than my last memory of my mother, who died at age 32. Ann was 52 with curly, graying black hair, likely permed. My mother had chestnut brown with auburn highlights flowing straight and natural past her shoulders. Ann was slightly overweight, as opposed to my mother's athletic frame. They were approximately the same height. Ann wore a polyester pantsuit that was popular in the mid-Seventies, and makeup that was slightly too heavy. My mother's makeup tended to be simply lipstick, and only when she went out.

I almost wanted to dislike Ann, but she charmed me from the start, and the attraction was understandable for my father. She smiled constantly and was extremely talkative. At first, I thought that her loquaciousness would- n't match well with my more pensive and terse father, but I saw how she helped bring him out of his shell.

She insisted on fixing dinner that night as my father and I talked more to get reacquainted. He had changed a bit in eight years, and felt slightly like a stranger at first. But as changes were inevitable in that length of time, it was interesting to get to know him again. As I was well into adulthood now— although I was likely very different to him as well at first—my father seemed more like a good friend than a father. The three of us shared the dinner that night and had a really good time. That night helped me feel much more re- laxed about my situation, where the past slipped comfortably behind me.

At the end of the evening, Ann said goodnight, and she and my dad furtively kissed goodbye at the door. I turned in to go to my old room shortly thereafter. And the fact that the bedroom was bare of all the childhood accoutrements helped me to keep looking forward, until I was comfortable enough to go to the attic and look through my old stuff. I felt nostalgic looking at things like my old high school basketball uniform, yearbooks, books on astronomy and such. I only pulled out one thing and put it back in my room—the telescope that my father gave me for Christmas in 1968 that I barely got to use. When it got a little warmer, I poked it out of my bedroom window, just like I used to in childhood, and pretended to look for my mother in the heavens—my own "Lucy in the Sky with Diamonds."

In short order, I also had to get my life back on track and get a job. Mr. Howe put me in contact with the only newspaper publisher in Rhode Island that he knew who ran *The Call* in Woonsocket, a small city on the north border. The state was so small that I could still live in Warwick with my dad and commute to work. I got a job as a reporter, and it was much like my old job in Hamilton, so it was easy to get into a comfortable groove soon after I started. I covered local events, such as fires and accidents mostly, but I moved on to covering the police beat and city government after a time. And because I liked sports, I filled in occasionally to cover high school sports. It was a small paper in a small community, and it was nice to belong to a new circle of professional friends. I was really enjoying my new life the first couple of years back. I looked back and thought how I never saw myself in this position. It never even occurred to me that I would be a writer—particularly good enough to make it a profession—until I tried it, nor how much I would enjoy it. But there I was.

Life sometimes settles into a comfortable routine, but then there are momentous occasions which help mark time's passage a little more sharply. In September 1979, my father and Ann announced that they would be getting married the following April. It seemed a natural matter of course for their relationship. They loved each other, and only seemed to grow closer with each passing year of their dating relationship. My father said I was welcomed to stay living with them at the house, but it suddenly occurred to me that I should finally get my own place. It was a great two years to get reacquainted with my dad, but I was then thirty. I enjoyed not paying any official rent, but when I offered to help pay some expenses, my father would usually take it to honor the offer, though he hardly needed it. But because of my low expenses, I saved quite a bit of my earnings, as I did before, without better alternatives to spend my money on, excepting my first new car that I bought—a Datsun 280ZX. It was an obvious appeal to my youth, much like my dad's Cougar, but it was my first splurge on myself. I also was in a good position to buy my own house, which seemed like a good investment as opposed to apartment living. So I started to look around.

In October of that year, I was out at a bar with a friend who worked at the *Providence Journal.* We became acquainted while we were covering the same story. Paul Marcoux was single and liked to go to bars to try to pick up women. I had thoughts about reentering the social scene myself at the time, but I would tag along with him for moral support mostly. I wasn't much of a drinker. I don't like beer. But I found whiskey sours—one of my dad's drink of choice—to be somewhat palatable, so I would usually nurse one or two during the evening he spent flirting. I don't know if my heart was fully into either on this or previous occasions, but I usually didn't feel much attraction to the women in the bars we went to. It was always too loud to converse with much intimacy, and I always struck out.

That particular night, however, I ran across a familiar face. It was a face that changed slightly over the years, and I didn't think I could be mistaken. I wasn't sure if she was there already when Paul and I arrived, or if she arrived with her friends sometime after. But after seeing her anonymously pass by a couple times to order drinks at the bar where I sat a slight distance away, I recognized her completely—none other than Allison Lambert.

She wore a slinky, black cocktail dress with spaghetti straps daintily draping her creamy, elegant shoulders. Along with her three-inch heel, patent leather pumps, her outfit was unlike any I'd ever seen her in. Allison's prom dress was the most formal attire I've seen on her, but it was much less sexy— a little too much ruffle and puff to adequately show off her fine feline-like frame. But this silky little number delicately clung to her lithe, still slender body, allowing a gentlemanly glimpse at what she had been endowed with by her creator. Knowing that she had once been mine, a pang of emptiness hit me in the chest, and the phrase, "Eat your heart out," materialized in my head.

I, on the other hand, was not dressed to impress. I was wearing my reporter's uniform: a non-dressy, white with blue pin-striped oxford shirt; a plain working man's tie; comfortable tan chinos, and scuffed brown shoes. Beyond just the clothes, my tie was jauntily loosened, and my sleeves were casually rolled up. Despite my appearance, I had to say hello to satisfy some of my curiosity.

When she came up to the bar to order drinks for her friends, a few stools down from where I was planted, sipping my first whiskey sour of the night, I stood up to approach her while she waited on the bartender's return. I looked at her a moment, hoping our eyes would meet, but she was oblivious to my presence, not likely expecting a familiar face in this crowd, especially not mine. So, I went over.

"Allison. Hi. How are you?" I said.

She looked up nonchalantly, probably wondering how someone knew her name, and then a sudden wave of recognition swept over her face. "Tommy! I don't believe it! How the heck are you?"

"Oh, fair to middling. How about yourself?"

"Just great. Wow! It's been years. I guess I should have expected to run into you again sometime. Just didn't expect it tonight. Are you living in the area again, or just visiting?"

"I'm back living in the area. Actually, living at my father's house for the time being, but I'm looking for my own place."

"Hey, how is your father?"

"He's doing real well, too. He's actually getting remarried come April."

"That's fantastic, Tom. He was always such a sweetheart. He deserves all the happiness in the world. Tell him I said so."

"Okay, I will." The bartender brought her drink order.

"Since you're here, do you mind helping me carry the drinks to my friends' table? They're right over there." She pointed them out, and I said, "Certainly."

Allison introduced me to her two friends, whom I couldn't recall their names five seconds after she said them. I was focusing too much on Allison.

"This is Tom Moore. Tommy was my high school boyfriend. We haven't seen each other in, what, about ten years?"

"Yeah, that's about right," I said. "I'd actually love to hear what you've been up to since I saw you last." I probably wouldn't have mentioned it had I recalled, but the last time I did see her was when we broke up.

"Yeah, I would, too. Maybe reminisce a little, also, about good old times." To her friends she said, "You two don't mind if I do some catching up with Tom, do you?" They said, of course, she should go right ahead. So Allison grabbed her drink, a white wine, and I gathered my unattended drink at the bar and we found another table in the corner where we could talk more.

I didn't feel too bad for taking Allison away from her friends for the moment because shortly thereafter I noticed that they attracted the attention of a couple of guys and seemed to be enjoying themselves.

"Wow, I still can't believe it," Allison said to me as we sat down. "I can't believe I'm running into you like this after all these years. So tell me, what are you doing now?"

"I'm working as a newspaper reporter for the *Woonsocket Call*."

"No fooling? How did you end up doing that? I thought you wanted to work for NASA and the space program."

"Yeah, surprised me too. Journalism is something that I kind of chanced into and found that I like it a lot. I quit school at BU not too long after I last saw you."

"I heard about that."

"Well, my college plans were kind of derailed, so I didn't get to study aerospace engineering like I planned, and I haven't had a chance to go back yet. So things happen; you move on with your next best options. It's hard to regret it, though. I love writing, and I don't know if I would have discovered it had something not taken me off the path I was on. So how about you? What are you doing now?"

"I'm a teacher, just like I planned all those years ago. I love it too. I can't imagine doing anything else. Maybe there's something else I could have found that I would have liked better."

"Maybe, but I bet the kids are glad you picked teaching. I always thought you'd be great at it."

"The kids are great. I work at a high school in Pawtucket. It reminds me so much of Warwick High. Remember our teachers there? How we would make fun of them all the time? I bet my kids still do that to us—anybody our age, really."

"Well, most of our teachers were older than Methuselah. But there were a few that were really good at relating to us kids. I'm sure that at your age you can still relate well to them."

"Oh, sure, I still remember vividly what it was like at that age, what I was thinking, and how."

"So, what else have you been up to?" I was probing about possible relationships without being too blunt.

"Let's see, I graduated in '71, got married in '72, and had a baby in '73—a beautiful baby girl." Another pang hit me in the pit of my stomach. The block of time I was missing with her was like a lifetime. She lived a whole other life during that time that I wasn't privy to, and it was crazy of me to think that she wouldn't have moved on, but marriage in particular seemed so final in terms of moving on. But as I lowered my eyes toward the table to disguise any sense of jealousy in my face, I noticed that she was not wearing a ring on the appropriate finger.

"You said you got married, but I don't see that you're wearing your ring right now."

"Good reason for that, I got divorced in '76." I hope my face also didn't show some glimmer of hope just then. "Must have been that spirit of independence going around that year. Just kidding. No, I thought I fell in love—with Brian was his name—but it wasn't long after we were married that I found him to be an extremely egotistical, selfish jerk. I should have seen it when we were dating, how he treated other people. But at the time, as he was courting me, he treated me wonderfully. After we got married, he treated me much the same as he treated everybody else, with arrogance and disregard. He was a star athlete in school, was becoming a lawyer—that type. Probably had a god complex or something. But hey, I'm over it. It's been a couple of years now, and I think I'm way better off now. And I do have my precious daughter as a result, which makes it all worthwhile. Her name is KC. It's spelled with just the letters *K* and *C*, but pronounced just like you would spell it out: *C-A-S-E-Y*. I wanted to do something unique and original, I guess. Would you like to see her picture?"

"Sure." Allison pulled out a wallet from her purse and showed me a few photos of her daughter KC. One was of her as an infant, and a couple in progression as she aged. The latest showed her mugging for the camera with an impish grin on her face. "She is absolutely precious," I said.

"So, how about you? Ever got hitched? Though I don't see a ring on your finger, either."

"No, I never did. I do have a son, though."

"Really? Congratulations. That's wonderful, Tom."

"Sorry, I don't have a picture of him. And the reason why I don't have a picture of him is quite a sad story really."

Allison looked concerned and patted my hand which lay on the table. "You can tell me, if you want. We're old friends."

"Well, this girl I met in Boston, we kind of had a relationship going, and one thing leads to another. I got her pregnant. Believe me, I begged her to marry me when I found out." I added that to make sure Allison didn't think I was some kind of cad. "But she wouldn't. Liberated woman, or something, didn't believe in marriage at all. Well, before she gives birth, she gets me to go to this farm commune in Canada. She says it's to help me get out of the draft, which was becoming more and more imminent when I dropped out of school and lost my deferment, but I don't know. I couldn't exactly let her go off alone, so I went along. Turns out she knew that guy who ran the farm, and not too long after she gave birth to our son, I catch her cheating on me with this guy. I don't know what exactly happened or why, but instead of leaving with me to fix things, she insists on staying. I think it's for the guy, but one day, she left us both high and dry. Me, more so, because she took our son and didn't leave one clue about where she went. I haven't seen or heard from her or our son since."

"That is sad, and terrible. But you couldn't trace her?"

"No. When we were first seeing each other, she was always mysterious about herself, her past, *et cetera*. She never even told me her last name, or what town she was from. Nothing. I thought it was curious, but perhaps a little hippie-like eccentric considering the times, but I don't think I could have ever anticipated that she would do something like that."

"Unbelievable. I mean, I got custody of KC when Brian and I got divorced, but he has visitations. To get back at him over some fight we had, I might have fantasized about cutting off all contact with our daughter, as some kind of retribution, but I never seriously considered it. At least he's still a good person to KC, so I have to put our differences aside. Maybe I'm biased about the guy, too. Maybe he's not all bad. He's seeing someone else now, so he's been able to convince someone that he has some redeeming qualities. He is a lawyer now, so maybe he has some sort of empathy. Let's hope, anyway, for his clients' sake. But I know you, and you're not some kind of monster who needs to be taken away from his son. What she did to you was evil."

I noticed that she had finished her drink, and I was nearly finished mine. I wanted her to keep talking to me, so I offered to get the next round. "Will you have another glass?"

"Sure, thanks. Zinfandel, please."

When I returned to the table, we continued to talk, but about more casual things. Allison was interested in the life of a newspaper reporter, so I related a few stories. She regaled me with a few classroom stories which I found humorous. She had another glass of wine before the conversation was drawing to an end. I had stopped in the middle of my second. I don't know how many she had before we started reacquainting ourselves, but I sensed she was getting a touch tipsy. Allison looked as if she were just getting into the spirit and enjoying our little two-person reunion. I enjoyed it immensely. A nice familiarity we had had with each other was returning, despite the absence of years. I still found her extremely attractive, and I never truly stopped loving her. It would have been easier for me to move on had I met other women who might equally fit the bill that she did when I was with her, but I found it difficult to meet other women who had the same effect on me. I saw that her friends were motioning to her as if eager to leave, so I simply asked if I could talk with her more another time.

"This was really fun seeing you again. I haven't enjoyed myself this much in a long time. I was hoping that you'd like to talk some more, sometime soon. Maybe I could take you out to dinner?"

"Oh, Tom. It *was* fun seeing you again, but that's all that it is. I don't know what you're thinking, but if you're expecting that we'll somehow pick up things right where we left off, it's not happening, and it never will."

"That's not what I was thinking at all," even though it was an inkling of my thinking, of what I momentarily saw in the future realm of possibilities. "We're old friends. Can't two old friends get together and see each other once in a while?"

"Oh, we're not really old friends, Tom. We're old lovers. And what's past is past. We can never recapture the past. I've moved on, and it sounded like you moved on as well. I was a girl when you knew me. I'm a grown woman now, with a daughter and a past marriage. I have a completely different perspective on life than I did back then when I was young and naïve."

"You don't look or sound that much different to me."

"But I am. I know I am. And I know you're different, although I don't know how much so. You're still a handsome young man, and any woman would be nuts not to investigate what you have to offer. But because of our history, I'll always be comparing the man you are now, to the boy you used to be, and the differences will cause altered expectations."

"What if I'm a better man than I used to be?" I asked, playing devil's advocate.

"I'm not suggesting you're not. But like I said, I've moved on. You have to find a way to move on too. Because of our paths diverging, we can't force them back to meet again. It's next to impossible. It has to be with somebody different."

"This is way more than I was expecting. All I wanted was to see you again, talk to you. I've really missed you."

"I know, I know. I know what's in here," she said pointing to my heart. "What can I say, Tom? You hurt me. You really hurt me. And I can't be casual friends with you because I can't forget how you hurt me. You devastated me."

"I'm so sorry for what I did. I was a know-nothing kid. I had no intention to do anything like that to you." My defenses were down, and I wasn't kidding around with her anymore. Allison got up to leave.

"And yet you did, Tom. You did. So forget the past, and please move on, for your own sake. Or remember the past fondly, as I do. But still, move on!"

Allison clutched her purse tightly and whirled away from me, leaving me standing in befuddlement. I couldn't understand how our pleasant evening developed into that scene. But perhaps she was looking for a closure that she never got in her own mind when I confessed my sin to her years ago.

I tracked down Paul after watching Allison leave with her friends.

"Hey, buddy," he said. "Who was that hot number you were with tonight?"

"Actually, she was an old friend," I replied.

"Yeah? Oh, so you struck out tonight, did you? Well, I pretty much did too." He laughed it off. "Although I did get a phone number. Say, you okay to drive? 'Cause I sure ain't."

"Yeah, no problem. Let's go." It looked as if I didn't have much choice. I had to move on. So I did.

VERSE 9:

"Will you still need me, will you still feed me when I'm sixty-four?"
Lennon-McCartney

"The long and winding road that leads to your door,
Will never disappear, I've seen that road before,
It always leads me here, leads me to your door."
Lennon-McCartney

"Number Nine; Number Nine; Number Nine; Number Nine."

The mile markers continued to roll on by, as the Seventies changed into the Eighties. Dad and Ann got married in April; and when she moved into the house, I moved out. I was ready. It was nice to live at home again to help make up for lost time I had with my father, but I was beginning my thirties, and the image of a thirty-year-old man living at his parent's house didn't seem very attractive. Although my father told me there was no need for me to move out if I didn't want to, I did want to. I told him I wasn't going that far this time, and we could still get together as often as he would like. And we did—for frequent dinners, all the birthdays and holidays, Pawtucket Red Sox games at McCoy Stadium on lazy, relaxing summer nights, or to Fenway on occasion for some big league excitement.

I bought my own house, which really made me feel proud. It seemed somewhat awkward for a single man to be buying a three bedroom house just for himself, but it was a good investment, and it gave me a chance to really enjoy the space. I bought a quaint old house not too far away in Lincoln. It was a little closer to Woonsocket and outside the city areas of Warwick-Providence-Pawtucket in the woods. It had a decent sized lot with the backyard trailing off to a river at the bottom of the hill. I, with the eager assistance of my father, discovered the joys of the manly pursuits of housekeeping—yard work, plumbing, and outfitting a decent garage with an assortment of tools that I might need one day for something or other.

My friend Paul kept trying to get me to apply for a job at his paper, *The Journal*, so that we could be co-workers. It was a much bigger daily, and we both realized that I would need to go back to school and get my degree in journalism or English to help propel my career. It was a good idea for the long run, so I began to take classes in the fall of 1980, after being out of school more than ten years. I picked up where I left off as a sophomore, this time at Providence College. It was a different experience from my first stint at college, being that I didn't live on campus and that I had a full-time job. With *The Call* being a morning paper, I generally worked in the afternoon and into the night. So I could still take a full load of morning classes on certain days and continue to work my way through school. It was hectic at first, but I adapted.

I even got a girlfriend of sorts—a cute nineteen year-old co-ed from one of my classes named Amy. As we introduced ourselves in the class, I mentioned that I was already working as a reporter for a newspaper. Amy, being interested in becoming a journalist herself, talked to me after class about my experiences. I had already felt a little bit out of my element because of my age, but I basked in a sort of celebrity status and reveled in the attention she was showing me, which emboldened me to ask her out. She surprisingly said yes. That first time, we went out to a diner for lunch after class. I regaled her with my grizzled veteran newspaperman stories, which I didn't realize I had until I spoke with her about them. We went out to dinner at nicer restaurants, for drives along the coast, our college's basketball games, and even for one weekend in the Berkshires. We slept together a few times. But as the age difference became more apparent—I felt awkward and uncomfortable around her younger friends—the relationship fizzled out. Also, I was with Amy the day John Lennon was shot and killed, which devastated me and depressed me for days. She was merely disappointed that someone would want to kill him. While she knew that he was a former Beatle, she wasn't a fan, and her reaction illustrated further our varied frames of reference. Maybe she just liked me for my car. Seriously, though, it was a unique experience to part amicably by mutual consent—no broken hearts, no crying, no regrets. I can't say that any break-up is enjoyable, but it was without malice as we both could see it going nowhere fast. She was a pleasant diversion, however.

I really enjoyed both the literature classes I was taking and the writing classes. I even ventured into a creative writing class. One assignment was to write a long descriptive paragraph on a significant childhood memory. I received an *A* for my written recollections of my mother's funeral, and the written comment across the top of the page, "Very touching," from the professor. At the end of the semester, with his encouragement, I thought I would try writing a short story.

After a couple of aborted attempts to come up with a story of complete imagination, I thought about the exercises in writing class and how they were connected to personal events and memories. I started delving into personal experiences that I could adapt, but many events in my life didn't feel like stories, with beginnings, middles and ends. I didn't know if I could convert something from my past and make a coherent story out of it, or have it have any meaning to anyone else but me. I wanted to write something about being abandoned by Lorelei, but it seemed too close to heart to simply retell the details. It wouldn't be fiction then. This is what I came up with. I started with a character—much like me in a lot of ways, but different—and placed him in the times of my young adulthood during the Sixties, on the road, hitchhiking. He's young, idealistic, carefree, and off to see America however he can. One day he gets picked up by a beautiful hippie chick driving a lima-bean green Karmann Ghia. I figure there is no harm in naming her Lorelei and describing her much like her alter-ego. Spending hours driving cross-country, the pair hit it off after sharing their similar free-spirit philosophies during their lengthy conversations. They stop for the night in the wide-open spaces (I set it in the desert Southwest, though I'd never been there, because it seemed warm enough to just camp out on a whim) and gaze at the dazzling stars and moon before getting some sleep. The main character's thoughts are expressed, especially how incredibly enamored he is with this woman. But he is reluctant to make a move on her to risk losing the wonderfully innocent feeling of the night. Unexpectedly, she makes the move on him, and they make passionate love to cap off a perfect day and night. The main character's thoughts drift toward making a life with this woman because of how she excites his imagination, as he drifts off to sleep. Expecting to continue his and her journey to California, he awakes only to find himself at their makeshift campsite. Lorelei and the car are gone. He only finds a small note pinned to his bedroll saying, "Remember me always." Not knowing enough about her—no last name, where she came from or her exact destination—she vanishes from his life, elusive to grasp as a wisp of wind. The main character is simply left to continue on as he planned before their meeting, to hitchhike on down the road and see where it takes him.

In creating something completely fictitious, something that never literally took place in my life, I infused it with a lot of my personal feelings to flesh out the character. I was very pleased with the end result, and I tracked down my creative writing professor during the summer sessions to get his thoughts on it. He was impressed, not just for a first attempt at short story writing, but overall. He thought it was good enough to get published, and even recommended a magazine to submit it to. I did, and awaited the results.

After somewhat putting that story to bed, and without too many thoughts about the past, I was getting ready for the start of my junior year in the fall of 1981. I went to the campus bookstore to stock up on my current semester's textbooks, and I ran into Allison who was doing the same. I literally ran into her, bumping into her as I was oblivious to the people around me and searching for my books. The English section was located right next to the Education section that she was looking in. As I launched into a clumsy apology for my clumsiness, I looked into the face that launched a thousand ships for me as a teenager.

"I'm so sorry. Please forgive—Oh, my God. Look who it is. Allison. I can't believe I just did that. I didn't watch where I was going. Please forgive me." I helped pick up the notebooks and pens and such that she had dropped.

"That's all right, Tom," she said with good humor and a smile. "Small world, isn't it?"

It was an extremely small state, that's for certain. "Yes it is. Funny running into you here. Are you a student here, too?"

"Yes. I'm a graduate student. I decided to go for my master's degree. It will really assist my career, and the extra money you get for having advanced degrees will certainly help out a lot. How about you? When did you start back to college?"

"Last year. I thought I should get my degree as well to help boost my career."

"You're doing the newspaper thing—reporter, right?"

"Yes, you've got a good memory. I'm starting my junior year. Wow, remember how much we had to convince our parents to let us go to Boston University together because we didn't want to be cooped up around here? We thought it too *provincial*."

"Wow, you've got a good memory, too. I do remember. And here we are, back at the same school, back in the old province."

"Yeah. Funny how things work out sometimes, even when you don't plan them. I just can't get over running into you again. You look fantastic, by the way. How's your daughter doing? KC, right?"

"Yes, that's right. She's doing great. You should meet her sometime. She's in school herself now—third grade she started this year. I can hardly believe it that she's eight years old already. How time flies."

"I know what you mean. I can't believe I'm thirty-two years old already."

"Shhh!" Allison playfully rapped me on the shoulder. "People might figure out we're the same age." We shared a few more chuckles, but then as I figured I should stop delaying her and let her get on with her shopping, I was about to excuse myself, and just say it was great to see her again, end it there and be on my way. But she caught me by surprise.

"Hey, where you heading off to?" she asked as she noticed me turning my head to look elsewhere. Her tone wasn't accusatory, but just curious. "Do you have a class right now? 'Cause I was wondering—"

"No, actually. I don't have to be anywhere soon. I just have to finish picking up some books."

"Me too. And I don't have to be anywhere right now, either. Maybe— if you don't mind—would you help me shop for my books? Then we can check out together so we can talk some more. Would you like to, perhaps, grab a cup of coffee with me at the student union after that?"

"Yeah, absolutely. That sounds great."

We breezily chatted while running our errands about the challenges of going to college while working full time and a bit about pop culture of the day. When we finally sat down at the union, Allison added a few details about her family life.

"I've been living with my father," she said, occasionally blowing the steam off her coffee. "My parents got divorced a couple of years ago, you know."

"Really? That's a shame. What happened?" I nibbled on a blueberry muffin and sipped an orange juice while listening to her reply.

"They kind of grew apart over the years, I guess. My mother grew into a more independent woman, which I think was great, but with my father being so old-fashioned, he had a hard time adjusting to her new self. At first she started a little self-exploration, taking continuing education classes in art and photography. She was a college graduate, but back in her day, she put all that aside to become a wife and mother. Even before my sister Bobbi graduated high school, she started talking about getting a job, to keep herself busy and to get out in the world more, interact with new people. My father was dead set against it, especially with Bobbi still living at home. But he relented after a bit, and she started with a part-time job as a saleswoman at the cosmetics counter at a department store. But then she got a promotion working in accounts receivable in the back office. It meant full time, but Bobbi had left the nest. Still my father objected. I guess he still wanted the stay-at-home wife he was used to, and like everyone else had down at the country club. He thought she started talking a foreign language when she started saying that her job helped 'improve her self-worth.' Beyond just the job, she wanted to do different things by going out to different social functions than they used to and pursuing more intellectual endeavors—museums, art house films and plays—all things he had no interest in whatsoever."

"That's a shame that they couldn't work things out."

"Yeah, it was a real shock to me at first. But then I could see things from my mother's point of view. Don't get me wrong, I still think my dad's a great guy, but I don't even think he's comfortable with his daughters being working women. I went into teaching. Bobbi graduated from college too, with a degree in psychology. Now she's working at a counseling center for troubled teens."

"That's wonderful," I said.

"Yeah, she's a real smart cookie. And my mom has worked her way up to office manager already."

"Fantastic."

"Yeah, well for all her success, my dad was devastated by the divorce, something he didn't really want but eventually relented to when he saw the writing on the wall. My mom seems so much happier and living in her own apartment in Providence. After my divorce, even Mom thought it would be a good idea, with me being a single mother, that I move back in the old house with Dad, not to replace her in a sense, but just to keep him company. And he loves to dote on KC."

"That's nice. It's hard though to see your parents in a different light than when you grew up." I talked a little bit about Ann, what she was like and how she was changing my father for the good. The conversation had a very pleasant tone, and when our cups were empty and we both had to be on our way, I said I really enjoyed running into her again. She said likewise. But then Allison caught me off guard again.

"Say, we should get together again, sometime soon. This was a lot of fun catching up with you. Maybe you'd like to catch a movie with me sometime?"

"Yeah, that would be great," I said, but perhaps my perplexed look puzzled her.

"What, you don't want to?"

"No, I do want to. The thing is, I didn't think that *you* would want to."

"Why would you think that?"

"Because the last time I saw you and suggested it, you said it wouldn't be a good idea, that it would be like trying to recapture the past, and that we needed to move on."

"I said that?" she said incredulously. "All I was suggesting was that we could hang out sometime, if you want. I have some teacher friends at school, but it's hard to get together to go out and do stuff like the movies because of everyone's busy schedules. The last movie I went to was *The Fox and the Hound* with KC. I just thought it would be great to have an adult night out with a good friend."

"You were making it abundantly clear that because of our past, we couldn't become friends again."

"I don't know why I would say that. I think we had a pretty good past overall. Don't you?"

"It was great."

"And I still think I could be friends with you, in spite of the past. Unless you don't want to?"

I gave her a reassuring smile. "Yes, I want to. I think it's a wonderful idea. I haven't had too many opportunities myself to do things that I really would like."

"Very cool, then. There were a couple of movies that I was interested in seeing, something like *My Dinner with Andre*, *Four Friends*, or *The French Lieutenant's Woman*. What about you?"

"Yes, indeed. I think we're on the same wavelength here. The last one I saw was *Raiders of the Lost Ark* with my friend Paul, definitely his suggestion. I don't think he'd be interested in any of the ones you mentioned."

"Okay it's a deal then," Allison said, offering her hand across the table to shake. I took it and sealed the deal. "Maybe you could call me later to set it up. Wait, here's my phone number."

She quickly found a pen and piece of paper in her purse and wrote the number down. I hadn't thought about it in years, but I knew the number by heart. It was the same old number from years ago.

"Okay, call me. And I'll see you later." Allison got up with her bags and headed out of the student union. I simply enjoyed watching her walk away this time, and smiled knowing I would see her again soon.

We made arrangements the next weekend to see *Four Friends* because it was the most convenient showing time of the ones we were interested in.

I picked her up at the scheduled time at the old house I was still familiar with, definitely not needing directions. Nostalgia filled the air as I approached the house, even though so many things had changed in the passing years. At least this time I had a car for our *date*. I parked in the driveway, and walked to the door, feeling almost transported in a time warp. I knocked as I had so many times before, and Allison's father opened the front door to greet me.

"Oh, it's you again," Mr. Lambert said a little gruffly to me. "Allison told me that she ran into you again, and that you'd be going out with her tonight to the movies."

"Wonderful to see you again, sir," I replied with apparent obsequiousness. "May I come in?"

"Yeah, sure." He moved back to allow me space to enter. "Come on in. Allison's not quite ready, though."

"How've you been, sir? Long time no see. How's business?"

"Business, ahh!" he said with a shrug and a dismissive wave of his hand. "I'm about to retire in a couple of years. I can't wait. Ally! Your company is here!" he bellowed off into the distance. "I hear you're a reporter, now? Is that right?"

"Yes, it is. I'm really enjoying it. Working up in Woonsocket. Been going to back to school, too. That's where I ran into Allison again, at PC."

"That's nice. Have a seat. I'll see what's keeping her." He left me in the living room to sit on the sofa alone, although a cat soon came in to investigate. Then shortly after the cat, a bouncy eight-year-old girl came bounding in looking for the cat.

"Hi, there," I said. "My name is Tom. What's yours?" Of course, I knew this had to be KC.

"My name is KC, like Kansas City, not Casey-at-the-bat." She giggled at her own apparently well-rehearsed line concerning her name. "And that's Chester the Cat."

"Hello, Chester," I said, putting my hand down to his nose to sniff, and then petting his head.

"Mommy says you are her first boyfriend."

"Yeah, well, I guess that's right," I said, taken aback slightly. I don't know how much information Allison passed on about me, but she had told her about me. "We used to know each other from a long time ago. We're old friends."

KC was a delightful child, with silky straight brown hair, with golden highlights that made me wonder about her father and what he might look like. He likely contributed to that blonde trait, I thought (later confirmed in a photo where I saw he was sandy haired). But she reminded me a lot of Ally's sister Bobbi, who was very close to KC's age when I first met her as well. KC didn't seem to have that bratty streak that Bobbi did, but maybe that could be attributed to the big age difference between sisters. KC was an only child, but didn't seem spoiled in the least. She charmingly kept me company while I waited for Allison. KC regaled me with what was currently going on in her third-grade circle when Allison finally did come in.

"Oh, Tom, I hope she wasn't pestering you."

"Oh, not at all. It was a pleasure to meet you, KC."

"The pleasure is all mine," she precociously said as she bowed down dramatically, which Allison helped explain.

"She's going to be in her first school play soon. She loves to perform as you can see." Then she turned to her daughter. "I won't be out too late, but you go to bed when grandpa tells you. And I'll see you in the morning. Okay? Give me a kiss goodnight."

"Okay, Mommy." KC gave her a big lip-smacking kiss, and then blew me a kiss, and blew kisses to an imaginary audience who enthusiastically applauded her stellar performance as she bowed again and exited the stage— er, room.

"She's quite a character, isn't she?" Allison said.

"She's delightful. Absolutely charming," I said. "Like mother, like daughter."

"Well, shall we? I'm ready if you are."

"Let's," I said as I offered my elbow formally for her to take as I escorted her out to the car. I continued in a playful mood and opened the passenger door for her with a flourish. Allison played along and thanked me for my gallantry. We had a pleasant night altogether, enjoying the movie and discussing it afterward. I don't know if she considered any resemblance in the story about a guy still carrying a torch for his female friend after many years of their lives going in different directions. But it wasn't a night for that kind of thing. I simply enjoyed the moment to gain back a little of the friendship I had lost with her. I didn't have any idea where things were going to lead after that first *date*. We both left things up in the air that night, but she suggested doing it again some time. We both had busy schedules, but she called me to chat not more than a couple of weeks after the movie. At the end of another nice conversation, I suggested that I take her out to dinner, and she approved. I took her to a nice restaurant, but the idea was that we were still just friends hanging out together. At the end of that night, she invited me over to her house to have a dinner that she would cook for the family—her father and KC. That worked out pleasantly as well, but I still wasn't sure that her father ever forgave me for breaking her daughter's heart, even though years ago now. Maybe I didn't look half as bad as the other jerk—the ex-husband—and he tolerated me, at least.

After the two dinners, we went to another movie, *The French Lieutenant's Woman*, and after that Allison invited me to attend KC's school play. She had two roles in the several fairy tales that they were dramatizing. KC was Gretel in *Hansel and Gretel* and the title character in *Little Red Riding Hood*. The drama teacher was the old witch and the grandmother, looking every bit as if she relished getting into character, makeup and costume. The set design was quite elaborate, including the gingerbread house, the cage for the children, and the oven that they pushed the witch into. Other children played roles of the woodcutter and his wife, the big, bad wolf—who also pulled a double in *The Three Little Pigs*. They did a nifty little switch so that the drama teacher was suddenly in a wolf's costume so that she could be saved by the woodcutter's ax (she unzipped the wolf costume and stepped out of it to fervent applause). The whole production was wonderfully cute, for what it was, an elementary school play. But as I was focused on KC's performance, she really did an impressive job, I thought. Primarily, she delivered her short lines of dialogue right on cue, while the other kids missed on the timing, or simply fumbled the lines. KC was a born actress it seemed.

Of all the times spent with Allison, I never attempted to kiss her goodnight or try to insinuate that we had anything other than a platonic relationship. Our times were carefree fun, and I didn't want to mess things up by trying to alter the relationship in any way. It seemed we were both comfortable in friendship, and that the past *was* the past, and that we had both moved on. But truthfully, I still had regrets about how I messed up such a good thing. The joy of our new friendship was a constant, if not slightly bitter, reminder of that. But I did my best to hold those feelings at bay and enjoy the present for what it was worth. Allison was making that incredibly easy for me.

After separately celebrating Thanksgiving Day, Allison was able to spend some time at my house that weekend for a casual supper and watching television to relax. KC was spending the remaining weekend with her aunt Roberta, the former Bobbi. We ended up reminiscing about high school days, with me pulling out the old yearbooks and other photographs I had of my youth.

I noticed the time and figured that Allison would be leaving soon. "Wow, it's getting kind of late. It was a really nice evening, though. I'm so glad that we can hang out like this, you know. It's been quite enjoyable for me. Maybe we can do it again soon. But you're probably ready to hit the road and call it a night. I don't want to keep you."

"Maybe I don't have to leave so soon," Allison said a bit coquettishly.

"Oh, for sure," I replied a little densely. "You don't have to leave right now. I mean, I wasn't asking you to go. I didn't mean to imply that. You can stay a little longer if you'd like."

"Well, I was also thinking that I don't really have to go at all. You know, um, I could, sort of, spend the night?" With the last three words, she morphed her declarative sentence into a question. "If you'd like me to." Allison's head tilted slightly down and her hazel eyes looked up at me searchingly. I was dumbfounded and flabbergasted. I put aside such thoughts so far away in the back of my mind because I thought that it would never happen. It couldn't happen and never would happen because I ruined it forever.

"Of-f c-course, I would love for you to stay the night. B-but I never thought that you would want to—not in a million years."

"Well, time flies when you're having fun. But you can't tell me that you never considered this option, after we got reacquainted."

"Honestly, I didn't. I thought that we were supposed to move on, and more specifically you moved on, that you would never consider me again."

"Is it that you fell out of love with me? It's okay if you did because I can't expect that after all these years your feelings would be the same. I guess, with girls, they say we never get over our first love. And you were mine. I never stopped loving you, you know."

"But *me* fall out of love with *you*, Ally? It never happened. Never. I made a mistake that I couldn't justify and could never reconcile, but it was never possible for me to stop loving you. But it was *you*, it was you who said that you had moved on, that I devastated you. And because of that we could never go back, never try to recapture the past. You said that we couldn't even be friends because of what took place, that we both had changed too much to go back. You said to forget the past and move on."

"I don't know what possessed me to say all that, but I think I must have done it to hurt you. I needed to reject you for my own sake after you rejected me, and I wanted you to hurt like I hurt. But after seeing you again these past couple of months, I don't see a monster in you. I don't know what exactly happened all those years ago that made you stray, but I think I've found it in my heart to forgive you. I've forgiven you enough to be able to become friends once again, but also I'm starting to believe that I have the capacity to forgive you completely and accept your word now that you will never do that to me again."

"I never will. I never wanted to in the first place. All I can say is that I got caught up in something that I didn't really understand. I didn't know what the consequences would truly be, and I rushed headlong without enough forethought about how twisted our lives would become afterward. My only excuse is perhaps my youth. I knew that you were great, but when I met Lorelei, I thought that she had everything that you had, and that elusive something else—that I don't even think I can define. Maybe the old cliché, 'the grass is always greener,' is apropos—the unknown being more exciting and desirable than the known. But through my experience, I've learned that Lorelei never had that 'something else.' I know now that she never even had what you had. I always thought that my realization came too late. But I've prayed for your forgiveness so that I could prove that I am worthy of it. Please know that I never stopped loving you."

"I do forgive you. Can we please somehow forget the past and start anew?"

"Yes, of course, darling." The emotions got the better of us. We cried a little together, and then we kissed as if to make up for lost time. We made love that night with wild abandon. It was both old and new. It was old as in a familiar comforting embrace, but it was new as in freshly exciting, an awakening. I sensed that Allison felt the same way, but I thought that there was nothing quite like finding a love you thought was irretrievably, irrevocably lost.

The next morning, I still couldn't quite believe that Allison's mind change was real and complete. I pressed her for her reasons for feeling so differently than that night two years ago.

"A thought occurred to me," Allison said. "If the past had some how worked out differently—if we had stayed together—things could have worked out several ways. We could have ended up marrying and at some point growing apart and divorcing, like my marriage. Of course, I didn't see that in our future because I always thought we were meant for each other. My actual marriage always felt like settling for second best, or not even that—just something else. Obviously, I wouldn't ever have been interested in Brian if we were still together at the time. So then the other alternative to us splitting up somewhere down the road is us staying together—for life. That means that today, we would be like this, together, enjoying a decade or so of marriage, maybe watching our own little girl grow up right before our eyes. That's what we talked about, planned for our future, isn't it?"

"Yes, it was."

"And you made promises to me that it would end up like that. You broke your promise to me to have that life by making that one mistake. It erased the entire future, or so I thought. Seeing you again made me think that we may have lost the last decade, but we could also still actually have the remaining future. I wasn't trying to think of us as a couple again, but I don't know if it was dinner at home with Dad and KC, or you going to KC's play with me, but it felt *possible*. You know what I mean?"

"Yes, I believe I do," I said. "Like I said, I never stopped loving you. My only thought was that I broke my promise for good with my stupidity."

"And I thought so too at first. I was sad and angry and jealous and all that stuff. But over time, I guess I've come to look at it as either one mistake, one broken promise, completely erasing our future, or a series of broken promises. Each day that we weren't together, our future didn't exist. Only a choice has to be made today: continue to be apart and go our separate ways, breaking more promises each passing day, or get back together and remake our future as we used to see it, fulfilling the original promises."

"I wanted that chance for so long now, but a lot of people might think you're crazy for giving me a second chance. They say, 'You can't go home again.'"

"You know where that came from, don't you? It's the title from a Thomas Wolfe novel. I read it for a lit class. It was basically a response to his first novel, *Look Homeward, Angel*, where he went back home and wrote about the locals in a way they thought was disparaging. So they gave him a lot of grief for it. And because of that one incident, people now say, 'You can't go home again,' as if it is an incontrovertible truth. How does one guy get to say for everybody? Maybe some of us can, you know? I mean, what do you do when you break something, like your car, your toaster, or this lamp here? Do you just leave it broken, or do you fix it?

She looked to me for an answer to her seemingly rhetorical question. "I—I fix it, if I know how," I said.

"Well, then why can't you be expected to do the same thing if you break a heart?"

"Yes, I suppose."

"I figure life is a gamble, right?" Allison continued. "I mean, I feel as if I've been gambling my whole life. Nothing is a sure thing. And it is just a feeling, but I'm feeling right now that—knowing you as I do—you're the closest to a sure thing as I've come across. My last gamble didn't work out too well, but that's the risk you take. Brian was no improvement over you, believe me. I fell for a lot of his *empty* promises. And as it goes, I haven't met anybody else who would be an improvement over you—your kind, loving nature that I see as ingrained in your character. I've met a few other men since Brian, but once they know I'm a single mother, it seems to make a difference. I mean, you know that I'm not looking for a new father for KC, right? She's got one already. All I would ask while you're in my life is to befriend my daughter, to treat her with love, care and respect, as I've already seen you do. You can accept KC in your life, can't you?"

"Absolutely. She's adorable. It would be the easiest thing in the world."

"So you're willing to give it all a brand new chance?"

"Yes, I am. All I can do is thank you for giving me that chance. I want to show you that I deserve it."

And with that, the transition from reunited friends to a couple planning a future together was complete. The word *marriage* wasn't uttered right away, but it was assumed. We announced that we were a *couple* again to family and friends. I told my father and Ann, and they were wholeheartedly happy for me. Allison told KC, who spontaneously hugged and kissed me the next time we saw each other. Even Mr. Lambert was happy enough, welcoming me back. We went to see Allison's mom, and she was overjoyed. Because of our past history, she was like a second mother to me, and she always seemed to like me, as a person and as a potential mate for her eldest daughter. We then told Bobbi, Roberta, and I was amazed at how much she had grown up. I hadn't seen her in many years, and instead of the bratty little sister, she looked much like Allison did in her early twenties. She had her share of attention from guys, but she wasn't looking to rush into relationships or marriage. She was seeing a guy casually at the time. Roberta grew up to be a very mature, level-headed woman, and I could easily imagine her giving great advice to kids in her counseling job.

I only thought that I may have messed things up again, however unintentionally. Two weeks after Thanksgiving, I received an acceptance letter to publish my short story in the magazine I submitted it to back in the summer. It was a magazine with nationwide readership, and at first, I was ecstatic. I didn't have strong expectations for it, and had nearly forgotten about it. The editor praised my touching portrayal of both characters, and my fresh take on a relationship by having the woman walk away unencumbered, when it's most often the man who departs, and the sense of longing it leaves on the man despite being essentially two ships that passed in the night. He even pointed out the symbolism of being deserted in the desert—the barrenness, the emptiness that it evoked—something which hadn't even occurred to me.

Naturally, I shared the news with Allison and gave her the story to read. At first she seemed a bit upset and jealous that I wrote about my old lover like that, naming the character after her making it completely obvious. I told her that it wasn't Lorelei; the story was complete fiction, and none of the events depicted ever happened like it was told. It was a name that evoked something a little exotic, and so I did use it for the character. Allison soon lost her annoyance with it because she really liked the story and was happy for my achievement. I also promised to write a future character named after her at some point if I continued writing fiction.

The story was to be published the following May issue, which actually came out in April—go figure. After the Christmas holiday, Allison and I formalized our future plans. I proposed on New Year's Eve, and she expectedly accepted. We both saw no need to waste any more time, and set the date for the first weekend after the school year ended in June.

So, after the wedding and honeymoon, our relationship quickly settled into the vision we had seen all along so many years before, almost as if we were married in 1972 instead of 1982. Allison and KC moved into my house in Lincoln. KC was easy for me to imagine as our own daughter. She continued to see her father one weekend a month, but in her own actions I could see that she accepted me as a step-father, treating me like a respected father-figure. So the transition was very easy all around.

I continued with school, graduating with a bachelor's in English in April of 1983, and soon after moved up career wise by getting a job as a city desk reporter at the *Providence Journal*, working alongside my friend Paul. Allison also soon after moved to teach at the high school in Lincoln to be closer to home.

I attempted to write more short stories after my initial burst of success, but no strong ideas came forth, especially to match the first story. I wanted to attempt writing novels because the ideas I was getting were more elaborate than short stories. My first book was actually inspired by a Beatles' song—"Paperback Writer." It came from years of mishearing the lyrics. For some reason I always thought it said, "Based on a novel 'bout a man named Lear," when it was actually, "Based on a novel by a man named Lear." I began envisioning this character, this dirty sort of man with the dirty story, and clinging wife who doesn't understand him. Because the name Lear evoked the Shakespeare play *King Lear*, I imagined that this character wanted desperately to become king. But I also thought about my limitations and how I didn't want to attempt to write historical fiction, and instead I set it in modern times. I had the character be a member of parliament who desperately wanted to be prime minister, using the term king as a symbolic metaphor for his ambition. My novel was titled *King Lear* for that effect. Also because I didn't think I knew enough about British society, I set the story in Canada. The son would be a newspaper reporter, which I knew something about, working for the *Daily Call* instead of the *Daily Mail* from the song. And while Lear's hubris allows him to seek out cheap, clandestine affairs bordering on recklessness while in his climb to the top post, ironically it's his son who discovers the truth and writes an exposé about his father before the big election, bringing his candidacy crashing down, which he does for his mother's sake.

When it was finished—and thankfully more than a shade under a thousand pages, give or take a few—I sought out the opinion of my trusted English professor, who had directed me to the magazine for the short story, and this time, as he liked my effort, directed me to a literary agent, who then helped me get it published mid 1985. It was the publication of the novel that inadvertently led to the next big change in my life.

The book was not a smashing success, but a modest success for a first novel. It received some publicity with newspaper reviews in the *New York Times*, *Boston Globe* and several others countrywide. Local publicity was handled as a news story in *The Journal*, the paper I worked for. They pointed out that a staff writer published a new novel, and they reprinted the *Globe*'s review to maintain journalistic ethical standards instead of having our reviewer write it up and give the impression that she was promoting it simply because she knew me. But after doing some initial local appearances at bookstores throughout Rhode Island and Massachusetts to promote it myself, I received a long-awaited phone call one night at my desk at work.

"Hello, Tom Moore here," I said into the receiver.

"Hello, Mr. Moore," said a young male voice coming through the line. "I'm not sure that you're the right person I'm looking to speak with, but I'm checking out some possibilities."

"Well, go right ahead. What can I do for you, then?" I asked, almost impatiently. I was always eager for specifics, just as journalism taught me: punch up the lead, grab the reader's attention in the first graph. I sensed he was beating around the bush in not identifying himself first.

"May I ask you a couple of questions?"

"Sure, if they're quick. Shoot."

"Well, I know that you have a very common name, but are you the Thomas Moore who used to know a Lorelei Sommerstag in the Boston area back in the late sixties?"

I only knew one Lorelei, of course. I unconsciously gripped the phone tighter.

"Um, yes. I mean I believe so. I never knew what her last name was. But how do you know that I—?"

"And you wrote a short story titled, 'Lorelei,' a few years ago based on her character?"

"Yes, I did. Who are—with whom am I speaking?" At first I thought the person could be a private investigator trying to track me down, which I more than welcomed concerning Lorelei, but the tone of voice didn't match my expectations for that. The voice was very young—a teenager, perhaps.

"It may sound funny—it does to some people—and I'm not sure if you ever heard it or not, but my name is Tranquility."

My throat clenched tight. I couldn't believe what I was hearing. My breath was frozen. I wanted to inhale to say something, but it didn't happen. Then I wanted to exhale, and that didn't happen. After an indeterminate number of seconds, the tight grip around my voice box finally loosened enough to speak. I was never able to hear him utter a word before, but I knew this was no joke, and it was my son that I was speaking to on the phone.

"I—I'm the person you're looking for. You don't have to convince me any more. I know it actually is you, son. You don't know how happy I am to hear from you. I—I didn't know—"

"Whew, pardon me a second." It sounded as if he were clearing his throat as well. "I wasn't sure that you even knew that you had a son with her, my mother, Lorelei."

"Yes, yes, I did. I was there when you were born. It wasn't too long after that she disappeared with you, leaving behind no traces of where she had gone. I'm guessing she didn't tell you much about me either, but she never told me much about herself, where she was from or her last name even. What was it you said, Summer-something?"

"Sommerstag."

"Sommerstag," I repeated. "It was that lack of information that kept me all these years from tracking her and you down. I wanted to. Please know that, I did want to know where you were, who you were. I wanted to be part of your life, but she hasn't let me. What did she tell you about me?"

"Not much," he replied. "Early on she said that you had died. Then later she said that you had left her before you knew that she was going to have me. Now, it makes sense with her different stories that she was lying to cover up something, for whatever reason. She did give me one piece of truthful information, though. She said that my father's name was Thomas. But that's all she would say."

"How did you ultimately track me down then? And does she know that you've been trying to contact me? Where is she now?" He then related the whole sordid story. Sadly, Lorelei passed away two years prior, but ultimately her death led to Tranquility's search for a father. I couldn't believe that she was gone, wanting to be angry at her for her brazen actions of the past, but instead I was very much saddened and upset to hear that she had died.

Piecing together Lorelei's story from our son and from what I gleaned talking to his grandmother later, whose care he was left in after Lorelei's death, I learned that she had a mostly unfulfilling life, before and after I knew her, and I was saddened by that as well. First of all, her proper name was Lori Sommerstag. I came to realize how tantalizingly close she came to telling me her real name all those years ago when she playfully said her name was *Lorelei Summer's Day*. She gave me the English translation to her German surname. *Tag* is German for *day*, and *sommer* is *summer*. She wanted something she thought was less pedestrian and more flowery. *Lori* as well sounded too plain and common, so she changed it to Lorelei. Even more amazingly, she grew up in Lowell, Mass., where Tranquility now resided, on the very street that Jack Kerouac grew up on. When she took me on that field trip of sorts, to see the birthplace of the great writer, I now wondered if it really was to surreptitiously show me where she grew up as well. The Kerouacs had moved long before little Lori Sommerstag was born, but just about everyone in the neighborhood knew of the house he did grow up in and looked at it with a sense of pride, knowing that someone famous came from those somewhat mean streets.

I don't know—and I don't know why—but I'm guessing Lorelei was actually ashamed to have come from where she did. Perhaps that's why she didn't want people to know. From her mother, I learned that she was always a rambunctious child, never being able to sit still for long. She was precocious as well, and always dreaming of a better life. Not a richer life, financially speaking, but she wanted a richer experience than the mundane workingman's world of Lowell of the Fifties could seemingly offer. Her parents divorced when she was fourteen, and she never seemed to adjust to life without both parents at home. Lori did very well in high school, despite the domestic disruption, and she was able to go to college on a scholarship at Lowell State. Even that seemed a bit too small and old world for her blossoming brave-new-world spirit. The Sixties seemed to fit perfectly with her need for self-exploration. She dropped out of school in her junior year and migrated to Boston and Cambridge where she found like-minded bohemians of the day in 1965, and became *Lorelei*. I also came to discover that she was a bit older than I originally thought. She was twenty-three when I first met her, and her attraction to me was sort of making more sense because of that.

Lorelei had a couple of years already behind her where she was influenced by a few guru, Svengali types who wanted to initiate her, to guide her, to teach her in their mystical ways—but most likely and most importantly to them, to bed her. Once these guys went by the wayside, though, likely on their own locomotion, she probably felt not only their equal, but even superior to them. She may have wanted to show them how to live and influence the blooming bohemian life. What better way than to have a fresh, young, naïve, pliable student of her own to mentor? I no doubt fit that bill early on with my eagerness to explore that strange, foreign world to me, but she likely found that I was more intractable than she realized—and yes, more stubbornly *bourgeois*. And perhaps her little planned unplanned pregnancy was her way to have an even more perfect—and more importantly, uncorrupted and unmolded—protégé than I.

In the subsequent years since she left me, Lorelei was something of a wayward soul. Immediately after leaving the farm, it was thought by her mother that Lorelei went to New York City to crash with another male friend. I figure he was one more Ziggy type who could offer the utopian life she was looking for. But likely this new guy wasn't looking for a girlfriend with a kid in tow. Hippies were looking to stay unencumbered, after all, not looking for attachments and serious commitments. Her stay in the city was brief, and it is known in more detail that she then went to stay with a group of friends on the Jersey shore, in a beach house in Wildwood with a set up that sounded a lot like the Pink House. Tranquility even had some vague memories of the beach. They stayed about a year, but the cohesive group for whatever reasons also became unglued. I imagine that it was tough for Lorelei to raise a child in these environments, and I think that she finally became frustrated enough that she sought help from a source that she wished to avoid—her own mother.

So with great reluctance, she and her toddler moved back home to Lowell. Lorelei may have meant it as a rest stop of sorts before moving on to greener pastures. Mrs. Sommerstag offered what help she could to her daughter, but life continued to be a struggle. Glad to have her daughter in her life again, she enabled Lorelei to reorganize her life. But as time passed, and with Mrs. Sommerstag pressing Lorelei to get a job to help take care of her son, Lorelei vigorously resisted all efforts to push her toward a life— much like her mother's—which she resented so much. Lorelei acted childish, like a teenager living at home. She would often leave the care of her son to her mother and then disappear for nights, sometimes whole weekends, to socialize with various questionable people. I easily imagined that she continued using drugs during these outings, but also she took to the more readily available and legal alcohol for escapism. Her mother did her best to raise Tranquility in a normal environment at her home, despite Lorelei's wildness, and secretiveness about who her son's father was and what was going on in her life. Occasionally Lorelei would come home with a new boyfriend, and they would go through the motions pretending to be a real family and plan for the future. Only her boyfriends never lasted long. Now and again, she would announce that she was ready to move out of the house, ready to raise her son again on her own, and then move in with a new male friend. Once it was to another section of Lowell. She also briefly moved with a new fellow to Boston, then with another to New Hampshire. It was always mysterious why she ended up moving back to her mother's house. Either she was still disillusioned, or the boyfriends dumped her after a while. At least two of them were abusive.

After years of this kind of behavior, there was a period when Lorelei tried to straighten up her act. In and around 1976, she sobered up for a time and then got a job as a waitress. It seemed to ease up life at home, with Tranquility going to school, and Lorelei keeping herself busy with work, the three of them—mother, daughter, grandson—formed a fully functioning family. For about four years, Lorelei stayed clean and took more parental responsibilities for her son back from her own mother. Perhaps the pressures crept back into her life, and Lorelei backslid into drinking again—drinking heavily, though mostly at home. Maybe it eased whatever pain she was in temporarily, but she lapsed into old, bad habits. She wasn't as reliable at work. Although, she wasn't abusive while drinking, she lost the ability to take on full-time motherhood, being lethargic and uncaring. Care of Tranquility again fell to Mrs. Sommerstag. Then even more sadly, Lorelei had an unknown liver condition, which worsened considerably with her heavy drinking, and she died suddenly due to a massive hemorrhage of the liver in 1983.

Now left with permanent care of her grandson, Mrs. Sommerstag watched Tranquility grow into adolescence. But in going through her daughters personal effects, she uncovered Tranquility's birth certificate, which listed the long-sought-after name of his father—a Thomas Moore.

That's the one lead that I overlooked, the midwife. Perhaps because the birth was not in a more formal setting such as a hospital, where they likely churned out official birth certificates, I failed to realize that one existed. Even for a home birth like Tranquility's, the midwife was required by law to create a birth certificate. As I was that naïve at the time, and with Lorelei providing the information—including the full name of the mother—a lead back to her hometown, where she did eventually turn up, was overlooked. Lorelei secreted that document, along with her other secrets, and pulled it out only when necessary, such as to get Tranquility into school or to get him a social security number.

Still, having my name wasn't much of a lead to Mrs. Sommerstag. At first, she wondered if she should share the newly found information with TJ. After trying to decide how to investigate my whereabouts on her own, she did think that he had the right to know if he still had one parent still alive. She shared the information with him, and when publicity started ramping up for my book, they naturally had to wonder if I could be the one and the same. They saw that I was somewhat local and, therefore, had some possibilities. Tranquility did some sleuthing on his own. He read my book's bio, which was brief and not very informative. He simply checked my name in the *Reader's Guide to Periodicals* to see if I had any other publications to peruse for clues. Of course, a name jumped out at him—the title of my published short story, "*Lorelei.*" He found the library's bound copy of the magazine it was in, read it, and was convinced that I was his father. Still, it could have been purely coincidental. He knew that I worked for the *Journal*, and eventually mustered enough courage to call me, and if nothing else, eliminate me from contention.

All that was left to do now, I thought was reunite. Way too many years had gone by already.

"Can I come to Lowell to see you?" I asked. "As soon as possible."

"Yes, Dad. I'm anxious to finally meet you."

I was anxious, giddy, nauseous, apprehensive, overeager, petrified, and elated all rolled into one.

REPEAT CHORUS AND FADE OUT:

"All you need is love, All you need is love,
All you need is love, love, love is all you need."

Lennon-McCartney

"And in the end, the love you take is equal to the love you make."

Lennon-McCartney

"We can go through our love, we can do things that they said were impossible."

McCartney

"To lead a better life, I need a love of my own."

Lennon-McCartney

"And woman, hold me close to your heart,
However distant don't keep us apart,
After all it is written in the stars."

Lennon

"Don't ever ask me why, I never say goodbye to my love, It's understood."

McCartney

"Girl I love you, Girl I love you, Girl I love you so bad."

McCartney

"But when I see you darling, It's like we both are falling in love again,
It'll be just like starting over, starting over."

Lennon

"She's the kind of girl you want so much it makes you sorry,
Still you don't regret a single day, ah girl, girl."
Lennon-McCartney

"But of all these friends and lovers, there is no one compares with you."
Lennon-McCartney

"If I fell in love with you, would you promise to be true,
And help me understand?"
Lennon-McCartney

"I've just seen a face, I can't forget the time or place where we first met,
She's just the girl for me, and I want all the world to see we met."
Lennon-McCartney

"Maybe I'm amazed at the way you love me all the time."
McCartney

"Bright are the stars that shine, dark is the sky,
I know this love of mine will never die, and I love her."
Lennon-McCartney

"Love is all, love is new, love is all, love is you."
Lennon-McCartney

"When love is all that stays, only love remains."
McCartney

Oh, did I mention that Lennon and McCartney wrote the best lines on love ever? And *Obla-di, Obla-da,* life does indeed go on, bra.

Needless to say, it was a tearful father and son reunion, at least on my part. Tranquility Jack—which is the name that he likes to go by now—was a little more reticent, but that's completely understandable. He probably had no clue to how I felt about him. He may have thought that he was going to be an intrusion into my life, and that I didn't want him in it. He may have thought I must have done something that caused his mother to flee from me. At least he was going to wait until I showed him otherwise. I tried my best to tell him the circumstances surrounding his and his mother's departure from me without going into the painful, embarrassing details. I told him as strongly as I could that it wasn't my intention to separate. I didn't leave him or desert him. I always wanted to be a part of his life. He said he thought he understood.

When he was born, I told him I had wanted to call him Jack. He thought about it and said he liked it. But he grew fond of his unique name as well. He also didn't mind TJ. In our first time attempting to bond, he told me of getting teased about his unusual name when he started school. It was perfectly normal to him before that because that's all he knew, but when he got all sorts of mispronunciations from his peers, and questions like, "How come you got such a funny name?" He came right back and said, "My mother named me 'cause she's a hippie. It means peace and quiet." And a lot of times, they would become more interested and say, "A real hippie?" or "What's a hippie?" if they didn't know. But it tended to lead to discussion after that. Even against the more belligerent kids, he learned to keep his cool and ignore their taunts, which would generally diffuse them, as well. Maybe it helped having a peaceful name. It just wouldn't cosmically fit to be named *Tranquility* and be some sort of hot head. Despite the tough single-parent upbringing, TJ seemed pretty well adjusted overall, no doubt thanks to the firm foundation provided by his no-nonsense grandmother.

As soon as we reached a certain comfort level, I offered to have TJ come live with me. I felt torn about it considering I was asking to take him from the only family he had known to now live with a complete stranger. But I pointed out all the years which I had already lost with him, in conjunction with the few remaining adolescent years before becoming an adult, and I was afraid I would never be able to bond with my son as a father should, during his developmental years. Initially, Mrs. Sommerstag was reluctant to let go her precious grandson, now the only living connection to her one and only child, but she realized the primary place a parent should have. I think I convinced her that I never abandoned him, and showed how much I wanted Tranquility in my life now, and she consented if he would also. It meant taking him away from established friendships, entering a new school, and entering a whole new family, complete with step-mom and step-sister. But with the upcoming school year having to advance to high school from junior high anyway, that decision was a little easier. And I insisted that close contact be maintained with his grandmother, allowing for as many visits back as he desired. Tranquility Jack carefully considered the proposal and decided to come to Rhode Island and live with me at the start of the school year.

The transition seemed to go pretty smoothly. Allison and KC welcomed him into our home and helped him feel at ease. And he soon was introduced to his second set of grandparents, Grandpa Jack and Grandma Ann. He even started out by having Allison as his freshman English teacher at the high school. He quickly settled into his new life, and said he was very happy how things worked out. He finally had a father. And I finally had my son.

It was easy for me to ponder how much this new, cobbled-together family life wasn't much different from the visions I had of a future family life with Allison all those years ago: two loving, adoring kids to raise, to love and adore. The only thing that might have made the picture a little more perfect would be if Allison and I had a child together. We had tried ever since we got married, but it just didn't happen. I suppose we could have sought out fertility specialists to figure out what the problem was, but as Allison's biological clock was ticking down anyway, we decided not to fuss and bother. We weren't greedy. We had a lot to be grateful for.

TJ was a reserved, sensitive teenager who delved into his artistic side by learning music. He had already started taking piano lessons while in Lowell, and he continued his study in Lincoln. Funny thing was he had an affinity for Beatles' songs. Lorelei's record collection provided the inspirational source. He learned to play some of their songs on piano because the well-known melodies were in his head already, and it was easy to remember by ear as opposed to reading the sheet music. He also said it was much more fun than playing those classical pieces that piano teachers tended to push on students. As his proficiency grew, he also began composing his own pop songs.

Bonding with him was also easy after finding out he was a big Red Sox fan as well. Even though they lost in ignominious fashion in the 1986 World Series, it was a great time to share history with TJ there. My father scored tickets for us boys, three generations of Moores, to a giddy Game 5 in Boston, the one that put them on the brink of their first championship since the departure of Babe Ruth. But while huddled around the television for Games 6 and 7, we bonded in despair and dejection after the Mets swept another Sox season away without a title. You have to be a fan to understand the closeness we achieved in sharing the moment, even if it was heartbreaking.

Tranquility Jack, my son, continued to develop as a musician as he joined a rock band as a senior in high school. He played keyboard, mostly a synthesizer, but a regular piano for some songs. They played gigs locally to start, growing from parties to paying jobs in clubs. In the years following high school, the band moved to Boston for more exposure, and they ultimately landed a recording contract. The band had a gimmick of sorts to help them stand out. In the era of *glasnost*, they used Russian/Soviet Cold War imagery and clothing as something kitschy, and the band's name was *Maximum Gorky*. Of all things, on the bands first album, the first single was a song co-written by TJ and myself. He wrote music to the poem I had written about twenty years prior, "Red, White and Blue." As a writer, he turned to me for advice on writing song lyrics, which he was struggling with. I had no experience writing song lyrics, but I told him that I wrote some "stuff," as I called it— attempts at poetry in my early college days. I pulled out the stuff I had saved, and he liked "Red, White and Blue," so much so that he decided to set music to it. His bandmates did a good job at arranging it as well, the first three stanzas being set to rhythm acoustic guitar, and then sliding into a piano ballad (featuring TJ), and then a rocking electric guitar, heavy drums instrumental break to come back to the final two lines in concluding piano ballad. The song got some radio play and actually cracked the top-40, peaking at number

36. It wasn't a huge hit, but a modest one, and something with which I could be extremely proud. I was more excited than when I published my first byline, short story or novel. I was a songwriter, after all, as I had wanted to be.

The band recorded a second album, but sales plummeted after the music scene shifted styles in the Nineties. The band broke up after creative differences amongst its members, and TJ was an unemployed musician at age 22.

But as life went on for him, he changed paths, going to college and ultimately becoming a middle school music teacher, which he loves, though he likely never saw himself in that capacity as a young musician with aspirations of grandeur.

In a case of crisscross symmetry, KC continued to develop her acting skills throughout her school years as she took all the drama classes she could and performed in many school plays. But in a stint on her high school newspaper, she developed a taste for journalism. I doubt that it was to somehow please me, but more a self-discovery. When she went to college, she majored in journalism, minored in drama, and with her looks, seemed a perfect fit for television news, which is what she ultimately did do, working locally for channel 6.

I'm not one to put much stock in life's little coincidences having some cosmic significance, but I do take note of them on occasion, and they have to make one wonder sometimes. It really helped me bond with TJ when I realized that both of our mothers died unexpectedly of hidden diseases when we were twelve years old. No connection, but there you are. And then, there was the fact that Lori Sommerstag happened to pick the name Lorelei and quite admirably filled the part of the sexy siren whose beautiful song draws the sailor's ship off course toward the rocks. And then, there was me running into Allison at the bookstore, which truly salvaged my life.

It was interesting that Allison made reference to Thomas Wolfe in her reasoning for us getting back together, for Wolfe heavily influenced the writing style of one Jack Kerouac. Wolfe wrote with the contemporaries of the Lost Generation. The Lost Generation basically begat the Beat Generation, which begat the Woodstock Generation, which begat Generation X. All of us have something in common, whether it's Eugene Gant who looks homeward, or George Webber who looks elsewhere, whether it's Jake Barnes who runs with the bulls of Pamplona, or Sal Paradise who hits the road; or Dag, Andy and Claire who move to the Mojave Desert in Douglas Coupland's book, *Generation X,* which helped name TJ's and KC's generation. We're all looking for something within ourselves—our soul, our identity. And Wolfe had it right when he offered his dichotomy. When you're on the road, you have two directions with which to choose. You can look homeward or go the other way, away from home.

I don't know what Lorelei found during her search, but she tried to avoid looking homeward at all cost. Perhaps she knew that what she was looking for wasn't to be found there and kept looking elsewhere. She truly seemed a child of the Sixties, as it was where her true nature blossomed and flourished. She found her identity then, her *chi,* her inner life force. She didn't fit in the old-fashioned ways of the Fifties and broke away from it as soon as possible and as cleanly as possible. She found herself with like-minded people who wanted something new and fresh, radically different, and she finally felt as if she belonged. But when the decade ended and Seventies cynicism shattered her Sixties idealism, she was lost once again, never able to recapture her spirit.

I happened to find what I was looking for—though after a long and fruitless search—right where I started, at home. And each generation may have different obstacles to face and overcome, but we all go on a spiritual journey to find our identities, our eternal truths, our dharma, the meaning of our existence. My dad had to overcome World War II, and I had to overcome the Vietnam War, which gave our generations its unifying themes. Some generations don't have wars to fight, and the unifying theme is not as obvious, but the obstacles are still there. Despite the peace dividend, many in Generation X felt the angst of a bleak future and searched for their own identities wherever they could. Pop culture seemed to be their unifying element, but as many saw pop culture as empty and meaningless, that too became a rallying point to move beyond that. The point is that our generations may have different experiences, but we all go through the same thing, ultimately. One of the voices of my generation, Bob Dylan, perhaps could have said it a little more precisely, for the times they are *always* a-changing, which is the constant thread running through all generations. My generation wasn't anything special for wanting to toss out the old and bring in the new. We all do it, and will do it for time immemorial. Simply, this was my story, and how the events of the day affected my life.

I haven't meant to gloss over Tranquility Jack's and KC's lives and make it seem that everything always worked out fine for them. They went through their own struggles, but that is their own story to tell. And life does indeed go on. They each eventually got married, a few years apart, and blessed Allison and me with grandchildren, the start of a new generation, whatever they'll be called. I always thought it would be great to be able to name a generation like Hemingway named the Lost Generation, Kerouac named the Beat Generation and Coupland popularized Generation X. I don't know who called us the Woodstock Generation or, even more commonly, the Baby Boom Generation.

As new generations arise, however, sadly old generations pass. My father died near the end of 2003, at age 77, perhaps finally reuniting souls with my mother. We had shared one more moment of history watching an intense, but heartbreaking Red Sox-Yankees playoff series in October, much like in 1978 after I was back home, only this time it was Aaron Boone instead of Bucky Dent who buried the Sox with a homerun. Dad suffered a fatal heart attack in mid-November. He lived a good life, though. He sold the business when he turned sixty-five, and enjoyed some nice retirement years with Ann, who passed two years after him. Among other things, he bequeathed the Carl Yastrzemski baseball I gave him in 1968 to Tranquility Jack, who cherished it as a precious connection to his grandfather. Unfortunately, the cosmos didn't align just right to let him experience a Sox championship in his lifetime, having finally come the next year. It's funny how people placed a lot of cosmic significance on the 2004 World Series win, however. Maybe I could say that my father was able to exert some heavenly influence in the outcome.

Now, when I get out the old telescope and scan the sparkling night sky of starry diamonds, I search the heavens for two: my father, as well as my mother—Lucille Mae Moore—Lucy. Any cosmic significance? I doubt it, but it's kind of cool. It's much like the sun and moon appearing to be the same size in the sky despite being vastly different sizes in actuality. There's no way to tell for certain whether it means anything, but there it is to observe and wonder.

My second novel used a lot of suggested cosmic import. I got the idea from one of Tranquility's bandmates, the drummer. He was a few years older, born in 1964, and he joked around that he could be the reincarnated John F. Kennedy, born exactly nine months after the assassination. I titled it *Amerigo*, after the character I created, Amerigo Vespucci Jackson, who was born exactly nine months after JFK died. I don't say that he is reincarnated Kennedy, but I have people in the book suggest it and believe it. Into adulthood, he becomes a rising political star, who runs for Congress as soon as he is of age at twenty-five, then runs for the Senate when he is of age at thirty. Almost because of his meteoric rise, he is pushed by some to become the new youngest president—after JFK—as soon as he is constitutionally eligible in the 2000 election, after he has turned thirty-five. He also becomes the first black president. Or he is half-black and half white. His father is African-American and his mother is Italian-American. They christened him after America's namesake because they saw him as the new future of America, where race would no longer be an issue. But as it was only their dream that this be the future, they and Amerigo are confronted with old strains or racism as he gets closer to the presidency. And in a play on cosmic significance, shortly after being elected to usher in a new generation, Amerigo is too assassinated, this time by a racist who couldn't stomach a black president for the United States. Amerigo had named a white running mate to be vice-president, who was then sworn in. But to honor the slain Amerigo, he names a black vice-president for himself and then promptly resigns, to elevate the second black president to office. He is urged to nominate a black vice-president as well, and he follows suit as a message to all bigots that they couldn't ultimately defeat progress, as the country begins to heal.

I am working on more writing, another novel and songs occasionally. I'd like to write a book that honors Allison for her beneficence and magnanimity for giving me a second chance, to ultimately fix what I had broken, or a song that expresses my love, something that more than balances the short story for Lorelei. For me, there is music in great literature, and profound words in many great songs. And I think there might be some cosmic connection between Jack Kerouac and the Beatles, as well, considering how *Beatles* is spelled. I know that the mop-tops were trying for a name that rivaled Buddy Holly's *Crickets*, and one early appellation was the *Silver Beetles*. (Another was *Johnny and the Moondogs*.) But the spelling came from the beat of music, as in the Mersey Beat sound that they were associated with. (Either that or it really was the man on the flaming pie.) Kerouac coined the term *beat* in reference to several things. Partly it was music related, referring to the beat of jazz music. But it also meant tired or worn out, like his generation may have felt after the Herculean task of fighting World War II. But supposedly it could mean upbeat, also, or—my favorite—beatific, which describes the spirit-state he was longing for and searching for out on the road. It's all cool, man. I can dig what he was saying.

I was also thinking that maybe I could write a "road" book. It's a great metaphor for the path of life we find ourselves on. You know, how we're all *on the road*, the *long and winding road* of life. And we're all desolation angels. We're all dharma bums. And we're all beat, man. We're all beat.

www.ingramcontent.com/pod-product-compliance
Lightning Source LLC
Chambersburg PA
CBHW031709170626
46808CB00005B/1675